A Spoonful of Malaysian Magic

An Anthology

Edited by Anna Tan

Published by:
Teaspoon Publishing
14 Solok Lembah Permai,
11200 Tanjung Bunga, Penang, Malaysia.
teaspoonpublishing.com.my

Anthology copyright © Anna Tan 2023
Copyright for individual works belongs to the respective authors.
Illustrations by Yura | https://yura-w.carrd.co
Cover art and design by Amita Sevellaraja | amitaseve.com

This is a work of fiction. Names, characters, places, and incidents either are the product of the author's imagination or are used fictitiously. Any resemblance to actual persons, living or dead, events, or locales is entirely coincidental.

All rights reserved. No part of this book may be reproduced in any form on by an electronic or mechanical means, including information storage and retrieval systems, without permission in writing from the publisher, except by a reviewer who may quote brief passages in a review.

ISBN 978-967-19634-6-3 (paperback)
eISBN 978-967-19634-7-0 (ebook)

Cataloguing-in-Publication Data

Perpustakaan Negara Malaysia

A catalogue record for this book is available from the National Library of Malaysia

ISBN 978-967-19634-6-3

CONTENTS

Introduction	1
Burong – *Ismim Putera*	3
Kampar and the Kings of Kedah – *Joshua Lim*	43
Visitor in the Night – *Zufar Zeid*	70
Moonlight City of the Hidden Ones – *Joni Chng*	95
Rosetta and the Fairy-in-Training – *Ilnaz A. Faizal*	114
Remembering How to Cook – *Sharmilla Ganesan*	140
The Rivers and Lakes – *Collin Yeoh*	154
Flower Fell – *Syazwani Jefferdin*	173
Up in Flames – *Stuart Danker*	180
Taxation – *Rowan C*	194
The Fiery Tale of Embun and the Prince – *Julia Alba*	231
The Dahlia of Hutan Kilat – *Hamizah Adzmi*	269
About the Authors	303
About the Editor	306

Introduction

Fantasy has always been my go-to genre. The earliest inclinations started with Enid Blyton's short stories filled with fairies and pixies, then progressed to CS Lewis' Chronicles of Narnia, before culminating in JRR Tolkien's *The Lord of the Rings*. By then, it was fantasy all the way, the more epic the better.

This is not to say that I didn't read anything else. I read plays, poems, romance, classics, science fiction, and almost everything in between—except for horror and erotica. I discovered I didn't always understand poetry, WW2 stories quickly became stale, and once I crossed thirty, I just didn't have enough patience for long-winded classics about long, long ago. I kept returning to fantasy over and over again.

When I started looking for Malaysian fantasy in English, however, I discovered that most of them were shelved under paranormal/supernatural stories and rooted in horror. There was hardly anything that came under the usual purview of "fantasy", as least, as I understand it. *A Spoonful of Malaysian Magic* is my attempt to address that lack.

We start with folktales and retellings with *Burong* and *Kampar and the Kings of Kedah*, then get a glimpse of ethereal beings and other worlds in *Visitor in the Night*, *Moonlight City of the Hidden Ones*, and *Rosetta and the Fairy-in-Training*. *Remembering How to Cook*, *The Rivers and Lakes*, and *Flower Fell* then root us back in the real—but magical—world. But would a fantasy anthology be complete without secondary worlds? *Up in Flames* and *Taxation* take you there before we end the anthology back in Magical Malaysia with *The Fiery Tale of Embun and the Prince* and *The Dahlia of Hutan Kilat*.

This anthology tries to capture many things—the essence of Malaysia, our multicultural and multilingual backgrounds, our shared experiences and identity, and that perpetual exploration of what makes Malaysian literature truly Malaysian. It probably fails on many counts—Malaysia and her peoples are too vast and complex to be captured in 12 stories—but it is a start, both for us in putting together this anthology, and for you, in picking up this book.

May this little spoonful of Malaysian magic introduce you to new and wonderful flavours, whether you're from these shores or from far away.

Anna Tan
Editor

BURONG
Ismim Putera

Shajat flung the blanket made of fine shreds of pomelo rind across his cavern and spread it on the floor. He sneezed when a mote of glittering dust powdered his face.

Kneeling on a small mat in front of him were two young burong warriors from the Pangkas tribe named Anta and Antiko. They were clad smartly in loincloths and headgears with colourful bird feathers, with chains around their necks and rings on their upper arms. Their eyes darted around, as if in search of clues in the cavern signalling whether to feel fear or relief.

"Embuas sent us down to train with you, Shajat," said Anta while placing a hornbill effigy carving in front of him. "This is our gift."

Burong

"Fear me not, my warriors. But before we start your training, let me tell you a story. When I lost one of my wings, I became an antu," he said, wiping his nose with his knuckle. "Listen, warriors of Sengalang Burong!"

༄

The world or the sky, maybe, is an inverted glass bowl. Its moist lips seal in the edge of the icy plains, hilly deserts, and mountainous ranges along with many innocent people and some prophets, not forgetting the three Sun Sisters—Selempandai, Selempeta, and Selempetoh—and the five Moon Brothers—Bunsu Ikan, Bunsu Tekuyung, Bunsu Lelabi, Bunsu Gerama, and Bunsu Baya. These are the children of Bunsu Petara.

The Sun Sisters walk hand in hand, fashionably dressed like three colossal prisms. During the day, they melt the sand into three pools of fresh blood, scorching the earth with their rigours. The sisters are strong enough to melt the icy giants into puddles of oases. The rivulets flow into the desert, fertilising the dormant dreams in it. At night, they lull children with their rosy breeze.

Poets often catch a glimpse of the sisters' pale faces every time they glance into their sinopia-coloured mirrors. Crimson red light that glitters like quartz fill the cave houses and shabby huts on the mountain. They call them *geronong*. These lights are as soft as the silk spun by the puss moth caterpillars at midnight after spending the entire day munching on angsana flowers. A two-hundred-page entelah from the *Papan Turai* says it is the three sisters' hair. A thousand years ago, there used to be five of them.

Geronong curls along your finger if you play with it. It can turn your hair peach red if it contaminates the water in the well. If you taste it, you can feel a strange salty sweetness. Foliage from the grapevines, beads of pomegranates, and feathery palms of dates and figs grow lavishly under these lights. Hence, their berries and nuts have a similar strange salty sweetness too.

The roots of those trees crave moisture from the sand. The sand often spits out fumes of mirages to trick the trees. Trust me, mirages in these deserts are real.

Alas! Soon, the three Sun Sisters will complete their annual astronomical cycle. They leer at the Moon Brothers from afar.

"Oh, sisters," says Selempetoh, "we are going to be buried in the ice."

Selempandai and Selempeta lower their gaze. Their fiery arms cling to the lowest curve of the arc. Their feet will soon touch the earth.

The Moon Brothers climb up the horizon. Their dullness paints a strong brush of azure blue on the northern horizon canvas. There, they begin their fateful journey on the celestial arc. The sky now has three crimson suns and five azure moons against a pale emerald sky. After a few hours of wiping and shedding their tears, the Sun Sisters inhale the earthy petrichor; their bodies dissolving quickly into the thin ice-like minute spores that burrow into the dust.

A thin ivory halo encircles each of the five brothers as they march towards the first quarter of the sky with boldness. They align themselves like a string of pearls, ready to illuminate those who wish to wear them like a necklace.

Turquoise light drips from the moons' rims like honey on the sizzling pot. The morning sky becomes night again. Bravely, the light fractures into stacks of purplish needles that rain down infinitely.

People call these magnificent light drops *telang*.

cg

The last surviving strand of geronong extinguished when Firazik leaned on the windowsill.

"The transition is too early. The moons have deviated quite far from their path," he murmured while wiping a triangular concave lens and securing it back in his ram's horn telescope. He'd pulled out the thin lens after spotting a small crack at the rim that blurred the image of the moons.

Firazik re-examined the illustration of the celestial motions on the palm leaf scroll, hoping his calculation was wrong again. "The moons should have been travelling in a row, but one or two are trying to run away from the rest," he murmured. He gripped his quill tightly. A gob of blue ink oozed out from the tip.

"Morning, Firazik," greeted Shajat, who had been perching on the branch of the old gaharu tree the entire morning, playing with the telang light drops childishly.

"Telang! Telang!" the children outside yelled while running barefoot in circles, hands twirling to catch the needles with their bare hands.

"Shajat! Come down from there!" hissed Firazik, lowering his tone as far as possible. He did not want the neighbours to see him shouting at no one in particular.

"I want to catch these rains. These needles are beautiful!"

"Those are light vapours from the moons. You might fall from the tree."

"I won't fall. I can fly." Shajat hopped from the skinny branches into the air and flapped his left wing to balance himself. He perched on the windowsill, showing Firazik a handful of fragmented telang needles in his hand. He stuffed the needles into his mouth, pretending to chew them painfully.

"I am going out now. Are you coming with me?" Firazik rolled his scrolls.

"Where? To the library? That place is boring. I see scrolls and scrolls and scrolls. Aren't you tired of reading those?" Shajat turned his sirat around his slim waist twice before looping it underneath the improvised belt.

"I am a High Scholar now. I need to work, like the others."

Fourteen months ago, King Sarizar had adorned Firazik's neck with a copper royal amulet to reward him for his diligence and outstanding works in Archaeology and Ancient Astronomy, with the Sun Sisters as witnesses. The oval egg-like amulet was flat but heavy, about the size of a clenched fist, made from stones unearthed from the pillows of lava in Lubok Antu. The royal seal engraved at the centre of the amulet gleamed. At merely twenty, Firazik was the youngest recipient of the prestigious award.

"I need to read and translate those works," Firazik continued. "The Council likes my translation of the *Songs of Bunsu Antu* and I pinpointed the exact location of the legendary Northern Niah Temple. The discovery was exciting. The twenty-day journey and the excavation were even more marvellous! We found many things in the temple—scrolls, weapons, artworks, clay earthenware."

"Sounds great to me." Shajat crawled into the room from the windowsill. He had been staying with

Firazik for the past ten years. He slept most of the time, but he helped Firazik roll the scrolls, arrange blocks of manuscripts on the shelf, brew black ink, sharpen the quills, and accompanied him whenever he went to the market.

"The royal army has found another temple buried next to the Niah Temple. There are lots of preserved palm leaf scrolls in it. They are shipping everything to the library this week to be studied. Now that we have new scrolls, maybe we can learn something from them about the war."

"It's always about the war," said Shajat. His wings tensed up when Firazik touched his wrist.

"There're simply too many things we don't know about our world," explained Firazik. "I want to know the secrets of the moons and the suns, ancient ruins, ancient wars, old palaces, and temples."

"Good. Then you can find out whether or not you are a prophet."

"Maybe…" Firazik gave an indifferent shrug. "Or…maybe not."

"You are a prophet, Firazik. That's why you can read those runes. Trust me, the runes are dangerous. I remember seeing them somewhere before."

"I am not a prophet and I think everyone can read those runes. It's just that everyone has their own interpretation."

"But only you can see me. Only prophets can see creatures like us, isn't it?"

The question stumped Firazik for the umpteenth time. Being a prophet, even a self-proclaimed one, is an arduous task. No one would choose such a task. Not even the king himself. A king cares for his people. A prophet, however, cares for both the people and the world. They receive omens from the sky and read them to the people. Firazik believed the omens recorded in the Songs of Bunsu Antu. Other than repeatedly reminding the people about a coming catastrophe, it mentioned things like birds of omen, or *embuas*.

Finally, he said, "I don't want to think about it. It is just a talent." He quickly fastened the string that bound the palm-leaf manuscripts together, slipping the manuscript into his cowhide sling bag. "Shajat, today I'm going to Mulu."

"Mulu?" Shajat's eyes widened.

"We found strange feathers there. The Council thinks something fell from the sky before the Moon Brothers made their first move a few days ago."

"Are they like mine?" Shajat spread out his left wing, displaying his obsidian feathers.

"Here." Firazik reached into a drawer and pulled out a feather.

Shajat gaped at it. The feather was no longer than a child's forearm and almost three fingers wide. The end of the bony shaft had a pointy ragged edge with a tinge of rosy blood smeared on it. It must have been ripped off its master's back. The rigid rachis was preserved and waxy, resistant to most earthly magic. The vane had a susurration of interlocking wavy barbs that allured every mortal eye, flexible enough to drown anything in its hues of powdered lapis lazuli.

"This is the primaries. It flies at the speed of the moon's light!" Shajat gasped.

"I kept one for myself when the army from the palace and the priests of the Council flooded the scene last week. I compared its textures with various other creatures from many books. What surprised me is that this is a—"

"A burong's feather! *Burong*, that's what your people call it! Right? Am I right, prophet?"

"Exactly! The runes on the feather are the main clues. These are old runes. It's almost like yours." Firazik flicked the feather with his thumb before dropping it into Shajat's hands.

"I have been here for hundreds of years. You're the first one who can see me since that night. If the feather belongs to a burong, he can help you ascend to the sky." Shajat grinned and flapped his wing gently.

"I will not fly to the sky. That's just the famous rhyme from the old book. Prophets are ancient historical figures. People don't read those nowadays."

"I've seen feathers like that in the war. Those belonged to strong burong that led entire armies." Shajat sniffed at the feather again. "The feather is calling its master. Our feathers will find us, no matter where we are."

Firazik dusted his shoes and headed straight towards the door. Shajat followed him.

"That poor burong must have hidden somewhere deep in Mulu's cave. I hope he's safe. I want to know where he comes from," said Shajat before returning the feather to Firazik.

"The burong come down from the sky. That's where they live," Firazik answered curtly. The feather gave off a faint glinting flash before he slid it into his bag. "But…can we use this to find him?"

"Can! Let's go find this burong!"

ঙ

The Kingdom of Santubong lived and thrived in the plateau mountains, flanked by flourishing rows of plantations and alternating patches of ice sheets and deserts as far as the eye can see.

The most intricate part of the kingdom was the Dome. Time had wandered under the Dome centuries ago and the prisms seized it as a floating fleck of frozen light. The architecture was, therefore, vaguely immortalised.

Rose-cut halite crystals patterned with copper-rich iron tracery formed the Dome's main body, making it the most expensive part of the palace. Glass smiths had boiled seven different grains of rock in a violent volcanic core that resembled a cauldron. The liquidated ore, the permata, was as clear as the air. Once it cooled, the glass smiths chiselled it with diamond axes into sheets of glass. The artisans assembled the glass sheets one on top of another, each staggered in a geometrical zigzag formation, forming an eight-pointed star. Silvery lava mixed with burnt volcanic ash glued the pieces together. Thirty bronze pillars clamped the slippery rim, each standing proud bearing the royal seal, lifting its beauty as an offering to the sky. The Dome blinked at moons in the sky, wishing to be one of those pearls.

Protected within the Dome, the Great Garden of King Sarizar was the best place to see the moons. The Dome gathered the lights and funnelled them into a straight column, like how sand falls from the top half of the hourglass into the bottom half. Not all kings can see through the Dome's kaleidoscopic machinery.

King Sarizar lifted his head, proud of having inherited the fine arts of star gazing from his late father. Light streamed through the overhead polygonal prisms, and dispersed into a flurry of fireworks, leaving only a strip of light dipping into his right eye.

"I can see the Moon Brothers, all five of them!" exclaimed the King confidently in front of his ministers and the High Priest. "I, therefore, declare tonight as the beginning of a new year."

On the mountain, the citizens of the Kingdom of Santubong sang and danced for hours and hours. Even the smallest passage was choked with royal manang, lemambang bards, soldiers, labourers, women, stone smiths, glass-smiths, farmers, dancers, and artisans. Shops, rooms, wells, markets, shrines, equipment, animals, and vegetable gardens added vivid colour to the ground. The crowd splashed telang light drops and flowers on each other, welcoming the Moon Brothers and the new celestial age.

༄

The expanse of spiky pillars near Mount Santubong is the last place anyone wants to set foot on. It is called the Spike as it resembles the legendary and forbidden northern mountain in the Mulu province. The mountain had towering metallic spikes protruding along the columns of limestone pinnacles before it was wiped out by an earthquake.

The pinnacles are mostly red and orange in colour, thanks to their iron-rich core. They look like skinny branches from a cermai tree. Salt from the icebergs makes them rust, turning them redder every day, while dust from the desert blotches some pillars with patches of golden yellow. Rope-like spikes hang loosely from one pillar to another, like tendrils of grapevine coils on a supporting rack. If a pinnacle is damp enough, mosses creep along its border and nest in it, turning the pillar a straight sheen of green. To make it worse, some spikes have smaller icicles branching off from the main stem, like a thorn upon a thorn.

Each spike on the pillar is cursed. If they grow high enough, they could puncture the sky. On windy days, they sway like whips. Any unlucky creatures who fly close enough could get impaled on the spikes; a moth is no exception. Once it snatches the poor creature's wings, it would ruin its feathers, disembowelling its chest, thus potentially stopping its warm-blooded heartbeats.

Frequently visited by scholars to study its history, the Spike is also a common site for the army to test their endurance. Only those who return alive are selected into the Royal Army. Over the years, as more areas of the Spike were explored, small caves were gradually turned into storage huts. Important pillars were marked and routes were paved for easy access. To prevent regular citizens from entering the Spike, a row of wooden planks fastened with spears fenced the outskirts of the Spike.

The closest building to the Spike is the library. It is only a three-hour journey on foot for those who have memorised the twists and turns of the paths around the pillars.

Firazik chose the least crowded tunnel and walked through it like wind, evading the citizens and their dances and chatter. Shajat followed him, flying up near the ceiling of the tunnel. After squeezing through the labyrinth, they reached the edge of the city and walked down towards the western shoulder of the mountain.

Knowing the area as if it was drawn onto his palms, Firazik climbed up a rocky limestone column and spied on the library through a hole from above, like a hungry hawk. The sight of a gigantic cage piqued his interest.

What's that for, he wondered.

Shajat, on the other hand, was no longer flying above Firazik. He sat quietly behind a rectangular rock slab on all fours, like a lizard. He had folded his wing in half, squeezing all his feathers into a giant ponytail that hung down his back, and covered it with a blanket, thick like a shield. It was the safest way to protect his wings from those demonic spikes.

The sky had been raining telang needles endlessly since the morning. It showered lavishly on their heads and backs, puncturing their skin and staining them with cyanic blue and purple rashes.

Several platoons of the royal army and masses of priests from the Council congregated at the entrance of the library. The soldiers had set up tents and were sharpening their weapons while the priests hummed amongst themselves like bees. They threw relentless questions at each other.

"I'm not going anywhere further than this. I won't fly near the Spikes." Shajat sat frozen, not twitching a muscle.

"You wait here, keep an eye on everything and don't play with the rain. I need to talk to someone." Firazik slid down along the slab. After dusting off his pants, he trod as casually as he could towards the library, ignoring the long, cold stares from the soldiers.

"Morning. I am Fira—"

"Freeze! Show us your amulet," yelled the guard, pointing an oily spear at his chest.

"Wait!" Firazik unbuttoned his shirt revealing the amulet.

The guard snatched the amulet from his hand and examined it thoroughly. Another guard grabbed his shirt.

"What are you? A manang?"

"No, I am a scholar."

"What are you doing here?"

"I am going to the—"

"Guards, let him go, he's the king's High Scholar!" shouted Amamun the High Priest from the overhead balcony. "Let him go! Don't you ever treat him like that!"

Amamun came down from the balcony and dragged Firazik away from the guards. The duo dashed towards the library's main gates, evading the falling telang needles.

In the central hall of the library, amateur scholars disassembled the stacks of scrolls and pinned them on the table for display. Tonnes of new manuscripts from the Sun Temples were being examined for the past few months after the excavation ended. The mustiness of the fossilised date palms scented the air.

A strong urge to touch the scrolls recovered from the Sun Temples bit Firazik's wrist. He'd noticed a bizarre scroll made up of feathers among the paraphernalia. Its hieroglyphs glinted as it was displayed on the main desk.

Hieroglyphs were like songs to him, singing the vast wonders of their world. If the weather had been fine, Firazik would jump into the mountain of knowledge and immerse himself in the mysteries of the past embalmed in those pages.

"This room please," said Amamun, snapping Firazik out of his reverie. The dim tunnel led them straight into a private study room.

"Tuan Amamun, what is happening here? Why are they guarding the library?"

"Fi, I am glad that you came here early. From now on, the library will be a temporary army campsite. The army is looking for the bird with the feathers that we found weeks ago. The king wants it badly."

Firazik froze for a moment. He had not expected the news of the mysterious feather to have reached the palace. "Is it really a burong, Tuan?"

"Yes, I'm afraid so. King Sarizar believes it is a burong's feather. It turns out that there were more feathers scattered in the Spike. The wind must have blown some of them into the caves. The army brought them to the palace several days ago. The king liked the feathers and ordered them to trace the bird. The first platoon went to the Spike yesterday. They found traces of blood leading to the cave on the tallest stone pillars but stopped at the ravine because it was too wide and deep to cross. They will bring more ropes to make a suspension bridge."

"Oh, they have found the burong! I want to see it." Firazik pinched his sling bag against him, hoping he would be the first to see the legendary creature himself.

"Let's hope it's just a regular bird." Amamun exhaled a deep sigh. "Forget about the burong. It's the moons that worry me the most."

"I agree. I think the moons are acting strange too," Firazik took out his scroll and showed Amamun his measurements. "These are weird signs."

"I see you have traced the moon's journey," said Amamun, studying Firazik's drawings with a magnifying glass. "Last night, I saw the moons through the crystal lenses at the Dome. They are restless and crazy."

Firazik nodded after wiping the sweat off his brow. "Yes, Tuan. They have deviated from their path. The moons have appeared too early in the sky and the telang needle rains have not stopped yet and it is still dark at this time of the day. Those needles are becoming more and more like arrows. I have a feeling that this is a bad omen. This is exactly what happened in the songs."

Amamun placed the magnifying glass down and stared at Firazik. "The *Songs of Bunsu Antu*?"

"Everything is like the songs from the book. 'The rain from blue moons is a rain of blue arrows, splitting the three piles of earth and two skies.' It's even written repeatedly on that big scroll too! What should we do now? Does King Sarizar know about this?" Firazik paced, eyes darting around the room. Spotting the telescope at the window, he peeped into the lens and began adjusting the knobs. "See this! The blue moons are becoming one!"

"I'm afraid that he refused to listen to me. This is not normal rain, Fi. I warned the king about this last night and suggested we hide deep in the tunnels underneath the mountain, but he kept on insisting everyone catch the bird. He kept a handful of those feathers with him and made a necklace with them!"

What if it's a real burong? King Sarizar might keep it as a pet and Shajat will not be happy about it. He will break into the palace and freak everyone out. But can they see Shajat? What if they catch him and lock him up in a big cage too?

Firazik hung his head low. After staring blankly for a moment and scratching his goatee, he sucked in a deep breath. "I think I'm going to look for the burong. Maybe it can tell us how to stop this strange rain."

Amamun pulled out a chair and sat down. "If you're curious enough, find it, but be careful. Sharp thorns and spikes are everywhere. Maybe...you're right. The bird can tell us something about these events. That's why the king is eager to find it. Did you see the cage?"

"Yes. I will go looking for the burong, too. Please, you must persuade the king to evacuate the people to the underground tunnels."

"I'll try. Be careful, Fi. Do you still remember the secret passages from the Spike to this library?"

Firazik replied with a smirk, "This library and the Spike have been my playground for years."

ଓ

Shajat had the body of an adult man with a stunning brown complexion, sturdy arms, legs, burnt umber hair—and a wing with obsidian feathers. The wound over his right shoulder blade protruded calloused flesh. Though healed, the forgotten wound looked like a fungating mushroom on a dead stump. No tentacles, no horns, or pointy tails. His eyes were embers. He ate, drank, kissed, slept, and laughed like any other man.

He had a comforting scarf around his chest and a loincloth worn tightly around his waist, covering half of his thighs. He carried a bag with many unfinished blankets in it and a dagger. He flew with his one wing in a rather odd pose: he had to tilt his head and body to the right. That would somehow balance his gait.

There is a canonical list of antu recorded in *Bunsu Antu* but none of the descriptions resembled Shajat. One of the ensera recorded that a burong had fallen from the sky after the last War of Heavenly Stars—the war that almost extinguished two Sun Sisters and had unfortunately stoned a prophet who was ascending to the sky along with his burong. No one was sure who the prophet was, or the purpose of his dire ascension.

There were, strangely, many prophets born after the war but no brave burongs to help them ascend for unclear reasons. Like Firazik, they too had minds brilliant enough to have dreams and envision catastrophes.

Shajat was gifted with the ability to see other people's dreams. According to him, dreams evaporated like bubbles at night. He could not explain such phenomena despite wondering about it himself. *Why bubbles? Why can't other people see it? Why do they only appear at night?* If the bubbles were broken by strong wind or insects, the affected person would wake up late and they would feel dizzy. Sometimes, the person would not wake up at all.

These bubbles are precious, he had reasoned once, *I must protect them*. Not wanting to lose sight of something so elegant, he would stay up all night to ensure all the bubbles stayed intact.

He had vowed, too, out of curiosity and compassion, "I will weave each of them a blanket to prevent their dreams from spilling all over the place."

A blind old woman had taught him to sew haulms into mushy sheets. She made many kinds of clothes from the sheets, simply by joining them together. She sewed scarves for the people to evade both the lurid rays from the Sun Sisters and the freezing patches from the Moon Brothers. People from the mountain came to her hut to buy her scarves. The old woman was happy. This was because she had an excellent, invisible helper.

For decades, the woman had mistaken Shajat for her son. She welcomed him into her hut joyously and nursed him with motherly love. Shajat went into the orchards to collect dried palm leaves, animal hides, and grain stalks for her. When she died decades ago from old age, Shajat buried her in the hut, cried for a day, and moved into a cave on the outskirts of the mountain. He now used the old woman's name as his own.

Alone, he sewed blankets in the cave. He gathered stalks and sheaths from dried palm leaves, thorns of sprouting acacia, and neglected barks of the tekalung tree. The *parang ilang* was his needle, Sempulang Gana's golden hair his thread. The old woman once used it to sew clothes. She had not known that she was holding sacred Celestial Regalia.

The parang ilang was once a fang from Nabau, the legendary snake nesting in the World Tree, before it became a blade that slew celestial beings. The fang was so painfully sharp that it had almost lacerated Sempulang Gana's neck. She was lucky to have her hair as a shield. All fifty thousand strands of her hair were piled beneath the tree, turning the ground golden yellow.

A few strands from the deepest hair roots coiled around the dull side of the fang. They immersed into the fang and embellished it with lemon-yellow cursive inscriptions. The hair would grow overnight, like a root, seeping out from the blade. Shajat coiled the hair around the hilt and the pommel to strengthen his grip whenever he used it in combat. The hair never turned grey or fell off.

At dawn, he plucked date palm leaves and sliced the rachis into slender fibres. One palm leaf is enough to make a warm and beautiful blanket for a three-year-old child. He threaded the fibre into the needle, along with the hair. He sewed the palm leaves by joining their margins, exactly what the old woman would want. The leaves were alternately layered with the resinous barks of the tekalung tree and clipped with the hooks of the thorns from the bidara tree. The tree barks were then smeared with the adhesive latex of jackfruit tree brewed with traces of gentle sweetness from areca fruits, thus tightening the square knots. At night when it is cold, the latex hardens and forms small silvery white beads, like a miniature mirror, gluing bubbles of dreams onto its surface.

He would sneak into the cave houses, and fling the invisible enchanted hand-sewn blankets to anyone who had too many dreams. Sometimes, Shajat wished to have his dreams again. But he had forgotten how to dream.

Ten years ago, Firazik had caught him red-handed when he laid the blanket on him. Strangely, he did not scream like any other child, thinking that he was a desert ghost.

"You can see me!" Shajat jumped a few steps backwards. "I'm an antu!"

Firazik gaped at him. "No! Antu does not have wings. You're a burong!"

"Burong? What's that?" Shajat spread his wing, casting a greyish shadow over the boy's face.

"What are you? I've never seen a burong like you."

"I don't know. But you can see me. So you must be a prophet."

"I'm not a prophet. Where's your right wing?"

"I cut it off. It was bleeding badly."

"Can you fly?"

"Can."

Shajat hugged the boy and brought him around the mountain, over the palace and across the Dome. They travelled for many nights, flying over deserts, oases, and paddy fields.

༄

Firazik put on his scholar's robe, hooded his head, and sneaked out of the library. He climbed uphill to where he'd left Shajat earlier on.

"Shajat! Shajat! Where are you?" whispered Firazik.

"I'm up here. What took you so long?"

"I had lots of things to discuss. Listen, we must go to the Spike."

"Wait!"

"What is it? Is anything up there? What do you see?"

Shajat jutted out his claws and climbed a block higher. Standing firmly on the top of another slender stone pillar, his eyes fixed eastward.

"I heard strange sounds from those tall rocks deep in the Spike. I can smell blood. The burong is up there! He's there! He's crying in pain. It's the same sound I heard from the feather. It sounds so familiar." Shajat flicked his ears to collect the sounds again. He nodded weakly at Firazik after confirming the source of the screech.

"Good! Let's follow the sound."

"How should I go there? I can't fly. There're too many spikes."

"Keep your wings down all the time. Try to walk and run like you used to do," Firazik said as they set off.

A snake-like rock studded with spikes marked the entry into the convoluted tunnel. Broken swords and rusty spears pierced its body as if acting as a deterrent. Firazik and Shajat scurried past like rats, scanning the ground for hideous spikes that might ensnare them. The spikes were indeed everywhere, pointing at them from head and toe. A wrong turn meant having a spike pierce through your eyeball.

Firazik and Shajat hid behind the buttress root of a stone pillar. Close by, a platoon was setting up tents along the cliff of the ravine.

"Prophet, the sound is coming from up there. He's in one of those caves!" Shajat said.

"Shhh! Wait! We can't just climb this rock pillar. There are soldiers everywhere. They might spot us and lock us up in the cage. How about we walk along this ledge? It's heading towards that pillar too."

"Sure!"

Shajat glared at the pillar when a cry pinched his ears. It flooded his auditory canals with memories, fervently echoing into his ribcage. His heart pounded wildly. The silence was older than his immortal soul. His ember eyes sparkled with joy, laughter, sadness, and sorrow. He had been waiting for too long, waiting for someone like him, someone with wings and feathers.

03

Shajat had fallen from the sky several hundred years ago. The Sun Sisters had ejaculated thick gooey exudates from their blistering skin. The mass exploded and a cocoon of molten ruby dragged him down. He crashed violently into an abandoned basin at the foot of the mountain. The impact destroyed almost a third of the king's fig orchards.

The bright red hues of the pillars reminded Shajat of the Sun Sisters. The cocoon had cracked open and melted like a molten candle. Suffocated with immense pain, he kicked the shell out and slumped on the ground. All he could remember was blood spurting out from his right shoulder ceaselessly, staining the stone slab red.

Fire and feathers were everywhere.

With only his two strong arms, he dragged whatever remained of his body into a nearby cave. Disoriented, he just wanted to die, be buried under the icy sand, and eventually become stone. The wound on his back was almost half the size of his body. The burden was unbearable. It pinned his ribs on the ground, rendering him completely motionless.

He lay on his chest, breathing unevenly to counter the pain. It felt like a thousand swords shoved directly into his spine consecutively for the millionth time. He growled and groaned for many nights, so corrupted that it scared the wild animals in the Spike. Voices wilted into echoes; tears hardened into salt.

After several decades of hibernating, Shajat was ejected from his dream, not knowing what had happened to his former self. He got up on his two feet, tilting towards his right to balance the loss. The sand in the cave had frozen into slimy stone. He was lucky he wasn't trapped in it to become an ember.

The air in the cave was humid, water dribbling from the coppery stalactites, hammering on his shoulder with the shushing *tick, tick, tick*. He kneeled and licked the water and, along with some traces of Sylvian salt, fed on the moss to nourish his new self. He crawled out on all fours, arms grabbing the fractured wing bone. One-winged, he hid in the tunnels of the caves, with no magic power and no memories of his former self.

༄

"Ohaaa! Ohaaa! Ohaaa!"

A new platoon shouted out their signature call before advancing further.

"Ohaaa! Ohaaa!"

Both platoons merged at the site, preparing to cross the ravine. The new platoon had brought supplies, mostly ropes and other climbing tools, plus the gigantic metal cage on a six-wheeled cart. The clanking sounds reverberated amongst the stone pillars, revealing their plan for the bird.

"Oh! They are going to catch him and put him in the cage!" Firazik exclaimed.

"Hurry prophet, let's go! I don't want them to catch him," said Shajat.

They leapt amongst the stone pillars to detour from the ravine. Each leap far and wide drenched their backs with sweat. The trip was longer but safer. What lay underneath the ravine was eternal darkness and pain.

The soldiers unloaded their supplies. They fixed ropes to metal hooks and shot them to the other side using their bows. The hooks coiled themselves around the receiving pillar, thus turning into many one-rope bridge-like suspensions. They secured the ropes, pulled them taut, and started crossing the ravine. Like ants, the soldiers trekked along the rope by wrapping it around their hands and hanging their legs mid-air.

"Ohaaa! Ohaaa!" Many soldiers successfully reached the opposite side. Some remained at the campsite to guard their supplies and the bird cage.

"Prophet! He's up there, I can sense it!" Shajat pointed towards a topmost cave on a stone pillar. "It's a burong!" he continued, hands clutching his chest. "And he's the *embuas*!

Firazik lifted his head. A whiff of organic blood filled his senses. He hoped to see the creature himself—not just a burong, but a bird of omen. The biggest challenge was none other than the thousand-year-old stone pillar.

The pillar had fewer thorns along its cylindrical body. Its body was firm, dark red metamorphic rocks carefully and creatively sculpted by the wind for years. It was the strongest of them, judging from its girth. The pillar had many caves in its grooves, and the top one was what might hold the bird. From where they stood, it looked like an old palm date tree, swaying gaily in a forest of stone pillars.

"That stone pillar is too high for us to jump. There's no other way to go there. We must go down and climb from below!" Firazik voiced his concern.

"There's no time for that. The soldiers are approaching. They have crossed the ravine. They are running towards him. Put your arms around my neck and grab my body tight! I'm going to fly now!"

"Can you fly in here? The spikes can kill you."

"No. There's no time to die." Shajat unfurled his right wing. The sudden change in Shajat's personality amazed Firazik for a split second.

Shajat was ready to fly and nothing could stop him.

One-winged, Shajat accelerated towards the cave like a nocturnal bat preying on a desert rat. Agitated, Firazik hugged Shajat's body tightly. Shajat flapped his wing and circled the pillars. He had forgotten about the spikes and their danger. His eyes were wide and clear, his wing flapped stronger every second.

"He's here! He's inside this cave!" Shajat landed at the entrance of the cave, the highest place in the entire Spike. Hundreds of other pillars of varying conformations and contours surrounded them. Each bore many spikes; all prostrating towards them as if they were new gods. It was breezy, as if the wind was trying to push them from the height.

"Let's go inside," Firazik said. "I need you to calm him down."

They trudged into the cave with small curious steps. For every step they took, they could hear a wail that shook their knees. Shajat remembered the pain, the pain of losing the left half of your worthiness.

What lay motionless in front of them was a wounded burong. A burong like Shajat. A young adult with a chest, head, neck, hands, and feet, two wings, and feathers both ultramarine and jasmine white. His wings were stained with crimson blood.

The three of them stared at each other awkwardly.

The burong leered at them, his hands trembling as he unsheathed his dagger. He pointed the blade at them. "Who are you?"

"I am Shajat. I present you, my wing." Shajat knelt in front of the burong with his right wing half erect, directing his obsidian feathers to bow towards the burong. Tears like boiling mercury beads blurred the corner of his eyes. This was the first time he'd seen another burong with wings.

The burong snarled furiously and gasped for air. More blood spurted out from his back as he strained. His wings swam in a pool of watery blood. The cave smelt like the flakes snowing down from rusted iron ores. The blood found its way out from the cave and dripped down along the pillars, giving the soldiers the bird's exact whereabouts.

"Don't worry, my friend. We are here to help you!" Shajat walked towards him and patted the deformed wing gently. His hand flickered when a gush of pale blue blood from the burong's wings stained his hand.

"He is actively bleeding!" remarked Firazik as soon as he knelt.

"The wound on his back is deep and I can see some metal bars in it." Shajat took out his needle and uncoiled the golden threads.

"Ohaaa! Ohaaa!" The clamour and sounds of footsteps echoed around the pillar. Firazik touched Shajat's arm and locked eyes with him for a second.

Firazik craned his neck slowly towards the edge of the cave. "They're here! They're climbing up!"

The soldiers marked the base of the pillar with a pole. Some gathered around it, discussing amongst themselves. The rest unpacked their belongings, choosing the best tools to ensnare the bird. Their bounty was what lay in the cave. At such a working speed, they would surely reach and catch the burong in a few hours.

Shajat sighed. "Prophet, please stay here with him."

"What are you going to do?" Firazik leapt to his feet. He gripped Shajat's arm tighter.

"I am going to fly down and distract those soldiers from climbing up."

Shajat charged out before Firazik could say anything. He flew downwards like a raptorial hawk, shed his invisibility cloak, and screeched like a bat. He leapt from one stone pillar to another, occasionally closing his wing to avoid the spikes.

The soldiers chased after him, shooting arrows and throwing spears.

"Ohaaaya! Ohaaaya!"

They shouted for backup and blew the ram's horn. More men crossed the ravine through the ropes.

Shajat flew swiftly around the stone pillars in small circles, luring them away from the burong. Suddenly, he thought of a ruse. He landed on a truncated pillar and drew out the blanket from his bag.

Maybe I can use it to trick them, he thought briefly. He tore the blanket into pieces using his dagger and dropped a piece on the spikes nearest to the ground. The piece expanded and covered the spikes underneath it, making them invisible. He took another piece and pasted it on the wall of the tunnel. The blanket absorbed the image of the adjacent spikes and morphed itself into it.

"Oohaa! It's here! That side! Oohaa! Here!"

The blankets performed all kinds of tricks by manipulating the lights and flashing out false projections. The soldiers were tired and confused by the mirages and shadow plays. They shot arrows in many directions and fought mindlessly. They punched at the rock thinking it was the bird's silhouette. The blankets kept fooling them. Some soldiers walked in circles many times, looking for a way out of the tunnel.

Perched on a stone pillar, Shajat observed them.

"It worked!" he murmured joyously when the spikes began licking their young blood.

The men ended up entrapped in the complex structure deep in the stone maze. Some yelled in severe pain. Several soldiers had their arms and feet stabbed and could not move. Their blood stained the ground red. Their howls sounded worse than a pack of dying wolves.

The soldiers lost their formation and blew the ram's horn. The resounding boom signalled the army to retreat. Cries of grief issued into the night.

"Run! Go back! We are cursed!" They hurtled towards the ropes and crossed the ravine, leaving the toppled birdcage behind.

When Shajat returned to the cave, the burong was lying on the floor, face down. The wound on his back was stubborn and tricky, even trickier than extrapolating the trajectories of the stars and moons. The wound opened and closed like a fish's mouth, puffing out blood like molten rubies. The spikes, in turn, continued to feed on his body like snake hatchlings.

"Prophet, what must we do?"

"I'm taking this out," Firazik voiced his plan. "But I need clean water and some cloth. Bring them here!"

Shajat flew out of the cave to look for water. The telang rain had become annoyingly strong, turning everything they touched blue and purple. From afar, he could see a huge crowd running helter-skelter into the underground tunnel beneath the palace. The Dome rattled like the lid on a boiling kettle.

Shajat brought back two urns of water and some cloths he stole from the empty street.

Krik! Krak! Firazik twisted the spikes and pulled out all eighteen foreign metals from the deep muscles. Lastly, he pinched the finger-like spicules entombed at the base of the agitated wound.

"Shajat, can you sew up the wound? I have taken out all the spikes. I've never sewn skin with that kind of flesh before," Firazik said. "You must do it now or he'll lose more blood. We are running out of cloth."

Without hesitation, Shajat unsheathed his dagger and uncoiled the thread. He dipped it in the urn and washed it.

"Start here." Firazik marked the entry points.

"Hold him down. This will hurt a lot."

Shajat grabbed two skin flaps and pulled them to meet the opposing edge in one attempt, like what he did with most of the ruined blanket. The burong shuddered in fear. Firazik assisted Shajat by dabbing away the blood that obscured the site of interest. Twelve deep and wild stitches sealed the biggest gap. Deep flesh reunited with their counterparts. Muscles were tethered back to the wing bone. All sutures were bowstring-taut. Broken vessels were ligated, halting further blood loss. Another twenty smaller stitches patched up the remaining glaring defect.

The medieval surgery took three hours to complete. Interestingly, blood crawled back into the burong and revitalised his partially lifeless body. His wings turned ivory white.

The burong slept for three days, nursed under the blanket Shajat weaved for him. Shajat flew out from the cave on the pillar early every morning to draw water from the well and find pua kumbu and cotton wool. He also stole herbs and food from the market to feed Firazik and his new angelic friend.

"What should we call him?" asked Shajat as he put down a gunny sack stuffed with clothes, a bedcover, leftover bread, and a small jar of water.

"I don't know. Maybe he has a name," Firazik answered.

"No, we don't have names. Only a prophet can give us a name." Shajat sat cross-legged beside Firazik.

Firazik pressed the burong's sling-tied shoulders against the rough bedcover brought by Shajat and prayed he did not wake up to blood-dotted, feather-covered sheets.

A thought crossed Firazik's mind. "How about Embuau? Because you recognised him from his weeping sound."

"Hmm! Perfect! Embuau means weeping sound!"

ॐ

Burong

"Has it ended?" asked King Sarizar, wiping the sweat on his chest.

Above him, the limestone arch hissed, spewing out small stones from its crack. His guards marched in and out of the tunnel. Sitting cross-legged on the cold floor, men murmured their prayers while women wailed and children slept soundly.

The royal magong performed the bedara with ritual poetic incantation witnessed by the village elders, while lemambang bards in traditional baju gagong sang and danced—all in the hope of pleasing Sengalang Burong.

Still, there was nothing, just whispers of the wind. King Sarizar's face was pale from hunger and fear. He tiptoed around the old throne as if it were a heap of glass shards. Limestone dust chalked his royal robe. His trembling hand still held the feather of the mystical bird. It glowed brighter each time he glanced at it.

ଓ

The prospect of stepping into the human world had been harrowing, but the burong had had no other choice. He must find the prophet to warn him about the catastrophe. While braving the telang rainstorm, a strong gust of wind brought him to the Spike. A dark green spike sneaked behind him and speared his wings. An intense dizziness bore its way into his consciousness as he plunged into a culvert.

Embuau awakened, feeling as though something had dragged him through a bramble of thorns. His wings had burst out of their slings, though Firazik tucked them back in day and night. The wound was still angry-looking, sutures struggling to shut the wound's hungry mouth. His fists opened to reveal pellets of mud-coloured feathers pasted together with dried blood. It had gotten so bad he tried to dislodge one of the secondary flight feathers bound to his hollow bones. Sweeping the feathers away, he prepared to face the sun.

Outside, the air smelt of rain-soaked, dark stone. Embuau shut his eyes tight.

"Prophet, I've come to warn you. This is a bad omen," admitted Embuau, rolling his aching shoulders. His scapular muscles twinged.

"Why?" Firazik stopped folding the bedcover.

"I came down here to bring prophecies. That's what burong do. Come with me. You must ascend. You have no time. Your land is in danger!"

"I…I can't—"

Thunder silenced Firazik. Strong winds blew into the cave. The adjacent stone pillars collapsed along with their mighty spikes.

"Firazik!" shouted Shajat, who was standing near the entrance of the cave. "The pillars are collapsing! The rain is destroying the houses and the palace. The Dome is almost gone! It's setting everything on fire!" Shajat pointed towards the mountain.

Firazik ambled closer towards the edge to gain a sharper view. Compared to yesterday, more streams of smoke rose from the cave houses on the mountain. The north wind fluted its reedy tune through the mountains. The needles rapped on the mountain and axed the earth into three large trenches. Ice sheets burst into raging seas. Sandstorms uprooted acres of plantations. The Spike, as mighty as it sounds, succumbed to the calamity. Half of its body was slowly sinking into a sea of ice and fire.

I must do something. We can't stay here forever. This pillar will soon crumble too, thought Firazik. Right above him, the Moon Brothers revolved into a giant singularity, occupying the northern half of the sky.

Klang! Klang! Klang! The Dome shrieked loudly, revealing a gaping hole in its belly. The rain slipped past the hole and tore the flowers to pieces.

"Look! The mountain is shaking. It's sinking into the sand!" warned Shajat while flapping his wing.

"Prophet, this pillar will soon fall to the ground. This land was destroyed once, many hundred years ago," Embuau said. He walked out of the cave, one hand gripping his right shoulder.

"Prophet, now is the time!" insisted Shajat. "He can help you ascend so you can stop the moons."

"Tell me, are you an omen bird?" Firazik asked Embuau.

"Yes! I'm one of the omen birds that sends guidance and warnings from Sengalang Burong. I'm from the *embuas* tribe. You don't have much time left," reminded Embuau again.

"But your wings have not healed yet."

"I can still fly even with one feather attached to my back. Flying comes from the heart."

"I…" Firazik kneeled on the ground. Both hands palmed the ground. Guilt rattled his ribs like a window shuttered in a storm.

"Yes! You are a prophet!" asserted Embuau, clenching his fist. "There's no mistake. You have those eyes. You need to restore order. You can save your people. Don't let history repeat itself. Don't make Shajat lose another wing again!"

Firazik's heart tried to wreck itself against his chest bone when he inspected Shajat's wing. Three of the burong's chief primaries—the feathers that power and orient flight—were missing. The dark-brown epidermis was rutted and irritated, bits of hardened flesh embedded in the sanguine depression, resembling freshly dug ground. The ugly wound on his back was the ultimate proof of negligence. He wondered who the previous prophet was. Did the prophet manage to stop the end of time then?

"Just go! There are no more burong left in the sky. Don't let Embuau become like me," Shajat said calmly. He rubbed Firazik's back.

Firazik glanced heavenward, hoping the divine spirit would rain down a paean to soothe his ears. A gush of wind splashed agony into his eyes, and old memories sparkled and bled like guilt-infested scars.

Rise, my prophet. Rise and reveal yourself.

Firazik stripped off his robe and kneeled before Embuau, his eyes red.

Fly with me, burong.

"I will fly with you, prophet," answered Embuau heartily.

"Prophet, are you ascending?" Shajat asked.

Embuau spread his wings. Each feather gleamed like sheets of diamonds. He placed his hand on the prophet's head while uttering celestial incantations that were alien to the prophet himself.

"Take care, Shajat, I'm going to the sky!" Firazik bid his friend.

A cloud of blue haze blanketed the duo. Firazik closed his eyes. Runes crisscrossed his skin, snaking down from nape to heel. Another stream of runes sprouted out from his chest and spiralled around his waist.

Embuau's feathers glimmered in deep blue like light drops. His wings elongated into a feathery cocoon, enveloping himself and Firazik. A swirl of circular lights morphed them into a crystallised entity.

Shajat flicked his wing and touched the cocoon. "Am I going to see you again?"

Firazik hugged Embuau as tightly as possible. The lights were so bright that he could no longer see Shajat from the cocoon. "Shajat, keep making those blankets and keep dreaming about me!"

Kaaassh! Embuau launched Firazik far into the sky. They travelled at the speed of light into the mouth of a rolling sphere of blue flame.

"Fiiiraaaaziiiiiiik!" shouted Shajat when a pebble of light punctured the moon, riddling the sky.

Kraaaaammm! The blue ball shattered. Seven rings of biblical cosmic waves formed ripples in the sky. The mountain stopped sinking; the sandstorm fluttered like a mote of dust and the Spike snapped half of its thorns.

A few moments later, the waves slowly ceased into thunderous rumbles.

౪

A sudden gale rushed into the chamber and woke King Sarizar from his slumber. Sensing the relative calmness, he ordered a group of soldiers to peek at the outside world. They returned swiftly with good news.

"The rain has ended! The rain has ended!"

Men crawled out of the underground tunnels to find millions of telang flakes drizzling down like shredded petals of periwinkles. Women and children scavenged whatever they could from under the rubbles of wooden chips and burning bricks.

"Crazy bird!" King Sarizar trooped wearily into the Dome. "I should've known it was a bad omen!"

He tramped about the messy room, dragging his frayed robe behind him. He cursed when he saw that half of the Dome was nothing but a pile of fractured rock pillars and malformed steel trellises coiled on the fissured ground. The prism in the observatory chamber remained strangely intact. He trudged up the stairs and stood still right beneath its pointy edge; his lips kissed the one strand of wavering light before leering at the sky.

"It's gone! The Moon Brothers are gone!" he shouted merrily.

☙

Firazik floated in a pool of milky stars. Oceans of divine knowledge surged in his body like a high tide. Memories bloomed again in his mind. He had embraced the duty of a prophet once before.

A prophet must protect his people.

"Where am I? What happened?"

"This is Tansang Kenyalang," replied Embuau. "You've ascended. You have reached the sky."

"Am I dead?" Firazik patted his chest like a drum, feeling for a heartbeat. He remembered how Shajat's warm hand used to wake him up by patting his chest and pinching his cheeks. Tears streamed down his face when he thought of Shajat.

"No. You ascended to the sky once, but you fell. Since then, you were afraid to fly."

"I did?" Firazik gaped at the runes that glowed on his hands, which reminded him of the runes engraved on Shajat's body. He sobbed loudly.

"You remember?"

"We…we ascended to stop the Sun Sisters from blowing up. Shajat was my burong. He sacrificed his right wing to shield me from the brimstones when the sun exploded. We fell and—"

Embuau scrutinised the glowing runes on Firazik's body and raised his head gently. "You are special. You reincarnated as a prophet again. That's a very rare case. We have never seen a prophet live two separate lives before. Usually, when a prophet dies, a new prophet will be born and a burong will be assigned to him. From time to time, the burong will deliver revelations from Tansang Kenyalang to him."

Many a time, Embuau had requested Sengalang Burong to arrange for the birth of a new prophet to guide mankind. Without any clear reason, his request had been turned down. It was later decreed by Sengalang Burong that the same prophet had been reborn and was currently living in the Santubong Kingdom. The burongs debated about the existence of the prophet as none of them had been linked to him. When the news of the catastrophe arrived, they couldn't warn him. To sort things out, Embuau had flown down from Tansang Kenyalang to see the prophet with his own eyes.

"I can't believe I'm a prophet," sighed Firazik. He sat up.

"I didn't believe it at first, too. But after talking with Shajat in the cave, we believe you are the prophet. He was the burong who held the link to you. He was supposed to return to Tansang Kenyalang but somehow his memory was erased after the fall. You doubted yourself too much and that concealed your power too." Embuau helped Firazik wade out of the water.

"How's Santubong Kingdom? Did the rain stop?" queried Firazik. His voice quivered.

"The rain has stopped," replied Embuau curtly. "It could have been worse if we hadn't ascended in time."

"Thanks, Embuau," Firazik hung his head. "Sorry for doubting you. You risked everything to help me save my people. How can I repay you?"

"Promise me to take good care of Shajat. He's a warrior from the *kutupong* tribe. We have been looking for him for centuries. You have been living with a burong for many years."

"Where can I find him? Is he coming here?"

Embuau smiled at Firazik. "No. But you can see him in your dreams."

☙

The sea froze back into towering icebergs, and the sandstorm settled down into idle deserts. The Moon Brothers fragmented into a string of five pearls and veered back to the right track.

Shajat's gaze combed the indigo horizon fleeced with cirrus clouds. When the five moons glinted above the stone pillar, he spotted the first dark smudge; a feeble trail of light left by Firazik's ascension.

He crawled back into the cave. His blanket was a fusion of Firazik's robe and Embuau's blood-dotted feathers. He trembled again, this time from relief, from heady joy, because he dreamt of Firazik for the first time.

Then one midnight, the Moon Brothers shed a tear. A bright glistening tail swept across the northern sky. Like a hungry moth, Shajat followed the trail.

A huge crater had formed in the eastern desert. Shajat dragged the icy egg-like cocoon out from the crater and stabbed it with his needle. It cracked open. Inside, Embuau and Firazik were hugging each other lovingly. Delighted, he carried them into his cave.

Embuau opened his eyes and stared into the glittering sparkles of light that flickered over the flames in the fireplace.

"Oh, Embuau! Welcome back! You two have come back!" Shajat put his knitting down and crawled towards him.

"Thanks for bringing us here."

"But why? Why fly down from Tansang Kenyalang?" asked Shajat.

"I come to bring news. Sengalang Burong will send down more burong to this dangerous place. He wants us to train them to be brave warriors."

"I see. There are some pillars left in the Spike. That place is still dangerous."

"The burong will come down soon. I've told Sengalang Burong about your bravery and flying skills. You will be their trainer."

"Amazing! Oh! How's Firazik?" queried Shajat.

"He's fine," replied Embuau.

Shajat prowled next to Firazik, his hand caressing every part of his face. Due to the cold and windy atmosphere in Tansang Kenyalang, his face was as pale as an eggshell. His coal-black hair had turned dark blue. With a giggle, Shajat patted Firazik's chest like he used to.

"My dream has come true, Embuau. I have been waiting for him for six moons. We talked in dreams many times."

"Here!" Embuau reached for Shajat's hand.

"What is it?" asked Shajat. He pinched the round object that looked like a marble.

"A seed. This will help you grow your wing again. Firazik climbed the Pokok Raya to get it for you."

Shajat held the seed in his hand. Curiously, the seed seeped into his palm and tufts of young feathers started sprouting out from his right shoulder blade.

"It's growing! My wing is growing back!" Shajat cried excitedly as he hopped in circles. His arm reached for the feathers repeatedly.

"You will become a burong again, Shajat!" claimed Embuau. "But it will take weeks to grow."

"Thanks, Embuau. I thought I was going to be an antu forever." Shajat wiped the tears with his fingers.

"A brave warrior like you will never become an antu!" said Embuau, followed by a smile that broke into laughter.

"Should I wake him up?"

"No, let him sleep. Let him sleep…"

ଔ

"And that's the story of Prophet Firazik," said Shajat proudly. He placed the sewing needle into a bowl. "It's getting late. Go to bed and rest. Tomorrow we will start our lessons by climbing and flying around the stone pillars."

"What garment is that, Shajat?" asked Antiko.

"It's going to be cold tonight. Use these garments to cover your body. I've made these for both of you."

KAMPAR AND THE KINGS OF KEDAH
Joshua Lim

Celebrations swelled through the city of Kedah all night. From the balcony of his ornate mansion, the Bendahara could hear singing and revelling echoing up from the streets. Sipping Indian spiced wine from a golden goblet, he recalled the events of that day and smiled, hardly able to believe that the Raja Bersiong was gone at last, feeling as if an overlong burden had been lifted from his shoulders.

There was a knock at the door. The panglima, the captain of his guard, entered.

"We've got him, Tuan."

"Did he resist?" asked the Bendahara.

"Not much. He said he was too weak and hungry to be bothered."

Dismissing the panglima, the nobleman stood staring out his window over the arched roofs and spired towers of the city for a moment longer, draining his goblet. Then he walked out of his chambers and descended to the visitor's room where his guards stood watch over the shapeshifter called Kampar.

The large man was seated in a chair, unbound. His long hair was in tangles, muscled body covered in grime. He looked even more dishevelled than he had been that morning when the soldiers of the Raja Bersiong had dragged him into the palace courtyard to face judgement.

Kampar looked up, frowning at the Bendahara through weary eyes.

"What do you want from me?" Kampar's voice was a low growl, an uncomfortable reminder to those present that he was capable of transforming into a fierce beast in the blink of an eye. A distinctly foreign accent belied his words.

"What do we want from you?" The Bendahara let out a short laugh. "Oh Kampar, there is nothing more we can ask from you—not after what you have done for our people today! For almost a year we have been suffering under the bloodthirsty rule of the Raja Bersiong. You have helped us drive him out of Kedah, and for that we owe you our utmost gratitude."

He could see confusion spread across the shapeshifter's face.

"What do you mean?" said Kampar, sounding surprised. "Your king was trying to kill me; I was just trying to escape!"

With his growing appetite for blood and human hearts, the Raja Bersiong had killed and eaten the prisoners in his dungeons, and when he had run out, he started capturing and executing people for the slightest offences. The most recent offender had been the shapeshifter, and had he not been endowed with magical powers, he might have ended up as the king's midday meal.

"Our people stormed the palace in rebellion after you escaped," admitted the Bendahara. "We expected a bloody struggle, but you wounded the Raja badly and he fled into the jungle without putting up a fight, still bleeding from his wounds. Without you, Kampar, we would never have dared to contest the king's fearsome strength. We feared that you might be injured after the fight, but—" he took a quick cursory look "—you seem to be unhurt."

Kampar shook his head.

"I am a man of Kerinci. Magic blood runs in my veins. When I am in beast's shape, even swords and spears cannot harm me easily." He glanced at the blood seeping from long scratches along his arms. "But I haven't eaten in two days. I was not at my full strength."

It had been a shock to see the foreigner transform into a tiger, then a boar, then a gigantic king cobra, then back into a man, all while skilfully evading the Raja's keris. The Bendahara took notice of the yellow-and-black striped sarong that Kampar wore around his waist, as well as the boar-tusk hanging from the snakeskin cord around his neck.

"You come from Sumatra, then? Why have you come to Kedah?"

"Looking to start a new life." A tone of annoyance slipped into Kampar's voice. "I had barely arrived here when a food seller tried to cheat me, and I punched him. That's when soldiers arrested me, and your king tried to eat me. I was about to leave Kedah, thinking myself a fool to come to this land of madness, when your men tracked me down and brought me here." Now his tone turned suspicious. "You haven't said why you wanted to meet me."

The Bendahara nodded slowly.

"You are a stranger in this land, Kampar," he said, deciding to get to the point. "By a lucky chance you have shown your prowess and done our kingdom a great service. Doubtless the council of nobles will present you with a magnificent reward very soon, but as the highest minister in the service of—well, our previous king—I want to offer you a position in my personal guard. You shall be paid well in gold if you decide to stay and lend your martial skills to Kedah. Do you accept?"

The shapeshifter was clearly bewildered by the request. He stared, waiting to see if the nobleman was joking. "You want me to fight for you?"

"Yes, if the situation arises," said the Bendahara with a smile. "If there are people who want to harm me, you protect me. If there are people who want to harm our kingdom, you kill them." His smile dropped. "There are still many enemies of Kedah out there, Kampar—and also within. The Raja Bersiong has many supporters who would rather suffer under his rule again than see another take his place. I need your help and I can supply everything that you need. Will you help me?"

There was a short pause.

"I'm starving to death," said Kampar. "If you bring me some food now, I'll do it."

The Bendahara discreetly let out a pent-up breath and smiled. "Excellent!"

And thus, Kampar of Kerinci became Kampar of Kedah.

༄

A mass funeral was held for the victims of the Raja Bersiong the very next day. Pits were dug outside the city walls near the jungle where their bones were laid to rest. Almost the entire city attended, and Kampar began to understand the plight of Kedah when he saw the rows upon rows of graves and crowds of mourners weeping for the deceased.

"What kind of king would do this?" he muttered.

The Bendahara heard him. "A mad one," he answered. "I believe the king might have been experimenting with dark magic, trying to obtain powers like yours, and something went wrong. It turned him into a monster." He shook his head. "What a shame. He was a decent king, loved by the people, before he started to grow fangs."

Kampar saw many people staring at them. In general, he hated attention, but a strangely-dressed foreigner standing beside the most influential nobleman in Kedah drew many eyes.

"Who is this man?" a fat nobleman dressed in red asked the Bendahara, who told him.

Word spread quickly, and everyone in Kedah soon knew that the Bendahara's new bodyguard was the one who had defeated the Raja Bersiong. The royal treasury presented the shapeshifter with sacks of silver as a gesture of thanks from the city. The fat nobleman—whom he later learnt was called the Menteri Merah—presented him with a gift of Siamese steel armour, but Kampar chose to remain bare-chested, wearing his magical ornaments openly.

Among the rich, he was treated like an honoured guest; on the streets he was met with respectful greetings.

Yet people also feared him. The other guardsmen in the Bendahara's employ were respectful, but they kept their distance. Nobles were polite, but Kampar noticed their uneasy glances in his presence. Whispers in the streets spoke of dark magic. He was a mystery to the people, a man who wielded powers as terrible as the ones that their recent king had possessed.

The shapeshifter minded little about what people thought of him. With his rough garb and reputation for magic, he was the type of man that the people of Kedah would have considered 'wild', but he was not barbaric; seeing the sorrow of the city, his compassion moved him to action. Having little use for riches, not being used to a lavish lifestyle, he secretly gave his silver to the families of those who had perished under the Raja Bersiong.

The Bendahara reacted in disbelief when he caught Kampar leaving with his last bag of coins. "Are you giving away all your silver? That's the royal treasury's gift to you!"

"They need it more than I do," said Kampar gruffly. "I have a soft spot for those who have suffered under the misuse of magic. Don't tell anyone that the silver came from me."

But word got out anyway, and people spoke in wonder of the foreigner that gave gifts of silver. Most people decided that the Bendahara must be behind these gifts, unable to imagine how a 'wild man' could be so kind. This led to an improved public opinion of the nobleman, who welcomed all the praise and decided to encourage Kampar in his generosity.

Then Siam came.

Kampar knew of the great sprawling kingdom in the north. Traders visited often, but royal Siamese delegations were a special affair, and there was much excitement when the great golden fleet came sailing into the Kedah harbour. The Bendahara received the Siamese warmly, but the shapeshifter, standing close behind him, noticed the dark looks and frowns that the other nobles directed towards the Siamese when their backs were turned. One of the rich merchants mumbled loud enough for Kampar to overhear, "...prefer the Raja, he didn't lick Siam's feet..."

The Siamese ambassador listened to the Bendahara's story and shook his head.

"We should have intervened sooner," he said. "The Raja Bersiong should never have been allowed to cause such suffering, especially in one of our vassal states. But now that it is all over, why is the throne of Kedah still empty after a year? Is no one going to take the crown? Who is running the kingdom at this moment?"

"If we had an heir, we would have placed him on the throne by now," the Bendahara replied with a sigh. "Raja Ong Maha Perita Deria had not yet married nor produced an heir when he started drinking blood and growing fangs. In effect, well, *I'm* the king right now, seeing what I'm doing to keep the kingdom together, managing all those quarrelling nobles—but I can't just claim the crown even though I've got a drop of royal blood. The people would never accept a king that wasn't appointed by the sage elephant Kamala Jauhari."

Kampar knew a little about the elephant. He had peeked into the royal elephant paddock and seen the old creature eating sugarcane. He could not see what was so special about it.

"Why haven't you conducted the elephant's ritual yet?" asked the Siamese. "You have had many chances to do so since the Raja left."

"We have not yet confirmed the death of the Raja Bersiong," answered the Bendahara. "If we conducted the king-revealing ritual now, Kamala Jauhari might lead us straight to the blood-drinker himself! Efforts to find him or his body are still ongoing. I have issued a bounty for the Raja—ten sacks of silver to the man who brings in his head."

The bounty had been announced almost immediately after the king had fled. Ambitious men had tried to comb the nearby jungles and mountains, but no one had any success thus far. The Bendahara had confided in Kampar his suspicion that someone might be hiding the Raja Bersiong, preparing to restore him to the throne. "Keep your eyes and ears open for any talk of rebellion," he said. "Inform me of anything at all—even the slightest show of displeasure."

Kampar waited until the Siamese left, then told the Bendahara what he had heard the merchants whispering. The whisperer in question fell sick and died two days later under mysterious circumstances.

The cold-blooded murder disturbed the shapeshifter. He confronted his employer, but the Bendahara gave him a grim smile.

"People like that merchant profited much in the reign of the Raja Bersiong, Kampar. They would gladly help the king's butchers drain the entire kingdom of blood if it meant an extra shiny coin in their treasuries. Given the chance, they would welcome the bloodthirsty king back with open arms. Remember what I said about enemies of Kedah from the inside?" His smile disappeared. "I know what I'm doing, Kampar. Do not question me."

For the next three months, Kampar did not question him.

☙

Legend said that the sage elephant Kamala Jauhari had chosen the location to build this palace back in the days of the first king of Kedah. She lived in a wide enclosure alongside other royal elephants behind the palace, where an elderly handler took care of her. The old man was the fifth person that Kampar visited when the Bendahara decided to purge the city of the Raja Bersiong's secret supporters.

The silent night was pierced with shouts and screams and the dying groans of those who resisted. Kampar strode down the corridors of the palace, ignoring the soldiers who were dragging nobles and servants from their beds, not casting a look at the Bendahara who stood on a high balcony watching the proceedings unfold. He walked out the back of the palace to the elephants' enclosure, following the tracks of the old caretaker that led through the mud to the shed where the black hulk of Kamala Jauhari stood. As he approached, the elephant stirred, and the shapeshifter saw the caretaker huddling by her feet.

"Stop where you are!" cried the old man. "Listen to what I have to say!"

"You have nothing to say," called Kampar. "You want the Raja Bersiong to return. You have been heard spreading sedition against the very same people who saved you from that terror." His fury rose. "I fought that monster for you! And you dare say that things were better under his reign?"

"Things were horrible under his reign!" cried the man. "All I said was that the Raja was doing good things before he developed his appetite for blood! He had started to change things around, trying to edge us out from the control of Siam!"

"Enough excuses!" Kampar stepped forward and began to transform, his fingers turning into claws, teeth growing into fangs.

The old man ducked between the elephant's forelegs.

"You are the Bendahara's dog!" he snarled. "Why have the gods let us escape the Raja Bersiong, only to fall under the Bendahara's rule?" He pointed at the elephant. "Ask Kamala Jauhari who should rightfully be the ruler of Kedah! I've asked her many times, and every time she points towards the jungle. Raja Ong Maha Perita Deria is alive out there, and if the gods will it, may they heal his madness and bring him back to save us!"

"You doom yourself with your own words, old man!"

Kampar transformed into a large king cobra that lunged between the elephant's forelegs and bit the old man in the foot. Seeing the caretaker drop and writhe in agony, the shapeshifter retreated and changed back to human, dodging Kamala Jauhari's flailing trunk.

Footsteps came pounding up behind him. Kampar turned to see the guards of the Bendahara approaching, their drawn swords red with blood.

The panglima noticed the dying caretaker and laughed. "Tried to get his elephant to protect him in the end, did he? Leave the body there, we'll send people to remove it later." He frowned. "What's that stupid elephant doing?"

Kamala Jauhari took a few steps forward out of her shed, her bulk swaying and trunk waving, outlined in silver by the moonlight. The guardsmen and

Kampar backed away. The elephant turned the body of the old caretaker onto its back and gently closed his eyes with her trunk.

"What an intelligent beast," said Kampar.

"Wait till you see her at the king-revealing ritual," said the panglima. "You'd be surprised how smart she is. Let's go—the Bendahara has summoned you to the dungeons."

Kampar nodded, but his gaze lingered on the elephant.

༄

Blood trickled down the stones of Kedah, dark streams seeping out through the gates to stain the silent graves outside the city walls. Hither and thither the soldiers of the Bendahara went, piling bodies in the city square, and Kampar saw fearful eyes peeking out from the slats of windows shut tight. Heralds marched down the streets, proclaiming that this was what happened to people who desired the Raja Bersiong's return, announcing a reward for anyone who turned in rebels plotting against the Bendahara.

The dungeons of the city were no more than a series of heavily guarded cells in a building near the palace. As Kampar walked down the row, he caught sight of several soldiers dragging a screaming woman and her crying children towards a cell. He broke into a run, shouting for them to halt.

"This is the family of the Menteri Merah, Kampar," said the soldier in charge.

"Only the Menteri Merah himself was to be arrested!"

The soldier shrugged. "Bendahara's orders. He said the families of the main players behind the new rebellion cannot be left free. He's in the last cell if you want to speak to him."

Kampar strode towards the last cell, hearing the Bendahara's voice grow louder as he approached. Just before he knocked, his instincts made him stop and put his ear to the door. His senses, heightened by his years of shapeshifting, had given him ears as sharp as a wild beast's.

"I'm no fool, I know your plan!" came a weak voice that Kampar recognised as the Menteri Merah's. "You have already gotten rid of everyone with more royal blood than you. Are you going to take the throne after you kill me?"

"Not exactly," said the Bendahara. Kampar could almost hear the smile in his voice. "I'll kill you, then your family, then everyone else that the elephant could possibly select as king apart from myself—*then* I'll take the throne."

There was a rattling of chains. "Kill me if you want, but let my family go. Please."

The answer was a vicious laugh.

"You think you're so smart, aren't you?" cried the Menteri Merah. "That ploy of yours to turn our gentle king into a blood-drinking brute worked like a charm. In a stroke, the whole kingdom hated him and you had your excuse to undo everything he did to free Kedah from Siam. Where did you get that magic potion that you put into his food? Did some Siamese bomoh give it to you?"

"Oh, Siam knows nothing about it," said the Bendahara. "I made the potion myself, if you must know—but my plan did not succeed entirely, or else there would be no Raja Bersiong supporters left in Kedah. As you can see from tonight, a surprisingly large number of you remained loyal. I'm impressed."

"That's because we suspected foul play from the start," came the growling response. "But you will never win, you black-hearted demon! The Raja is still alive out there. You will never receive the blessing of Kamala Jauhari!"

"I've heard enough," said the Bendahara. "Guard, kill him."

Kampar leapt away from the door. A few seconds later, the Bendahara emerged, a cry of pain cut short behind him. He noticed Kampar and gestured for him to follow, walking briskly back to the palace.

"Is everything done?"

"Yes," said Kampar, hurrying along. "Tuan, some women and children were arrested. They aren't the leaders of the rebellion, why are we doing this?"

The Bendahara sighed. "I've told you before, Kampar, I know what I'm doing. Man, woman or child, they're all Raja Bersiong supporters, and they seek to undo everything that we have done for the good of the city. Leave a few of them free and they will never stop plotting against us. But now I've got a new assignment for you—we have the Raja's last whereabouts."

The shapeshifter stopped in his tracks. "He has been found?"

"He was last seen in a valley to the northeast a few months ago. One of the rebels confessed that they suspect he dwells there." The nobleman turned to face him. "I need you to kill the Raja Bersiong, Kampar. Finish what you started and there will be no more trouble in Kedah. Bring back his head, claim the bounty silver, give it away to the poor if you want—all I want is the certainty that he can trouble us no more. I have some strength-enhancing potions that may help you defeat the Raja Bersiong in combat."

"I don't need any potion." Kampar hesitated. "If there are people sheltering or protecting him, do you want me to get rid of them too?"

The Bendahara smiled, and Kampar could have sworn that he saw the glint of fangs among those teeth.

༶

In a remote valley under the noon sun, the man formerly known as the Raja Bersiong stood in the middle of his paddy field and surveyed his work in satisfaction. He pushed back his straw hat and wiped the sweat off his forehead, revealing a young face darkened by exposure. Picking up his basket, he trudged off towards his house at the other end of the field.

Unnoticed, a king cobra slithered after him.

Kampar had come prepared to hunt down the king like a beast in the jungle. The shapeshifter had only met Raja Ong Maha Perita Deria once, but he had gotten a good look at the young king's face. He remembered features distorted with an inhuman bloodlust, gnashing red fanged teeth eager for human flesh, wild eyes that belonged on an animal. And here was this honest-faced farmer, chatting and laughing over his meal that mercifully did not resemble human flesh, kissing his...*wife and child*.

The child in his mother's arms could not be more than six months old. He was squealing with laughter, his parents clapping and cajoling him in their quiet corner of the jungle. Kampar realised that he was looking at the heir of Kedah.

Kill the child, he could imagine the Bendahara saying.

He waited until night. When he was certain that the household was fast asleep, he slithered up the steps and into the house, making his way to the couple's bed. There he turned into a human again and stood looking down over the sleeping form of the king.

His first feeling was disgust. The rows upon rows of graves outside the walls of the city sprang to mind, and Kampar had the urge to slash the Raja's throat right then. *The deaths of hundreds on his hands, he is a monster—*

He must have made a sound, for the Raja groaned and turned in his sleep, mouth hanging open. Kampar peeked inside at his teeth. The canines were of normal length.

Then he noticed the empty space on the bed beside the king.

"Don't move," came a woman's voice. "Who are you?"

Kampar ignored her command and turned to look. The king's wife stood in the shadows beside the baby's cot, her face obscured, clearly waiting for him. The air shimmered around her, as if a layer of concealment magic had just been withdrawn.

"I mean no harm."

"Are you sure?" said the woman, sarcasm slipping into her voice. "Are you not a warrior in the service of Kedah, here to slay the Raja Bersiong?"

There was something strange about how this woman knew everything. It made Kampar wary. "You know about your husband's past?"

She laughed, her dancing voice eerily reminding the shapeshifter of the deep mountains of Sumatra where he had first obtained his magic.

"When the Raja Bersiong came stumbling in, starving, the dark magic having long since worn off, I personally nursed him to health." She stepped out into the moonlight that poured in through the window, revealing the keris that she had been concealing in her hand. "I made the magical girdle that hides us from the outside world. You will have to get through me if you want to kill him or our child."

As she spoke, the flash of her pearl-black teeth showed.

A memory resurfaced in Kampar's mind: an image of the dark fairy who had handed him his striped sarong ten years ago, her shining black teeth bared in a grimace.

"You're a fairy."

"And you are no mere human," said the fairy. "Only people with magic can pass through my girdle. I noticed that someone had entered. I was unsure if you were friend or foe, or else I would have slain you without hesitation. You reek of fairy magic. Where did you obtain it?"

"Kerinci in Sumatra."

"And you are in the service of Kedah?"

Kampar looked at the sleeping king and paused. He had been wrestling with his thoughts for the past few days, arguing within himself, and he decided that he finally had his answer.

"If I remain a servant of Kedah, I will have to slay this man and bring back his head. I would have to kill his child as well." He faced the fairy. "I have made mistakes in the past. I have slain many men, for good and bad reasons. But this—I cannot do. Thus, my answer is no; I am no longer in the service of Kedah."

The fairy's expression showed that she did not trust him, but she lowered her knife.

"Some men passed by not long ago," she said. "They seemed to be searching for the Raja Bersiong, but they were talking about bringing him back to rule Kedah."

"Those were his loyalists," said Kampar. He felt a surge of guilt and regret. The old caretaker lying in the mud in the elephant's paddock. The fat Menteri Merah. The bodies in the city square. "They're all dead now."

"Even if they had found him, he doesn't want to go back," said the fairy, gazing at her husband. "The bewitchment of the dark magic broke him. He is happy here, he says, far away from those who wish to destroy him. I can wake him up if you wish to speak to him."

"No need," said Kampar hurriedly. He did not know if the king would recognise him, and he did not wish to find out. "I shall return to Kedah and say nothing of this, fairy lady. To the world, the Raja Bersiong is now dead."

ଔ

The Bendahara was in a good mood. Everything was falling into place at last, the nobleman told himself as he adjusted his expensive robes in front of his mirror.

Kampar had returned from the northeast a week ago bearing the skull of the Raja Bersiong, claiming that he had stumbled upon the corpse. The Bendahara had personally inspected the skull to be sure. The bone had been stripped white, all the flesh rotted away, the teeth falling out of a crushed jawbone, among them four unnaturally long canines. The hair attached to the skull resembled all accounts of Raja Ong Maha Perita Deria's hair. Satisfied, he had given Kampar his ten sacks of silver.

He admitted to himself that he had doubted the loyalty of Kampar several times. The shapeshifter had shown a little too much compassion for his liking and the Bendahara had once considered getting rid of him. But bringing the skull of the Raja Bersiong was more than enough to redeem Kampar in his eyes.

The shapeshifter had tried to resign. "Consider this my greatest service to Kedah, Tuan," Kampar had said. "Let me take my silver and leave with goodwill. I have grown bored, and I want to seek a new life elsewhere."

But the Bendahara insisted that he stay until the coronation. "After that, you may leave with my royal blessing."

Few hours more and the crown would be his. The Bendahara could not wait. Even now the Siamese bomohs and ambassadors were gathering in the courtyard of the palace. The elephant Kamala Jauhari had been brought out of her paddock and decorated with gold ornaments and painted flowers. The entire city would witness the king-revealing ritual—although there was little to reveal when only one person in Kedah could lay claim to the throne.

"The king of Kedah," the Bendahara whispered, savouring the sound of the words.

ೞ

The midmorning sun shone bright on the coronation of the new king. Kampar stood beside the Bendahara in the shadow of a pavilion, watching the bomohs conduct the ritual.

He realised that he had no idea how the ritual worked, and he had also never asked. All the while, he had supposed that the elephant would draw names out of a jar like a regular lot-drawing. It seemed that there was a lot of singing, dancing, drum beating, and chanting needed before the selection. The elephant calmly ate sugarcane throughout the ceremony. Kampar wondered if she was even paying attention.

The magically modified skull—courtesy of the fairy's magic—had convinced the Bendahara, but Kamala Jauhari had showed no response when Kampar waved the skull in front of her large face, whispering that the Raja Bersiong was dead. Kampar hoped that the elephant understood. *She's supposed to be smart*, he reminded himself. *She should understand.*

The Bendahara would not be thrilled if he found out that the Raja was still alive. Kampar planned to be far away when that happened. He had his silver sacks and his belongings packed and ready to leave, but the intrigue made him stay to see what would unfold.

The leading bomoh's dance ended.

"Wahai Sang Bijaksana, Kamala Jauhari, anoint the rightful king of Kedah!"

The elephant lifted her forelegs and trumpeted. The people cheered.

Kampar slipped away into the crowd.

Kamala Jauhari lumbered forward, took the royal crown of Kedah from the hands of the bomoh and approached the pavilion where the Bendahara stood alongside a cluster of nobles. The minister lowered his head, prepared to feel the crown's weight pressing on his scalp—but the rumble of the elephant's feet did not stop, and people began to scream.

The Bendahara threw himself sideways as Kamala Jauhari ploughed straight into the pavilion, tearing cloth and snapping tentpoles, sending people scattering out of her way. The elephant tramped through the crowd, heading down the streets of the city without slowing.

Surprise ran through the gathered multitude as they grasped that the Bendahara was not to be crowned king. Then the surprise turned into cheers. The people of Kedah began to fall in behind Kamala Jauhari, marching and shouting: "Raja Kedah! Raja Kedah!"

"What's going on?" roared the Bendahara.

"I should be asking you!" said the Siamese ambassador, still sitting in his seat of honour, taking in the chaos around him with a look of amusement. "You seemed so certain that the elephant would choose you! Is there another candidate for king that you did not know? I would like to meet this special man!"

All the blood drained from the Bendahara's face. He swung around, looking for Kampar, but the shapeshifter was nowhere to be seen.

"KAMPAAAAAAAAAAR!"

Under the ruins of the pavilion, a cobra lay hiding, panicking.

Now Kampar understood why the king's death was so crucial. The blasted elephant was now plodding its way to the valley to place the crown on the Raja Bersiong's head—or his child's. Clearly the people and the Siamese ambassador would not contradict the elephant's choice.

The Bendahara's hurried whisper sounded directly above Kampar's hiding place. "Panglima! Follow the elephant and kill whoever she finds!"

"In front of all the people?" asked the panglima.

"The elephant is travelling in a straight line, fool!" raged the Bendahara. "Overtake her and kill the candidate before she reaches him!"

Kampar cursed. In a burst of fury, he lunged out of his hiding place, fangs bared, and struck the Bendahara in the foot. The nobleman screamed and fell. Kampar looked around for the panglima and saw him running away, calling for his squadron of soldiers.

Without waiting, Kampar turned into a tiger and disappeared into the jungle.

☙

They were in the house when Kampar arrived. The fairy was rocking her baby, her husband fixing a broken basket when a tiger came bounding through their paddy fields, splashing through the water up to their house.

The Raja Tidak-Lagi-Bersiong leapt to his feet. His face paled when the tiger transformed back into Kampar, but a strange calm quickly settled over him.

"My sins have caught up to me at last," he said, his voice firm but sad. "I remember you, shapeshifter. If you are here to kill me, grant me some time to say farewell to my fam—"

"I'm not here to kill you!" cried Kampar. He pointed behind him. "Kamala Jauhari the elephant is coming here right now, leading a crowd to crown you as king again. The Bendahara's men are on their way to kill you before the elephant reaches!"

The fairy glanced towards the jungle, worry on her face. "I feel people entering my girdle," she said. "Men with magic!"

"The Bendahara must have given his men some of his magic potions!" said Kampar. Bleeding cuts ran across his bare arms and chest. "I tried to waylay them, but they were too strong for me. There is no time left—you must run or hide!"

"Or go to meet them," said Raja Ong Maha Perita Deria. He asked no questions, seemingly accepting that Kampar was on his side. "If they have indeed conducted the king-revealing ritual, Kamala Jauhari will be coming for me. If I die, she will search for my son."

His wife stared at him.

"No," she said. "Please don't."

"It is the only way," said the king grimly. "You must deliver our son straight to the elephant. Both of you will be safe with her. I will hold the Bendahara's men off as long as I can."

And die in the attempt, Kampar realised.

"You don't know how to fight!" cried the fairy.

"I have the shapeshifter with me," said the king. He turned to Kampar. "Good man, you have my deepest thanks for delivering this warning to us. I regret that we first met when I was under the control of the Bendahara's dark magic. If we survive this day, you will have my friendship and gratitude forever. What is your name?"

"They call me Kampar of Ke—of Kerinci, Tuanku."

"Will you stand with me, Kampar?"

Kampar stared at the rightful king of Kedah, barefooted, wearing a simple sarong, a straw hat on his head.

"Yes, Tuanku," he said. "I will stand with you."

Raja Ong Maha Perita Deria kissed his wife, then his child. "May you rule long and well, my son," he said, tears in his eyes. Then with Kampar at his side, he strode into the jungle.

The Bendahara's soldiers were nearer than they had thought. Barely had Kampar entered the jungle when shouts rang around them and arrows came slicing through the air.

The king ducked, then steadied himself and shouted, "If you seek the king of Kedah, he is here! Come and get me!"

Men came charging through the bushes, sunlight glinting off spears and swords. The king ran off in the opposite direction, Kampar following, the soldiers thundering after them. As the shapeshifter glanced back, he glimpsed the fairy sneaking through the trees, clutching her child in her arms, a thin veneer of concealment magic around her.

But he had no time to react before the soldiers came bearing down on him. Kampar had seen their bulging muscles and bloodshot eyes, doubtless the effects of the Bendahara's potion. He dreaded the thought of facing them again. The king was yelling and drawing all the soldiers to himself, about to be cut down. Kampar leapt into the fray.

The battle between Kampar and the Raja Bersiong in the palace of Kedah almost two years ago was nothing compared to the frenzy of this struggle. Man, tiger, boar, cobra, tiger, cobra, man—Kampar was four beasts all at once, slashing, goring, tearing, biting, grabbing the weapons of fallen men and using them against their comrades. Yet the soldiers never seemed to die, and wounds simply made them stronger and wilder. They were no longer men but ravening monsters with gnashing teeth and a feral light burning in their eyes.

Kampar soon found himself standing over the Raja who was huddled on the ground in a pool of blood, surrounded by a dozen dead soldiers. He did not know if the king was dead. He saw the Bendahara's panglima hanging back, shouting orders.

"Is this the same potion that the Bendahara put into the king's food?" roared Kampar.

"Just a small dose, Kampar!" shouted the panglima in reply. "Witness the power of the Bendahara—you shouldn't have betrayed him. You could have tasted this strength too. Forward, men! Ten sacks of silver to the man who brings home the Raja Bersiong's head!"

For the first time, Kampar fought for his life.

The remaining soldiers fell, but the panglima entered the battle. He was the most hideous of them all, his natural leer almost becoming the grimace of a snarling dog, back arching like a wild beast. He leapt on Kampar, casting aside his sword, striking with his fingers which had lengthened into claws. The shapeshifter switched from boar to snake to tiger in desperation, but the inhuman speed of the panglima outpaced his tired body. A hard blow struck Kampar on the jaw as he was changing back into human, and he crumpled.

His head throbbed. Crawling up, eyes bleary, he dimly saw the panglima draw a keris from its sheath and raise it over his head.

Everything happened in slow motion.

The Raja Bersiong pounced on the panglima's back, dragging his arm away. The panglima roared and lashed out with the keris, the two men tumbling into the undergrowth.

Kampar tried to clear his head. *The king needs me, he is wounded...*

The panglima let out a final cry of pain that faded abruptly. With a sob, the fairy shoved aside the panglima's dead body with her own keris transfixed in his neck, pulling her dying husband free, calling out to him.

Kampar staggered up and went to them. Both he and the fairy quickly saw that the king's wounds were too grievous to be healed, even by magic.

"Tuanku, you saved my life," said Kampar, hardly believing it. "Thank you."

The king's breathing was ragged. "Where is our son?"

"The elephant has taken him," wept the fairy. "He is safe."

The Raja's face was filled with relief, and Kampar gave the couple privacy for the king's last moments. Later, they put the king's body in the little farmhouse with all the weapons of the soldiers and set fire to the building. They stood and watched from a distance in silence.

"And thus, the Raja Bersiong passes into the next life,' said Kampar, staring into the flames. "On a funeral pyre fit for a king."

The fairy nodded through her tears.

"You need to go to Kedah as the mother of the new king," said Kampar. He was still a little dizzy in the head, but it no longer hurt. His body ached and he was utterly exhausted.

"What about you?" she asked.

"I'll escort you back to the palace. After that—I do not know."

"Stay with my son," pleaded the fairy. "You protected his father and he will need your protection too. He will have many enemies, both inside and outside of Kedah. As king, I'm sure he will be able to provide all that you need in return for your skills."

It was too familiar. Once again, he was hungry, tired, and someone was trying to hire him as a protector. Kampar laughed softly.

"I've had enough of kings and kingdoms, dear lady. I'll take my belongings and seek a new life someplace else. No amount of riches can convince me to stay in Kedah any longer."

They watched the flaming farmhouse crumble into ashes and sink into the waters of the paddy fields as the sun went down over the western hills.

The *Kedah Annals* tell us that the elephant Kamala Jauhari brought the child back to the city, where he was crowned as Raja Phra Ong Mahapudisat. Following the death of the Bendahara due to a snakebite, Kedah freed itself from Siam within ten years, and the young king and his fairy mother lived happily ever after. The royal bloodline of Kedah has carried fairy blood in their veins till this day.

As for the shapeshifter called Kampar, the *Annals* do not tell us of his fate. Legends say that he gave away most of his silver and headed southward with only a single sack of coins, but it grew distasteful to him and he buried it by a riverbank in a peaceful valley. If you ever visit the Kinta Valley in Perak, Malaysia, be sure to check out the town that bears his name, where you may behold the numerous tin mines that yield the fruits of his labour.

VISITOR IN THE NIGHT
Zufar Zeid

The ceiling fan creaked as the blades swam lazily through the air. I grimaced at the stifling humidity and wondered why I had never invested in an air-con. Groaning, I made my way across the messy room—clothes strewn everywhere, half-smoked cigarettes forgotten on window sills, a copy of *The Buccaneers of America* gathering dust on the floor—yet strangely organised to my eyes and mine only. I knew how to differentiate one pile of clothes from the other; were they truly dirty or were they clean but just left to fold themselves? The cigarettes were left there for ease and convenience; I disliked pacing around whilst smoking but when one absolutely had to do both, it just made sense to leave them at strategic thinking points.

I drew the curtains back and threw open the shutters dramatically, hoping that a gust of cool air would march into the room and wage war with the stifling heat. Instead, I was greeted by the low trumpeting calls of banded bullfrogs and the high-pitched stridulations of male crickets, eager to mate.

The humidity remained unchanged.

Resigned and annoyed, I went to the fan control box—once white, but now yellowed—hoping against all odds that it had somehow been erroneously set to the lowest speed, cursed as I saw that it was, in fact, at the highest setting. Not quite willing to call it quits, I did what many would: I wrenched the knob down to zero and watched the fan blades slow to a crawl and then, without warning, turned it all the way back up to five. The logic was sound; perhaps the supreme being that controlled all the fan movements in the universe would be preoccupied with fan-related business in other parts of the world and wouldn't realise what I've done. Thus, my fan would be free of its shackles, free to spin however rapidly it wanted to, free to push itself to the very precipice of physics, free to fly unhindered by man or god.

The exact same creaking informed me that no, the supreme being that controlled fan movements across the universe wasn't so easily fooled. I finally slumped down onto my bed, tired, sweat drenched, and utterly defeated. I went to the window, absent-mindedly reached for one of the half-smoked cigarettes and lit it up, watching the cocktail of three thousand hazardous compounds incinerate and meld together to form blue-tinged smoke that rose in a near straight line. The trees that made up the forest that bordered my house stood silent and passive, grieving the absence of the wind that would have spread their seed, rustled their leaves, and cooled their aged boughs.

I have always been enamoured by the forest. The city-folk and those who stay by the sea, the unfamiliar ones, they see darkness and peril and danger nestled in every corner. Wild animals, venomous snakes, fangs, claws, deep dark pits, roots that snare, swarming insects, even demonic beings that delight in waylaying. They aren't wrong, but I'd argue that there is so much more to it.

It is the delight one gets being in a terrain that teems with life in every single corner. It is the way it pulls you in, deeper and deeper, appealing to man's insatiable desire to be part of a greater existence. It is the non-verbal conversation that echoes through the forest: the branches sighing in the wind, the crushing of dead leaves on the floor, the dull thud of fruits falling from up high onto the ground, and above all, the scent. The scent! A unique perfume blended by the animate and inanimate alike, carried forth by the wind, beckoning one to enter the verdant green boudoir and lay eyes on the most beautiful creature alive.

"A beautiful thought," a faint voice whispered. "If not completely naive."

I was about to retort but my voice failed. The crickets and bullfrogs fell silent. My eyes frantically scanned the tree line only to see the vague shapes of trees standing still.

A small laugh floated to my ears and against my will, alarm bells ringing, my head turned in its direction. Reclining on the thin branch of a monstrous Cempaka tree, I could barely make out the shape of a person. Rapid fire thoughts stormed my brain: *How could that branch support any form of weight? Why would there be a person here in the middle of the night?*

I squinted, hoping to gain some visual prowess against the dark. A clear mistake; while it did improve my vision somewhat, I noticed that whatever was on the tree had its eyes trained on me.

The fear that had slowly been accumulating in me burst forth torrentially, and I leapt away from the window. *What in the holy hell is that*, I asked myself, before realising how stupid a question it was. Horror stories I heard in the past resurfaced; accounts of visitors in the night with long claws and hair falling to their feet assaulted my mind. I took a few steps back, hoping to leave my room and flee some other way. As I turned to grasp the door knob, my hand only felt emptiness. My feet felt the moist touch of grass. In confusion, I looked up to see the forest, only much closer now. I was outside my home, the light of my room shining out of the windows.

I stood there, in the darkness, rooted to the ground. Reluctantly, I looked at the Cempaka tree and shivered as I saw the figure still in its position. It was toying with me, enjoying how afraid I was. Childhood memories of studying religious scriptures meant to ward off evil made themselves known but I've forgotten most of them.

"Why do you flee, son of Adam?" the voice asked, now unmistakeably feminine and, above all, haunting. "Why do you fear what you don't know?"

I kept mum, largely because the adrenaline that coursed through my veins had fried the circuitry of my brain. As my eyes slowly grew accustomed to the dark, I saw the figure rise from the branch and slowly float down to the ground, light as a feather. It walked towards me with small, rapid steps. As it came closer, the air seemed to explode with the scent of jasmines. I whimpered and grit my teeth, imagining the horror that was to come. The figure stepped into the weak light that emanated from my room and I gasped.

It was a woman.

She was garbed traditionally in a black kebaya and batik sarong, an intricate red and gold shawl draped across her shoulders. Her hair was long and black, coiffed up into a bun through which she had pierced two golden hairpins. Both hilts were designed in the likeness of a mousedeer. She had ivory earrings in both ears and an elaborate golden necklace around her slender neck. I stared in a mixture of awe and surprise as silence found a home in between us. She turned her face to me, sun-kissed skin that was radiant to behold, and frowned.

"It's been years since I've had to walk, I fear I've gotten somewhat clumsy," she said, adjusting her shawl to rest on top of her head. "I ask again, why did you flee when I made myself known?"

"Be–because I was afraid," I replied, stuttering. The muscles in my legs began to ache from standing still. "And because you came from…there." I pointed to the forest.

She looked at the forest and smiled. "It used to be so grand. Trees so large you could build castles on them. But you have a point. Best not to trust things that come from the deep, dark woods." She floated over my head and landed on a mango tree. She tiptoed across a branch which, similar to the Cempaka tree, should not have been able to hold any sort of weight. "Well then, now that you've seen me, is there anything to be afraid of?" She hopped off the branch and whispered words foreign to my ears.

Zufar Zeid

I watched in amazement as inflorescence began to grow and the flowers bloomed. "I...I don't know. I'm more confused than afraid right now, and honestly, just how exactly did you do that?"

She looked at me with wide, amused eyes. Eyes the shape of perfect almonds, eyes lined with kohl, eyes that shone as if they were made of diamonds, eyes that held years of sadness and misery. Beautiful eyes. She raised a hennaed palm to cover her mouth in an elaborate manner; she raised it from her side, palm inward and at the level of her neck, and smoothly twirled it so that it faced outward. Then she giggled. It was girlish, but at the same time, echoes of wisdom and maturity emanated from it, as if she had lived a thousand years and survived only by being joyful and aloof.

"Some things just need to be nudged in the right direction. The desire is there, but quelled because of fear and insecurity. All I do is encourage. Pretty boring way to explain what magic is, but I can't think of another explanation." She pondered silently for a moment and a sudden maliciousness stained her face. "For example," she said, uttering words from the same language but the inflection was harsher, coarse and malignant.

The ground trembled and the grass that had been crushed beneath my feet sprang to life, growing endlessly and snaring my legs. They snaked up, entangling my body, rendering me immobile. Only when they curled around my neck, accompanied by my terrified screams, did she give the command to stop. Immediately, the blades of grass and their tendrils lost their power, collapsing to the ground impotently. I, too, felt my knees buckle, falling onto my back.

"Don't be offended now," she said, offering a slender hand. "I was just trying to illustrate a point."

I took her hand and was instantly filled with warmth. She helped me to my feet and with my hand still in hers, she gestured to the forest. "It seems like a good time to take a walk."

Nothing could have prepared me for what was to come. With my hand in hers, she led me into the forest, but each of her small steps seemed to cover great distances and the trees whizzed past us blindingly. Once in a while, we crossed paths with animals, all of them moving out of her way and displaying some form of reverence. Eventually, it dawned upon me that at the rate we were moving, it shouldn't have been possible for us to still be in the forest. She seemed to have read my mind.

"Once upon a time, your people knew of the secret paths. They walked them with respect and took only what they needed. But they were corrupted by their greed and the paths became closed to them. They were cast out, and their descendants became lost, doomed to live life with their eyes half closed. A fitting end, perhaps."

While her steps remained the same, the speed in which we travelled slowed. She let go of my hand and I followed her into a clearing in the centre of which stood a giant Cengal tree. I tried to peer to the top but gave up when midway up the bough, the darkness became impenetrable. I stumbled to the ground after tripping on a root and I heard her laugh. A whisper in the dark and droves of fireflies convened around us, illuminating the clearing with a pale yellow light.

I sat on the ground and sighed.

௸

"I must ask," I said, breaking the silence. A few of the fireflies landed on her shawl, giving her a halo for a brief moment. "Who are you?"

"Who am I? Who. Am. I." She repeated the words as if giving them a thorough taste. When she was satisfied, she smiled—that smile, how it burned a hole in my essence—and then she danced.

I'd seen the dance before at a cultural show once, when I was a child—but this was different. The ones who'd danced before had had joints that were mechanised by cogwheels; their bodies, while perfectly slim and toned, were chiselled from stone; their faces stoic and emotionless. They performed. They smiled and curtsied at the end. They received an otherwise unremarkable applause, bowed, and left the stage. The lady from the forest however...

She *danced*. In the purest, truest, sincerest sense of the word. Her movements were smooth, delicate; her body slithered and twirled and arched in ways that I never thought was possible. Each flick of the wrist seemed to tell a story, each sway of her hips, each smile, each pause, each gesture—they all had a tale that needed years of interpretation to be fully understood. As she danced, the miniscule bells attached to her anklet jingled merrily; carefully controlled by each movement, they provided a rhythm amongst the sounds of the creatures lurking in the night.

Here she beckoned for me, there she forbade me to come; here she laughed at me, there she mourned for my loss. Everywhere she danced. She ended it all with a slow, almost painful, twirl, hands extended fully. When she faced me again, she flicked her wrists and brought her left leg forward, raising her left hip slightly against the fabric of her batik sarong. She tilted her shoulders, the right raised higher than the left, and finally, finally she brought her palms together in front of her chest, all in one fluid movement. An aura seemed to radiate out of her, something that I could not describe; so sensual yet extremely modest, exposing yet concealing, everything and at the same time nothing.

I could only gape. Mouth ajar, an expression of pure confusion and ecstasy glued onto my face. The sudden cessation of tinkling bells was deafening, and she laughed at my utter disbelief.

"I have not danced with such vigour for a long time now. I used to be better, so much better. I used to be a lot of things. Prettier. Stronger."

"That was...sublime. I'm at a loss for words," I said, desperately trying to think of some way to compliment her. "I have never seen... No, never thought that it was physically possible for..." I trailed off, completely stumped.

She smiled, enjoying the response.

"Once, my beauty and power were famed throughout the old country. Sultans, admirals, even the poor beggars...they all came and they all offered me unimaginable things, gifts fit for the greatest queen the world had ever laid eyes upon. I laughed in their faces and reminded them how they could never measure up to my standards. The truth was that I had no need for anything physical. It was their adoration and devotion that I needed."

"Whatever for?" I asked.

She sat down beside me and brought her shawl down to her shoulders. "To be worshipped. To constantly be in their thoughts, in their dreams, on the tips of their tongues. All that they did in my name became a prayer. There was power in that, pure energy, and it used to give me everything I needed."

All of a sudden, it seemed as if the burden of years and years of anguish had descended upon her; she looked haggard, the youthful sparkle gone in an instant, her lips curled downwards. She looked sad; the world had loved her once but now it cast her down to be forgotten. I could not bear to see that. There was no longer fear in my heart, its place taken up instead by pity and, surprisingly, wrath. Wrath at the world that was so used to carelessly disposing of things it no longer needed, wrath at mankind that freely labelled others as idols only to forget them—almost deliberately—when they were no longer interested.

"As for names, well, I had plenty of those. When you're a few thousand years old, you tend to live multiple lives and if you did anything noteworthy, the mortal mind would attribute them to different characters. Once, I cursed a fisherman for being a lecher but his brother brought gifts and appealed to me so I lifted the curse. Next thing I knew, they made a whole story out of that but in their version, I had six sisters and we desired the lecher instead. Absolutely rubbish! What use did I have for a perverted fisherman?"

We laughed and the fireflies shone brighter. I urged her to tell me more. I needed to know her, to learn her story.

"I resided in the north once. I was in a bit of a warring phase, you see. It comes around every other century or so. So, I got on a horse, started absolutely wrecking entire armies. I guess the sight of a woman on horseback was just astonishing. Some other women banded together and joined me; women who were too often overlooked by their fathers, husbands, and sons. What happened was just a societal problem these women were trying to escape from and what did the men do? Twist the story where I was somehow a Queen and the ladies were of my army. Because when royalty comes into play, the rules change. It wasn't strange anymore for women to lead or go to war and fight."

"Never been a big fan of the idea of royalty myself, to be honest."

"You can't imagine the insanity I've had to deal with. There was a Sultan once that so wanted to possess me that he sent a man to ask for my hand. Imagine that. So conceited was he that he thought he was above common decency and decorum."

"What did you do then?" I asked, anxiously anticipating her answer.

"Had a bit of fun, naturally," she chuckled. "I asked for a bridge made of gold built to connect where I lived to where his palace was. And another made of silver just for fun. Then I told the envoy I wanted a barrel of virgin tears, a barrel of betel nut juice, a tray of mosquito hearts, a tray of germ hearts, and finally, a bowl of the prince's blood."

"What? Mosquito hearts? Blood? What were you going to do with all of it?" A gnawing feeling welled up in me. The story sounded familiar, yet I couldn't pinpoint where I'd heard it. A distant relative? A teacher? A brief memory flashed in the plains of my mind. Old, yellowed pages from a book left forgotten at the bottom of an equally-forgotten shelf.

"Beats me. I just sort of said the most ridiculous things I could think of. I was impressed with the envoy, though. Stoic, didn't even bat an eyelid. I thought that if they actually brought me the items, I'd throw them away or give them to someone else."

"What did the Sultan do when the envoy went back?"

"Oh, I don't know, threw a fit maybe. Apparently, he tried to get the bridges built but couldn't do anything about the rest of the tasks. Eventually, he fell from grace and his kingdom fell into ruin like so many others."

The crescent moon cast its glow through the spaces between the crowns of the surrounding trees. I turned to look at her, observing the faint creases on her face that did nothing to betray her age. An infinite wealth of knowledge lay dormant within her. Surrounding that was a mountain of grief, carefully hidden. Her stories were astounding but she told them wistfully, as if the end of her own tale was coming.

I shook my head out of the melancholic clouds and cleared my throat. "Why did you not accept any of the proposals? Did you not want any children? A companion? A life?"

She looked at me and there was a profound sadness in the look; a sadness that could only be achieved after a life well spent, a designated look for the wise, a look that broke my heart.

"I had a husband once…" Her voiced trailed away, as if the Lord of the Wind wanted it all for himself. "And children, oh yes." She frowned and scoffed and the air smelled of petrichor. "The earth was young then. The land itself was nothing but a baby. If you listened closely, really closely to the slow tumbling of the waves, the silent gusts of wind, the patter of the rain as it fell against the earth, you could hear the land asking itself, 'Am I doing it right?' and you could tell it, 'Yes, you're doing just fine'. The land still whispers. Nobody ever listens to it, though.

"There weren't many of us back then, and even now I can feel them returning to the earth—unwilling to face the changes of the world, dwindling. Do you know what it feels like to belong to a race where most of the already-minute populace refuses to carry on? Of course you don't, child… Of course you don't." She looked up at the moon with a look of resignation; as if she knew that she too would one day drift away and submit to the fact that the world that she lived in no longer knew her.

"He was a hunter. A great man who towered amongst others. Tall, muscled like an ox, and intimately connected to the land. It would talk to him and he would listen. He survived on whatever the land gave him. Anyway, he knew of the secret paths and on one of his journeys, he came upon me bathing at a waterfall."

At this point, her eyes darted seductively to me as if to say, 'Oh yes, you'd love to see me in that state, wouldn't you?', and then back to the forest again. "I ran from him because I wanted to see how much he wanted me, how far was he willing to go. I ran, I flew, I let the wind carry me, and yet the land betrayed me. It favoured him more; the trees shied away and created a path for him, the birds flew high in the air and told him where I was, rivers and streams changed directions. You'd find this ridiculous, but he ran after me for ten years.

"I was young then, and obviously foolish. I wanted to see what this man wanted, this man that scaled mountains and crossed ravines just to meet me. I pretended to be tired eventually and he chanced upon me while I was resting in a clearing not far from this very place. He knelt in front of me and he offered me his soul, a prayer of sorts—and then I felt it. The power, the fuel, the addiction that washed over me. It tasted like the dew on the first bloom of a Starpetal Jasmine."

"What's a Starpetal Jasmine?" I asked, wondering if my small store of knowledge on flowers had really been that minute.

"Oh, it's a type of jasmine that went extinct about two thousand years ago. It could only grow in fire and its petals shone with the light of the Sun itself. It bloomed once every five hundred years and the dew…oh why do I bother? It no longer exists."

She cast her eyes downwards and absent-mindedly ran her hands around the hem of her shawl. The memory of the flower must have opened doors to memories that she had kept shut for aeons. I felt the urge to reach out to her, to comfort her, but as soon as she had allowed herself to be visibly vulnerable, the steely countenance returned to her posture.

"We got married with the land as our witness. We made love under the open sky and the moon herself blushed. I did not bother with anything others associated with the marital life; all I wanted was that submission, that endless fountain of ecstasy… We built a life together, had countless children, and his strength remained for centuries, a boon from the earth.

"But it could not be denied that he was and had always been a mortal. The long years had only served to cloud my eyes from the inevitable fact. While I grew ever fair and strong and famous, he withered and collapsed into himself; muscles shrank, skin wrinkled, and his eyes lost its gleam. I sat beside him as he whispered my name for the last time. My children and I buried him where we first consummated our love, and then I watched my children and their children die, and their children's children—until finally the very last of my blood passed into the void.

"By then, my eyes were no longer wet, my heart no longer ached, and my strength no longer wavered.

Yes, I had had a husband, children, a home. But the price was far too great for me to pay." She sighed and I thought I saw her eyes line with tears and her face flush, but it was only my imagination. She could no longer cry; the years of pain had eroded her senses and she had been left with nothing.

It struck me then: that was what immortality truly meant. To be a constant in an ever-changing landscape, unable to grasp anything as it would surely disintegrate in one's hands.

"It must be terrible," I said. "I'm sorry, truly."

"I'm not so disgraced that I'd need the pity of a man," she retorted acridly.

"I'm just trying to put myself in your shoes, that's all. I didn't mean to be patronising."

"In my shoes?!" The air around us had grown cold. The fireflies fled and took the light with them, plunging us back into darkness. I gasped, for when I looked at her, she had gone white with fury. "If you so want it, I shall grant it. Take this boon now, mortal, and we shall see how you fare."

She brought her thumb and index finger to her forehead, the movements exaggerated and elaborate; another dance. She then touched the corner of my right eye and—

The world exploded. I felt the warmth and the love of unity, and then the intense pain of separation. Felt the earth underneath my nails as I awoke, naked and alone and afraid. The constant fire in my belly, fuelled by fear and the absolute intense desire to survive, making it day by day by a hair's breadth because in the early days, there were oh so many things that could have destroyed me. The scream I let out still lingered, echoing in the deep places thousands of years later.

I hid and cowered and feinted until an immemorable act of kindness to an insignificant insect granted me my first prayer. The power. The ecstasy. The insatiability. With that understanding came my meteoric rise to power. I was powerful. I ruled. I was a Queen, with the world grovelling at my feet. Civilisations flourished if they favoured me. Entire cities snuffed should any displease me. I brought fire and death and misery!

I felt the joys of existence, yet they were fleeting. Centuries flew past like pages of a book blown by a gust of wind. And grief, unlike joy, was eternal. They scarred my soul and remained permanently. My husband's last breath that I caught and kept in the back of my throat. Pain lancing through me because one of my battle maidens had perished and I wanted to cry and weep for her but I could not display any form of weakness.

And my children. All my children returned to the earth, till the last of them, with names I could no longer remember.

The prayers ceased. Slowly at first, negligible, unworthy of attention. Then came days where I no longer bathed in the waves of power. I tried to mend the situation but it was far too late. The memories of mortals were short, and with their deaths, my name was silenced, never to be taken up by their children for they had found other gods. I grew weak—without worship, I was as naked as the day I came into existence. The cycle was complete; once again I was alone and afraid, but old now, older than most and I—

I took a deep breath and vomited the contents of my stomach out onto the ground. I waited for the world to stop spinning and I realised that my face was wet from tears. Once I recovered, I realised that she had brought me back to my home. She stood next to me, the fury that tore through the sea of her emotion absent. All that was left was a hollow dullness in her eyes.

I walked towards the wall and leaned against it, waiting for strength to return to my legs. I wiped my mouth with the back of my hand and thought of lashing out at her; what she did was completely unnecessary! But the agony of her existence came flooding back and it quelled my anger. I stared at her demure face as she smoothed her batik sarong and sat down on the concrete floor outside my room. How did one live in such agony?

I reached out to touch her, to embrace her perhaps, to tell her that it was all right and she had me to talk to, no matter how meagre my existence weighed upon her scales—but just as I began to extend my hand, I knew that it was foolish. She had it once, a dalliance with a mortal, and it broke her. Never again would she allow somebody to take her by the hand into the night sky, only to leave her plummeting to the ground.

She didn't need me. I was temporary. After living for thousands of years, she saw my life as something that wasn't even worth commenting on; it was too bleak, too muddled by bad choices and rash decisions, too vulgar. I knew that, and when I saw her eyes boring into my very essence, I knew that she knew. We were separated by a gap that was wider than anybody could possibly imagine. I could not run after her for ten years, I couldn't even run for an hour. I could not give her gifts so lavish that they'd make the richest men and women pale in desire. I could not live with her in the wilderness. I could not go to all the places she could. I simply could not. I was bound to what I could see and touch and feel, while she could converse with the earth itself. She was the moon while I was the wolf; she had the freedom to dance across the night sky but my paws were set on the ground.

"Your company is good enough," she said.

"And that too must eventually come to an end."

Her hand sought mine and she gripped tight, with purpose. I looked at her questioningly and she in turn smiled.

"Thank you," she whispered. "For tonight. For trying to understand. And for sharing my grief."

I clasped her hand in mine.

"You know I've been wondering," I broke the silence. She raised her eyebrows inquisitively. "The spells you utter, for your magic…what language is that? It's unlike any I've heard of."

"I don't know what to call it. Maybe it had a name once, but I've forgotten it. It's the language of all things, the primordial one. It's the one we all used when the moon was but a babe and the earth sang her lullabies."

"And when you moved around and met other cultures with their own languages, how did you communicate? Did your magic help with that?"

"No, you don't need magic for something as simple as communicating. Language comes easily to us. Some are naturally gifted, some go into the minds of mortals and absorb the information, and some, like myself, learn it. It's not hard for us. Once you've studied a few ancient languages, you see the pattern and then it's a matter of gathering some form of vocabulary." She chuckled. "Remember the king I mentioned?"

I nodded. How could I forget about the list of practically insane demands?

"So after his kingdom fell and the *farangi* occupation began—"

"Wait, *farangi*?"

"Whites," she replied curtly, clearly annoyed by my interruption. "Anyway, there was a Dutch merchant who heard of me. So captivated was he by the impossible tales that he decided to come and see me. He brought a Malay man, a slave of his, to act as a translator. Now, this slave clearly was terrified to see me—which is also a pretty good source of power—so he refused to speak and spent the whole time in prostration. The merchant was so angry he started to abuse the man in front of me."

I shook my head, disapprovingly. "What did you do to him?"

"Nothing, really. I told him, in Dutch, that if he were to continue, I wouldn't be responsible for anything that happened. He continued and well, in that moment, the slave prayed for help. To me. Not to the new gods. But to me. So I granted his wish. He left with the Dutch merchant as a cloak."

It was strange watching her reminisce about flaying someone and making a cloak out of them. The act itself was inconsequential to her, but the memory, the story—that was what she derived pleasure out of. I shivered at the thought. We truly were ants in her eyes.

"Why have you come tonight? I've been pondering the question but I just can't make sense of it."

She laughed and, as always, executed the elaborate hand gestures to cover her mouth. "Need I a reason to walk the lands I once ruled?"

"No, I don't mean it that way. It's just surreal to me. Of all the places you could have spent the night at, of all the things you could have done, you ended up here. I'm just curious if there was a reason behind it."

She stared at me with her piercing brown eyes as one would before chastising an impudent subject. I felt the fear sink its teeth into my bones as I anticipated death through blades of grass. Instead, her expression softened, not out of weakness but of exhaustion.

"Fair enough. I don't have an answer to that, honestly. I go where the wind takes me. There isn't a rhyme or reason or motivation behind it—I just go. Perhaps it's my destiny. Perhaps I am just a figment of your imagination, one wrought out of overuse of drugs or even mental illness. It would make sense, wouldn't it? A beautiful, immortal creature visits you in the night and spirits you away to a fantastical realm. Tells you stories of ancient kingdoms and magic and secret paths."

"Wha—"

"Or maybe I just wanted some company, a reminder of a life that is about to come to a close."

I frowned. If it really was an illusion, then it was a damned good one.

"An inquisitive nature is almost always good but there are times when one should just accept things as they are. Immerse yourself in the moment and enjoy every second of it. The questions serve to distract you from what's happening and in moments like these, the devil is in the details."

I acquiesced and let my questions remain unanswered. We talked instead. Well, I mostly listened because when one told a story about the earth a few thousand years ago, there wasn't much that I could contribute. She recalled the glorious days when her kind roamed freely and there was magic everywhere; as she talked, a sliver of light returned to her eyes, as if the stories helped regain a measure of herself. She told me about a world extremely different from what I knew. How the trees moved in herds through the open land. How beast and man lived and thrived together. A time when the dark nature of man was kept in check by her and her kin, acting as teachers and guides in exchange for devotion and worship.

"Things changed, as they naturally would. Human nature cannot be caged, this applies to both the good and the bad. The knowledge that we gave them was used against us. Our roles changed; where once we were guardians and teachers, we became tools to be utilised. Some—myself even, at times—punished them for their ingratitude, their brazenness. And so the mutual dependency was broken, and we found ourselves with the short end of the stick. They turned away from us. And we lost everything.

"The spirits of the forest and the water left first. They were the ones who suffered the most as man grew in numbers." She sighed, and the wildflowers growing at her feet wilted. "It was heart-breaking to see. One by one, they returned to the One Mother, battered and broken."

"One Mother?"

"Where we originate from. The sum of all personifications of the earth. We are all just different facets of the great jewel that is Her and to Her we shall eventually return, where we can rest, free from pain, forever in her loving embrace. All of the characters; guardian, protector, herder, fighter, hunter... Back together, united in perfection.

"I truly am going to miss this place," she said shakily as a single tear fell onto the ground. She looked at the forest and a wan smile etched itself onto her face.

"You're always welcome back here, you know. I enjoy your company immensely." I managed the words without stuttering. In fact, I wanted her to stay and never leave, for me to serve her forever more. Such was the abyss of obsession I had fallen into.

"That's sweet of you." Tears flowed freely then, from her perfect eyes and mine. "But no, I don't think I can. Not even if I wanted to." The sun had begun its climb and the filtered light shone through the branches of the trees; innumerable lances of light washing over her tearful face.

In that moment, I understood.

"No," I attempted to argue. "You can't."

"All must come to an end, after all." Was it my imagination or was her breathing more laboured? "Countless years. I've drank freely from the infinite well of experience and tasted all that was offered. I've done it all. I've laughed, I–I've despaired. I've loved and I've warred." She grimaced.

"I don't know what to do!" Panic set in and my hands trembled. The colour had drained from her once-radiant face. My vision blurred and no amount of blinking or wiping could stem the raging flow of tears.

She lifted her shaking hand to my face and caressed my cheek. "There is nothing left to do. All these years of–of fighting…I cannot go against the current any longer… No more. Forgotten. I am forgotten."

I took her into my arms and held her tight. Her breath was ragged, and she held on to me.

"There…" she whispered, pointing to the forest. "Take me…"

I carried her in my arms, and felt my heart shatter into a thousand pieces. She weighed nothing. I whispered sweet nothings, not knowing if it helped, and felt her breath grow weaker with every step. As we approached the forest, she asked to be let down.

I obeyed, reluctantly. She held on to my arm while she steadied herself, mustering what little strength she had into her legs. Gingerly, she let go of my arm. She turned to face me and struggled to smile. I wiped my face with my hands and forced my emotions down. The tears halted momentarily. I understood what she wanted to say. A Queen must not show any weakness.

"Your name," my voice came out in broken pieces. "Tell me your name."

Gracefully, she turned to face the trees and began walking. The same tiny steps, but with each, she became progressively more translucent. The wind began to pick up, as if it was there to solemnly carry her essence away. I could see the shape of the trees through her, and before she disappeared in the darkness, she managed the strength to raise her shawl over her head.

A light breeze washed over me and carried with it her voice, albeit just a whisper.

I was left by myself with the brightening sky looking down on me. Grief wounds the soul, and mine had been torn and shredded. I returned to my home with its illusion of safety and collapsed onto a chair. Events of the night played over and over in my mind. I whispered a prayer and dedicated it—with a somewhat foolish and childish thought—to her; the lady of the night, the beautiful forgotten goddess. She who had Sultans, Kings, admirals, and beggars alike begging for her hand. She who rode a warhorse into war with her maidens. She who scoffed at gifts and was content with simple acts of devotion and belief. She who held my hand through the night.

And I wept again, mourning the passing of she who fought tooth and nail to be in the present, she who was forgotten, she who finally accepted her fate.

I wept for Melur.

MOONLIGHT CITY OF THE HIDDEN ONES
Joni Chng

Bram Kinlan's Travel Journal – Kuala Lumpur, Day 11

10:30pm — There is definitely something otherworldly about the Bulan Café, with its rustic wooden furniture, potted plants hanging from the ceiling, and creepy crawlers at the edge of its raw brick walls, illuminated by the warm glow of incandescent lighting.

The mystique of the place has a peculiar effect on me I can only equate to that thrill of being on the verge of discovering something pivotal in a journalistic investigation; that excitement of finding a new lead to a story.

For over a week since setting foot here in the capital city of Malaysia, I believe I'm closing in on that career-making story that's been eluding me. My hunch is telling me it's here in this quaint little cafe.

I chanced upon this place a few nights ago. On my way back to the guesthouse from getting some snacks at the 7E around 3am, I noticed bright lights from an open door in a pitch-dark alley I passed by. I wouldn't have given it a second look, had it not been for the sandwich board sign outside bearing a familiar logo. Imagine my excitement at not only discovering a hangout for people who live in opposition to the natural cycles of the sun like myself, but also the probability of having found what I'd come all the way for.

The cafe is open every day from 9pm to 6am. It's located at a Chinatown back alley, in between rows of old colonial shophouse buildings, tucked away and secluded from the city's nightlife hotspots. Hardly anyone walks past its front door; no hawker stalls nearby and the closest 7-Eleven is a 15-minute walk away. A rather odd choice for a business premise in one of Kuala Lumpur's most touristy parts, isn't it?

'Bulan', I was told, means 'moon' in Malay. How fitting. The owner, Yapin—a friendly gentleman in his late forties—told me he opened this place for night owls, like everyone in his family. His daughter, Izati, works there as a barista and his son, Izam, helps in the kitchen.

Here's the strange bit: for the past four nights I've been coming here, I've hardly seen any customers. I would be engrossed in my reading until the wee hours of the morning, past 5am, having my first and second meal here, and I'd never see a single soul come through the door. The cafe even uses an analogue cash register and issues handwritten receipts. I suppose that's only possible because the place is never packed. How then, I have to wonder, does it stay afloat?

On my third night here, there was a young couple sitting at the corner table, looking very much in love. A few minutes later, they got up to leave, not out the door, but into the curtained doorway behind the counter I assumed led to the kitchen. After about half an hour, only the woman emerged from behind the curtain and walked out the front door.

Also, the family running this place is almost never around. One of them would take my order—the food is heavenly, Malaysian-western fusion; definitely one of the things I'm going to miss—and a few minutes later, it's served fresh and warm from the kitchen. Then, all the staff would disappear behind the curtain. They would emerge, often immediately, whenever I rang the bell on the counter to ask for something. Other than that, I hardly see them.

Last night, when Yapin brought me my order, I reached into my journalist's bag of tricks to see what I could uncover. I made a casual remark about how quiet the place always seems and wondered if this was usual.

"This place is for those looking for a quiet place to chill at night," he said, briefly looking in the direction of the curtained doorway. "By the way, nice ink." He changed the subject by pointing to the half-sleeve tattoo on my left arm, which I explained was my twin brother's work.

When your livelihood for the past decade has you interviewing countless people on just about everything under the sun, you sort of develop a detective's eye for when someone has something to hide. But before I could venture another question, Izati called out to her father and Yapin seized the opportunity to excuse himself.

The father and daughter talked over the counter in a tongue I couldn't identify. Then, Yapin was about to go behind the curtain when a young woman emerged from behind it. She appeared to be in her early twenties, with a headful of thick straight jet-black hair tied up in a high ponytail, and was dressed simply in a plain long-sleeved fuchsia t-shirt and blue jeans. They exchanged a few words in that same language before the father and daughter slipped behind the curtain. The young lady greeted me with a smile and nod when she caught me glancing her way.

"Are you always out this late?" she asked.

I told her in all seriousness that I'm a chronic insomniac. My nights are days and days are nights. I explained that I used to have a healthy circadian rhythm, until I quit my day job and started travelling. The absence of a structured routine and office hours got the better of me.

She spoke English with crisp enunciation, free of any identifiable accent, unlike most of the locals. She asked about the book I had with me, and I held it up to show her the *Tales of Magic and Wonder from Borneo*, an old travelogue anthology that contained a piece written by my grandfather. That seemed to pique her interest as she came around from behind the counter and introduced herself as Munirah as she took a seat at my table.

"Your name is Bram? Like Bram Stoker, who wrote *Dracula*?" she asked with the amazement of a book nerd after I introduced myself, what I do, and where I'm from.

"Yes, it is short for Abraham, just like the author. It's not a penname," I said. My mother is a literature professor, and my father is the editor of one of the oldest speculative fiction journals in Ireland. He is also the author of some twenty horror novels with a cult following. When my folks found out they were expecting twin boys, they decided to name us each after their all-time favourite Gothic horror novel authors. *Dracula* is Dad's and *The Picture of Dorian Gray* is Mom's—both authors happened to be Irish. So, my brother and I were named Abraham and Oscar. They made it a point to call me Bram since I was a kid. It was not often I met people who could identify my namesake without me deliberately telling them.

"Is your brother in the literary field too?" she asked.

I explained Oscar's like the odd one out. He's a tattoo artist. He lives and works in the States. We normally only see each other twice or so a year, whenever both of us happen to be home. The only thing we have in common is our unrelenting belief in the fantastical.

She looked amused. It could just be me, but the way Munirah carried herself made her come across as someone older and wiser in years than her youthful appearance let on. Something about those dark eyes made me think twice about the questions I wanted to ask her. I decided to go against my gut feeling anyway and seized the opportunity to pry—for want of a better word—about the cafe.

"Where did you come from, by the way? I saw you coming out of the kitchen door," I asked with as much casualness as I could manage.

She said Yapin is a family friend. He invited her over, so she came in through the back door for convenience.

Moonlight City of the Hidden Ones

I repeated the "Is it always this quiet here?" question to her.

She didn't answer immediately but gave me a look like I'd asked a forbidden question. She then said, in almost a whisper, that I'm not supposed to be coming here. For a moment there, I thought I was about to learn that this place was a front for some illegal activity. But what she said next made even less sense.

"This is a liminal space." *A what?* "It's a threshold between the physical plane of reality and the realm of infinity. We chose a discreet location for a reason. It's so the uninitiated won't stumble upon it," she explained. "But you are not among the uninitiated, are you? You seem to have a keen interest in the Hidden People."

She slid my book back to me across the table, having flipped to my grandfather's story, which I had bookmarked with a piece of old ephemera. Munirah picked up the bookmark and unfolded it to reveal a vintage menu for a Café Luna in Italy, which bore the exact same logo as the Bulan Café.

"Come here tomorrow. At an hour before midnight, go behind the curtain. I'm sure you're going to love what you're about to see." With a smile, she got up and left.

And so here I am, soon to find out whether I am about to uncover the biggest story of my career, or I'm just the biggest idiot for traveling all the way to the other side of the world in pursuit of a childhood bedtime story Granda used to tell.

Excerpt from the bookmarked page of *Tales of Magic and Wonder from Borneo*, 1959:

The Kingdom of the Hidden People
by Clarence B. Atwood

What was of great fascination to me about the locals was their general acceptance of modernity, whilst effortlessly preserving many of their folk customs and traditions, with their superstitions and beliefs intact.

A story that was of particular interest, told to me by more than a few local friends and travel companions I met along the way, was the legend of the Hidden People—the *Orang Bunian*, as they are known in the local tongue. These mythical beings are the equivalent of fairy folk or elves of our own myths, but unlike pixies with wing and pointed ears, the *Orang Bunian*, according to local folklore, look very much human in stature and all manner of appearance. They were said to possess exceptional, ethereal beauty, with a lack of philtrum as an identifying mark.

These supernatural beings were said to be highly skilled in magic and possessed powers beyond human imagining. They inhabited forests, caves and mountains, occasionally venturing into the realm of mortals to assist mankind in various matters of healing and performing enchantments.

Legend has it they were the descendants of the supreme deity, Kinohiringan, creator of the sky and clouds, and consort of Umunsumundu who created the earth and shaped the mountain known as Kinabalu. A tribe at the base of Mount Kinabalu, which I had the fortune of mingling with, claimed that the Hidden People once lived among humans and that a tribe of them still inhabit the mountain summit. There were medicine men and women in villages within that proximity, known in the local language as the *dukun* or *pawang*, who were able to communicate and request an audience with these fairy folk should the need arise.

The legend has it too that *Orang Bunian* do intermarry with humans, whisking their beloved away to their mystical land and granting them eternal youth and immortality. Sometimes, encounters with the *Orang Bunian* were used to explain away sudden mysterious disappearances in the community. Such was the story I heard of a village elder by the Kiulu River, whose son had gone missing at the age of nineteen and never returned home, nor was the young man ever seen or heard from again. After countless futile searches, the village folk concluded that the youth might have fallen in love with a *Bunian* woman, whom he had taken as a bride, and gone off to live among her people.

As interesting as such stories were, they seemed—if I may be frank—to be nothing more than a means of consolation for a lost loved one. Perhaps the young man merely drowned in the river by complete mishap, was mauled by a wild animal in the woods or had fallen off a cliff to his death. Nevertheless, some form of closure was needed, and what better way to seek comfort than in a fairy tale?

Bram Kinlan's Travel Journal – Kuala Lumpur, Day 12

7am — Turned out there wasn't a kitchen behind the curtained doorway; just a short hallway to a red wooden door with some kind of symbol. In place of a doorknob was a circular keyhole.

Munirah was already waiting for me there. She took out a circular gold pendant from her pocket, fit it into the keyhole and turned it. What I saw behind that door…well, I think I finally get what the Pevensie children must have felt when they stepped through the wardrobe into Narnia.

I'll try to note down everything I saw and heard to the best of my memory, while it's all still fresh in my mind. This is something I would not ever want to forget.

First, we stepped into an identical hallway that led to a similar curtained doorway. Behind the curtain was the same cafe; the same the brick walls and rustic furniture, down to the creeping plants—except everything was on the flip side. Everything that was on the right was now on the left and vice versa. I just walked into a mirror version of the Bulan Café. But unlike the empty place I came in from, this one was almost a full house.

Izati was there, taking orders from table to table. Outside the café, however, was not a back alley, but a patio with an open-air kitchen and grill where Yapin and Izam were serving the orders. They both looked up when Munirah passed by and bowed their heads with their right arms placed across their hearts, which she simply acknowledged with a nod.

Beyond the café was a bustling part of town that remotely resembled Kuala Lumpur's Chinatown after sunset. Unlike that part of town that I had become so acquainted with over the past few days, the buildings here—like the local shophouses, with a touch of colonial design elements in their architecture—looked brand new, like they were painted over yesterday. There were hawker and vendor stalls along the roadside. All the establishments were up and running, and there were people everywhere.

I didn't see any cars or motor vehicles, though I did spot a few bicycles and rickshaws parked by the curb. The road was paved with cobblestones instead of asphalt, and at the roundabout where several roads converged was a huge fountain. Modern streetlamps were replaced with those black lamp posts you still see in some parts of Europe. I could smell flowers in the air, and oh, there were plenty of them lining the streets and balconies of the shop houses, in all their vivid colours. It was all so surreal that I was half expecting to be jolted out of a dream any given moment.

"Welcome to Moonlight City, the place where it never dawns," Munirah said.

I took my phone out to video the place, but it appeared out of power. I was sure it was fully charged before I went out.

"Your gadgets will not work here," Munirah said, seemingly amused. She led the way while I followed. "We are in another dimension," she continued, "one between the physical world we came from and the realm of spirit. It is a complex magical construct created by the lesser gods to provide a safe space where all beings of matter and spirit can coexist."

I wasn't sure I understood what she meant by that, until I spotted the couple I saw a few nights ago. They were sitting on a bench by the fountain, holding hands and talking, looking as happy as ever.

Munirah pointed them out to me as she explained that the man passed on last year. The woman came here to spend time with him. "Only in a liminal space like this can she still feel his warm touch. In here, disembodied spirits will solidify, all manner of magic and curses nullified and rendered ineffective."

We took a stroll along the avenue and I couldn't stop looking around me. So, this was what Granda sought in his extensive travels but never found. *Wondrous* would be an understatement. A few of the people who walked by us bowed to Munirah in the similar gesture like Yapin did.

"Are you a celebrity around here?" I voiced my observations.

"Why, I am Lady Munirah, Chief of the Hidden People, Mr. Kinlan." That wasn't the answer I was expecting, but it was hardly surprising. Though I could have easily taken her for a college student at first impression, I now saw an unmistakable regal dignity in her demeanour. When I pointed out she certainly did not lack a philtrum, Munirah laughed. "We had to make up something as a misdirect for us to blend in when we walk among mortals."

Munirah then went on to explain that long ago, in peaceful times, the Hidden People used to be a prosperous civilisation with a well-organised social order and thriving culture. Now, they are a scattered race. Those who live in the Moonlight City, herself included, are descendants of a lost tribe that once dwelled at the top of Mount Kinabalu, living in harmony with nature and neighbouring tribes of their own kind. They keep their distance from human civilisation, only occasionally meeting mortals who happened to chance by them or the select few who had either earned their trust or invoked their ire.

Their limited contact with humanity is necessary; they are entrusted with secrets from the gods that cannot simply be shared except with a few worthy ones. They lived peacefully atop the mountain until the early 19th century, when interest in Kinabalu grew among the colonisers after several Englishman made an expedition up the mountain that garnered attention. Then, more commercial expeditions up the mountain were organised and peace was disrupted. Some of the locals even sold the secrets they had been entrusted with by the Hidden People for their own gain.

Knowing they could no longer reside safely in the world of mortals, their elders appealed to the lesser gods—deities whose duty was to ensure that order in the universe was maintained—for aid. Thus, they were granted refuge in the liminal and tasked with governing and safeguarding these spaces.

The only drawback, Munirah lamented, is that sunlight and rain cannot reach this place. In fact, nothing living can ever be birthed or grown here. To my surprise, she explained that all the greeneries and flowers we saw were nothing more than magical constructs created for the purpose of adornment; they would neither grow nor wither. It saddens her that her people can no longer live among the flora and fauna they are so fond of.

But the Hidden People never completely severed their link with the world of mortals. "The natural world which we had a hand in cultivating and preserving is too beautiful, too wholesome, for us to leave behind for good," Munirah said, "even after much of it has been desecrated in favour of manmade wonders. Hence, physical entry and exit points to this place has been established in the premises we own and occupy, right here and on the physical plane. It enables us to sojourn to the world of mortals and to stay abreast of the latest happenings in human history. Besides, spending days on end in long stretches of darkness without feeling the warmth of the sun or walking among the trees can be maddening."

How about the stories of people going missing that were attributed to the Hidden People? Any truth to that?

"There have been instances whereby our people would whisk mortals away to our land, not for romance, but to punish them for disrespecting and desecrating certain spaces that were sacred to us," Munirah said. As to what kind of punishment that was dished out, I need not know. "There were also those who tried to obtain our secrets, and they had to be duly dealt with. We are a race endowed with a long lifespan. I'm talking about three to five thousand years, give or take. Time is not of the essence for us, but an abundant commodity. We are also immune to mortal ailments and age very much slower. We do not feel hunger and often eat only to indulge our sense of taste."

At this point, I couldn't resist asking Munirah her age at the risk of offending her. She gladly revealed with a smile that she had just turned 2007 this year. No wonder she didn't seem to mind at all.

She went on, "Many mortals covet these attributes, which is all the more reason for us to keep our distance. Nevertheless, it has happened whereby love manages to bind those of our kind with ordinary mortals. But for such unions to succeed, it would necessitate the mortal to leave behind their world to join ours. Unions with fairy folk are rarely a fairy tale affair, unlike how you mortals like to romanticise them in your stories."

We made our way further into town, stopping at some of the shops just for Munirah to show me around. She even led me across a stretch of indoor marketplace reminiscent of the historic Tabriz bazaar in Iran.

The city appeared to have a fully functioning economy. The Hidden People collected 'treasures' from our side of the world—from books, food items, exotic plants and flowers to household items and objects d'art—and brought them over where they would barter amongst themselves. Cash sometimes exchange hands, though cash that is of value in our world is treated as nothing more than another form of replaceable currency by merchants of the Moonlight City.

The air there was clean; nobody smoked, and everyone commuted either by foot, on bicycles or rickshaws. I even saw a horse-drawn carriage or two. On the streets, you could see people in clothing from different parts of the world and periods in history walking around, like extras on a movie production lot.

I professed, half-jokingly, that I might have found the right place for my nocturnal lifestyle. I'd be willing to risk Vitamin D deficiency to live here. Imagine the number of books I could read and the writing I could churn out!

That made Munirah laugh. "Unfortunately, the circadian rhythm of your mortal coil is rather dependent on the sun's cycles. It would do you a lot more harm to spend too much time here, if your current way of life hasn't already."

That, I can't deny.

According to Munirah, some 5,000 people—living, dead, and in between—come and go here. Less than half of them are permanent residents. Without the sun, how then, do the city's residents keep track of the passage of time, I wondered.

"They don't. Those who live here have chosen to let go of the very concept of time, something not easy to do for mere mortals with limited amount to spare," she said, then brought my attention to the waning moon in the sky, explaining that the moon's phases can give an indication of the days and months passed. Those visiting from the other side, like that woman with a dead lover, would have to do their own time keeping. For that, an analogue watch would suffice, since digital ones won't work here. They could then leave through one of the doorways—and there were many of them, hidden in different premises around the city—that would get them to somewhere in the physical world.

So, there were doorways to this place in other parts of the world. That explained the old menu Granda had kept from his trip to Italy in the sixties. But the doorways can only be opened after sundown, by those entrusted with a key like the one Munirah has, I came to learn.

She took me to a restaurant with immaculate white walls (then again, everything there looked spotless and new), with a patio seating that reminded me of a street side eatery in Greece I'd once been to. As soon as we sat down, a waiter brought us fruit juices with some fried finger food and bowed to his chief before leaving.

I had to ask Munirah the burning question: why did she bring me here? Was she not worried about revealing too much of her secrets to me? I reminded her that I am a journalist, like my grandfather before me, always in search of the next sensational story. For fame and fortune, I could write a piece that would send people flocking to the Bulan Café in search of this place.

That made her laugh again. "That is if you could convince enough people of your story to sell it in the first place. You mortals are so caught up in the rapid progress of civilisation that many have lost their sense of wonder, the ability to even entertain the possibility that there is so much more your sciences can never decipher. Your grandfather included. That's why he never found his way here."

I instantly felt foolish to not have thought about it that way. She appeared deep in thought for a moment, then said to me (noting it down as verbatim as I can recall):

"You are a person who can wield power with the written word, Mr. Kinlan. But unlike your grandfather, you seem to have retained enough of that innocence to believe that the world is more than the sum of its parts. That's why I let you see this place. Call me an idealist if you will, but I believe mortals need something to remind them of us fairy folks and what we have contributed to your world. We have no history books, no annals in the written word that enables the legacy of the Hidden People to live on, besides bedtime stories—if those are still being told.

"A day will come when we are no longer in vogue, so to speak, even in the innocent minds of small children. If mortals stop believing in beings like us, I dread to think what would become of your world in the hands of a generation so self-absorbed, so self-serving, that they can't see beyond the utilitarian function of everything in the world around them. Mortals need to be reminded that there is magic in every element, creature, and plant—and that all living things are being watched over by beings who will not look kindly on their destruction."

I wholeheartedly agree with her. It gives me enormous comfort to know there is more to this world we live in than the sum of its physical parts, and I meant it when I told Munirah what an honour it had been to have met her and be given a tour of the Moonlight City. I gave her my promise that I would do my best to see to it that her message gets out and the Hidden People's existence are not forgotten—without turning this place into a tourist attraction, of course. Though I confessed I didn't have the slightest idea how to go about that without running the risk of ruining my own credibility.

That elicited another laugh. "I am sure you will find a way, in your own fashion."

She then revealed that it was Yapin who went to her a few days ago, asking her to deal with me. He didn't know what to do with the clueless mortal who had stumbled upon one of their premises. But after she spoke to me, she knew I could be trusted with their secret.

I thanked her again. We then made our way back to the red door from which we came in, and I had to ask if I would ever be allowed back into the Moonlight City. She said to look under the pillow I slept on for a pair of feathers from the Great Argus, which is the sacred messenger of the Hidden People. That should serve as evidence that this visit was not a dream.

"Should you require further proof," Munirah said, "keep the feathers somewhere locked up where no one can get to. In three days, they will be gone. But if you don't need any further convincing, keep them as mementos. If you do find yourself in a liminal space again, produce a feather and you will be welcomed in with open arms."

Like the past few days, it was close to dawn when I left the Bulan Cafe and made my way back to the guesthouse. Of course, before I even sat down to write all this, I looked under my pillow—and there they were, a pair of foot-long black-spotted feathers. I'm keeping them safely between these pages. When I get back home from this trip, I'll keep one and lock away the other to see if it would really vanish in three days.

In the meantime, I have a killer travel story to start writing. I already have a headline in mind: *Moonlight City of the Hidden Ones*.

Rosetta and the Fairy-in-Training
Ilnaz A. Faizal

Prick, pull through, prick, pull through.

Rosetta's hands moved like clockwork as she sewed the lace applique to the lilac ballgown's hem. Working with fluid tenderness, she handled her materials just as delicately as she had the previous five ballgowns she'd worked on. With one final pull and a tight knot, she set down her needle and held up her handiwork. The skirt twinkled under the glow of the workroom's candles and was attached to a well-crafted bodice with a sweetheart neckline and flirty, puffed sleeves. It was the textbook example of what every young woman in the kingdom was desperate to have in their closet.

"You've done it again Rosetta," she whispered.

Gazing around the workroom, she took in its disarrayed state. Patches of silk, cotton, and lace lay scattered across the floor. Tall shelves filled with rolls of fabric in every colour imaginable lined the walls. Mannequins stood around the messy workroom; some naked and others covered with garments in varying stages of completion. At the far end of the room, numerous clothing racks held up the finest gowns, suits, and shirts in all the land—each one tailor-made with the utmost care.

Making her way over to a rack packed with ballgowns—each one as vibrant and stunning as the next—Rosetta hung up the dress and released a contented sigh. She allowed her fingers to toy with the sleeve of an indigo ballgown, then smiled as she stepped away and stretched her arms. Despite the stiffness in her neck and spine from hunching over all day, she basked in the satisfaction of wrapping up yet another order.

After three long weeks of painstaking work, the five ballgowns Mr Barnes had ordered for his daughters were finally complete. Silk, tulle, lace, crystal beading—these gowns were nothing short of showstoppers. Rosetta mentally applauded herself as she stared at the glimmering gowns. She couldn't wait to see the girls' faces brighten when they came to pick them up.

The workroom was soon shrouded in darkness as Rosetta blew out the candle on her table. As she exited, she shut the door behind her softly, careful not to make a sound.

The popular yet humble storefront of *Madame Miriam's Gowns & Garbs* provided illumination onto the dark and silent street, and Rosetta hummed a cheery

Rosetta and the Fairy-in-Training

tune as she ambled in. She dusted the displayed garments and ensured that nothing was even a centimetre out of place. This had become her nightly routine ever since Madame Miriam had graciously taken her in as her apprentice. Rosetta was always the first to enter the store in the morning and the last to leave at night, allowing her mentor the bliss of sleeping in and going to bed early every day. The young woman fussed over every little detail—from her tailoring work to the store's appearance—never allowing herself to slack from the esteemed image Madame Miriam had of her.

Rosetta made her way behind the counter to grab a wooden step stool. Before she could retreat to her fluffy bed in the apartment upstairs, she had one final task to complete: once she blew out the store's candles, her day would officially be over.

Strolling towards the front door with the step stool in her arms, she looked up and spotted a tiny, pink butterfly fluttering around the doorbell, its luminescent wings standing out against the brass bell.

Rosetta stopped in her tracks. But as soon as she blinked, it disappeared. Her head swivelled around the room. It was nowhere to be seen. The glass panes of the shop window couldn't be opened so there was no way it could've flown out. Looking up, she checked to see if it had been just as startled at her appearance and perched itself on the ceiling.

No, not there either.

Chuckling, she wondered whether her routine of burning the midnight oil had finally caused her brain to melt.

Setting the stool down by the door, she carefully climbed up and proceeded to blow out the candle mounted on the wall. As she turned back towards the room, the rapid fluttering of butterfly wings caught her eye, and she watched as the striking insect flew behind the shop's counter on the other side of the room. She hastily climbed down and rushed past the display tables and mannequins, rounding the counter to stand behind the till. Yet once again, the butterfly had magically vanished into thin air.

Turning around, her eyes desperately searched for what she was beginning to think had not been just her imagination. Bending down onto her hands and knees, she checked to see if the butterfly had settled on one of the shelves below the counter, but all she could find were Madame Miriam's ledgers. Letting out a huff, she was about to rise when the butterfly flitted right past her eyes. With her breath held and eyes glued to the tiny creature, she watched as it flew above her head and stopped next to another butterfly.

Rosetta's eyebrows furrowed as she stood and watched them float around each other. Distracted by the sight of not one, but two mysterious butterflies, a sudden tickling sensation at her nose had her jumping in shock. Her confusion grew as a third butterfly zipped around her head, and she instinctively stepped back to avoid it. Her eyes trailed back to the store in front of her, and a loud gasp escaped her lips.

An abundance of butterflies flew about the store, all emitting a light pink glow. Rosetta was frozen where she stood, mouth agape as she watched the butterflies rush the room, flying under tables, behind clothes racks, and in and out of dresses and suits. They flew around the mannequins and perched upon folded shirts and trousers on the display tables. She rubbed her eyes but discovered that instead of the butterflies going away as she'd hoped, they doubled in quantity.

The longer she stared, the more butterflies seemed to materialise out of thin air.

Rosetta suddenly found herself overwhelmingly outnumbered. The invading insects filled the space and left little to no room to breathe. She waved her hands around her to prevent them from getting close, but it proved pointless. The more she tried to shoo the butterflies away, the more they flew towards her.

A handful of butterflies whizzed around her face causing her to splutter. She had to get rid of them. Quickly. But how?

Spotting the front door through the thicket of pink-winged intruders, she dashed through the store, swatting her way through the butterflies as best as she could. As she reached the front door, she grabbed the handle and twisted it hard, but it refused to open. She let out a loud grumble—she'd forgotten that the door had been locked by Madame Miriam hours ago.

She silently cursed herself for forgetting to grab the key from behind the counter. When she turned around to begin her journey back, the butterflies began converging in the middle of the room.

They flew in a large circular pattern, creating a flurry of wind that swept through the whole room. Rosetta grabbed onto the door handle to steady herself as garments were sent soaring through the air. Though her vision was impaired by her hair being blasted into her face, she watched in astonishment as the butterfly tornado shrank, and shrank, until it formed a pink sphere of wings, flying so close together that their bodies began melding into one another.

In one quick moment, faster than Rosetta could comprehend it, the butterfly sphere erupted in a grand flash of light that blinded her—knocking her off her feet and sending her crashing down onto the hardwood floor.

Rosetta and the Fairy-in-Training

The first thing Rosetta registered was the throbbing sensation in her head. The next was the darkness. Third, she was lying face down on the ground.

"Oh god," she groaned as she cradled her head in one hand and pushed herself up with the other. Kneeling on the floor, she blinked her eyes several times to fight against the dizziness.

"Be careful! You had a nasty fall."

Rosetta froze.

That wasn't Madame Miriam's voice. Madame Miriam didn't have a high-pitched, twangy voice that sounded like a pesky toddler.

Rosetta's head slowly turned to where the sound came from. She was now confident she had concussed herself during her fall, because how else could she explain what she was seeing in front of her?

Standing in the middle of the room was a girl, probably not much older than Rosetta herself, with the palest skin and tightest red curls Rosetta had ever seen on a human being. She was dressed in a baby-pink ballgown with long sleeves, tall shoulder pads, and a ginormous, poofy skirt that formed a barrier around her.

"Are you all right? Do you need help standing?" asked the mysterious girl.

Rosetta slowly shook her head. Her hands fumbled for the door handle behind her as she slowly pulled herself up, never taking her eyes off the fancily-dressed stranger.

When she finally made it back to her full height, her brain slowly drank in the state of the room. Items of clothing lay strewn about and racks had been toppled over. Mini mountains of dresses and slacks were scattered across the floor. Display tables that used to occupy the space where the mysterious girl now stood had been blasted backwards, now laying on their sides. She pictured Madame Miriam's horrified face upon seeing her precious store turned upside down and gulped. She couldn't allow that to happen.

The mysterious girl followed Rosetta's line of sight and looked around the chaotic storefront.

"Oh, don't worry about this!" she said. "I'll fix it when I'm done."

"You'll…what?"

"Yes, I'll just," she smiled as she waved her hands around the air, "restore it all back to how it was before I got here."

Rosetta felt no comfort from those words, much less the smile the girl gave her.

"Don't you worry. You'll be feeling like a brand-new woman when I'm done with you. You'll look in the mirror and go, 'Hello gorgeous, come here often?'"

Rosetta discreetly pinched her arm behind her back in an attempt to wake herself up. When the peculiar scene in front of her failed to disappear, she pinched harder.

"Now, I'm sure you're worried that this process will be drawn-out and painstaking, especially with the haggard way you look now, but trust me when I say that this will be the best thing to ever happen to you," the girl rambled.

Rosetta looked down at her 'haggard' outfit—a knee-length, brown cotton dress and black flats. She didn't think it was that bad.

"What are you talking about? Who are you?" she asked.

The girl's smile and shoulders dropped as her eyes widened, "Oh god, I can't believe I forgot to introduce myself!" Throwing her head back, she let out a loud, guttural groan. "Rule number one, Genevieve! Always introduce yourself! Why can't you ever remember?"

Rosetta watched as Genevieve paced back and forth whilst berating herself. With her short steps and flouncing skirt, Rosetta thought she looked much like a wind-up doll tottering about. After a few moments of grumbling, Genevieve sighed and straightened her spine before turning back to Rosetta.

"I'm sorry, let me start over. I'm Genevieve, but you can call me Vivi."

Rosetta raised an eyebrow. "Vivi?"

"Yes, all my friends call me Vivi. And since I'm going to be working very hard on you, I thought why not skip the awkward formalities and jump straight to the friendship part?" She grinned. "Besides Genevieve is an old grandmother's name, I hate it when people call me that." She stuck her tongue and made a gagging noise. Regaining her composure, she smiled. "And you're Rosetta, right?"

"Yes. How did you know that?" Rosetta asked.

"Well, I know everything about you! I know that your name is Rosetta and you're twenty-three years old. You work in this shop, and…" A thick silence filled the air as Vivi's smile turned downwards. "Okay, I didn't manage to read everything on your profile sheet but that's not what matters! What matters now is that I'm going to give you the best makeover of your life."

"Profile sheet? What's a profile sheet?" But Rosetta's question fell on deaf ears as Vivi reached behind her back and brandished a long, silver wand. She shook it around until sparkles spurted out of its gaudy star tip. This seemed to please her as she smiled and turned back to Rosetta.

"Let's go!" Spinning around, Vivi began strutting towards the workroom.

"Wait, a makeover?!" Rosetta exclaimed, running to catch her.

Vivi flung open the door of the workroom with Rosetta right on her heels. With a flick of her wand, the candles around the room ignited with fire and Rosetta staggered in surprise at the sudden brightness.

"What on earth?" Rosetta mumbled.

"Now," Vivi said, parking herself in the middle of the workroom, "where should we start?"

"With what?"

"With your makeover! Hello? Have you not been listening?" Vivi gave Rosetta an exasperated look.

"No, no I heard you. It's just…" Rosetta held her breath as she tried to find the words.

"Just…what?" Vivi asked.

"Who exactly are you? And how did you get here? *Why* are you here? I never asked for a makeover. Especially not from some humanised cupcake."

"I beg your pardon!? Cupcake!? How dare you? That is so—actually, no, cupcakes are rather cute. I love cupcakes. That's a rather cute comparison." Vivi giggled as she twirled her hair, gazing off into the distance.

Rosetta furrowed her brows as she observed Vivi's erratic behaviour. Vivi noticed her staring and straightened up again.

"Well, you already know my name, it's Vivi, and I arrived here in that big ball of butterflies. It's how I get around. Secondly, it doesn't matter that you didn't request a makeover, because you've been specially chosen! And I've been personally assigned to you by my superiors. Tasked with giving you the most mystical, magical, makeover ever." Waving her wand above her head, a mini-shower of sparkles rained down over her.

"Chosen by?"

"My superiors! The high council of fairies! They see everything and everyone. And they have graciously granted you a makeover so you'd no longer have such a drab appearance," Vivi explained, eyeing the seamstress up and down. "They pitied you."

Rosetta frowned. "Okay, I'm going to skim over the part where you said mysterious beings are watching over everything for a second, but what you're saying is, your superiors took pity on me for looking shabby and assigned you as my fairy godmother?"

"Godmother?!" Vivi spluttered. "I am not your godmother! How old do you think I am? Really!"

"Well, how old are you?"

"I am nineteen," Vivi proclaimed, sticking her hands on her hips. "And for your information, I'm not a fairy. I am a fairy-in-training. That's why I don't have my wings yet. Fairies only receive their wings once they've passed the final test."

"This concussion must be getting worse," Rosetta mumbled.

"Oh, please," Vivi grumbled. "Look, I have an assignment to complete, and the assignment is you. So you are going to be stuck with me until I'm finished. Got it?"

Vivi didn't wait for a reply as she turned around and raised her wand. "Now, the first thing we'll need is an entourage."

"Entourage? I thought you were giving me a makeover."

"Yes, but in order to impress people you'll need to change more than just your appearance. It's all about presentation nowadays. You need to show up and show out! As my teachers say," Vivi declared.

A curdling sensation zipped straight through Rosetta's throat down to her stomach.

Vivi carefully surveyed the workroom. "Ah, yes! This is perfect!" she said, turning back to Rosetta with a grin. "We'll use these mannequins!"

"What do you mean?" Rosetta's question went unanswered as Vivi closed her eyes and took a deep breath.

With a long exhale, Vivi waved her wand in a circle above her head, then pointed it towards her target. Sparkles exited the wand, soared through the air, and landed on the several mannequins positioned around the room.

As the sparkles cascaded down, the mannequins became wrapped in a glowing, pink whirlwind. Behind the veil of pink light, Vivi's true powers began to take shape. Arms and legs spurted from the mannequins' torsos, pale cotton evolved into tan skin, and thick hair sprouted from the top of their heads. The whirlwind's light grew brighter and brighter until one last blazing flash of light caused Rosetta to turn her head away and shield her eyes.

When she looked back, her mouth dropped. Ten men with snow-white hair and strong features now stood where the mannequins had been seconds earlier. But despite their charming looks, their expressions resembled month-old babies, wide eyes curiously taking in the new world before them. Rosetta's eyes trailed down and horror filled her soul as she realised their unfortunate predicament.

As the men had been the mannequins Rosetta and Madame Miriam worked on, they were now in various states of dress—and undress. Some wore dresses, some just shirts or just trousers, and some wore nothing at all.

"Oh my god!" Rosetta screamed as she covered her eyes. "What have you done?"

Vivi turned to her. "What? I made you an entourage."

"Yes, but they're naked!" Rosetta hissed. Using her hands as a shield, she beelined for the clothes racks and hurriedly pulled garments off their hangers to throw at the men.

"Rule number thirteen of being a fairy: you've got to work with what you're given. I apologise for not yet being able to conjure up stellar outfits out of thin air," Vivi huffed.

"You could've at least given me a warning," Rosetta grumbled as she threw a pair of trousers at the last man, her eyes glued to the floor.

Rosetta looked up and sighed in relief when she saw the men were all finally decent. Under different circumstances, she would've found this image laughable—the men before her were clumsily dressed in gowns adorned with loud ruffles and shiny sequins, and in mismatched suits of navy, ruby, and cream. They shifted about in their spots as they stared at the two women, adjusting to their new bodies.

"Splendid! Let's move on." Vivi smiled. "Our next step is ensuring people will like you."

"I'm plenty likeable."

"Oh yes, I'm sure you are!"

Rosetta glared at the girl's sarcastic tone.

"—But we want your likeability to be invincible."

Vivi hummed as she pranced about the room, inspecting every object and clothing in sight, as Rosetta shook her head in disbelief. Vivi happily opened every cabinet she came across, quickly dismissing its contents when she disliked what she found.

Flinging open a large cabinet by the workroom door, she squealed in delight when she saw what lay inside.

"This will be perfect!"

Rosetta peered over Vivi's shoulder. "Thread?" she asked.

Spools of thread in every colour of the rainbow were packed neatly on each of the four shelves. Tucking her wand under her armpit, Vivi grabbed an armful of spools and chucked them onto the ground.

"Hey! Be careful with those!" Rosetta exclaimed. "Were you never taught any manners at fairy school? Or by your parents?"

"Shh, fret not. Everything will be fine. This is all part of the process. Now don't distract me."

Standing over the pile of thread spools, Vivi closed her eyes and waved her wand until another stream of sparkles appeared. Though not as grand as the mannequin transformations, a pink dome of light encased the spools and Rosetta lost against the urge to look away.

Turning back around, her heart shot to her throat at the sight of thirty-odd squirrels with the heinous abnormality of brightly-coloured fur. Squirrels of red, yellow, orange, and more began scampering about the room, their little claws tapping against the floor as they ran. Several squirrels ran to the mannequin men, scaling their bodies like trees. The mannequin men, eyes filled with bewilderment, began jumping about as if performing an odd dance, scratching at themselves as the squirrels nestled into their clothes and hair.

Rosetta let out a piercing shriek and bolted to a nearby chair, climbing it and clinging to the back.

"Squirrels?! Why'd you turn them into squirrels?!" she cried.

Rosetta and the Fairy-in-Training

"Because if people see you being followed by a group of cute animals who adore you, then they'll see you as a trustworthy and charming person! Trust me, using adorable little animals has been proven to boost likeability by at least thirty per cent." Vivi grinned.

"No, no, no, not squirrels. Anything but squirrels!" Rosetta pleaded. As a small scurry of squirrels scampered over and stopped in front of her seat, she screamed and pressed herself against the chair even harder, avoiding contact with their beady, inquisitive eyes.

"Why not? Everyone loves squirrels! They're adorable! Plus, I don't know how to transform objects into any other animal," Vivi explained sheepishly.

"No, I hate squirrels!"

"Why? They're harmless."

"A squirrel bit me on the arm when I was a child," Rosetta heaved.

"Is that all? Come now, don't be overdramatic."

"IT BLOODY HURT!"

"All right, just give me a second," Vivi sighed. Raising her wand, she pointed it towards the floor, and in a split second, the squirrels were all teleported to the middle of the room and trapped within a large, glass box with small air holes. "There. Now it's perfectly safe."

Wobbling as she climbed off the chair, Rosetta used the fairy-in-training as a makeshift shield and peeked from behind her shoulder. They watched as the squirrels fought to run about in their cramped confinement, squeaking out their displeasure.

"For what it's worth, I did try turning them into normal-looking squirrels but my magic's not quite there yet."

Rosetta groaned and rubbed her face with both hands. "How much more do we have to do?"

"Not much! There are only two more steps to completing your big makeover!" Vivi turned to face Rosetta and tapped her wand against her chin.

"What?" Rosetta cocked an eyebrow.

"I'm trying to decide between freshwater pearls or peacock feathers," Vivi said as she smushed Rosetta's face between her palms, moving it left to right. "You've got good bone structure, so you could probably pull off either." Releasing the seamstress' face, she began to circle her.

Rosetta yelped as she was pinched and poked at by the fairy-in-training. "What are you doing?" she asked, but Vivi ignored her.

"No, no I can't do that, that's a terrible idea. Or maybe I could—yes, and then I'll—oh, no, that's stupid. But what if I—yes, yes that's perfect!" Vivi muttered to herself, beaming as she returned to her original spot.

"Ladies, gentlemen, and squirrels. The moment you've all been waiting for! The pièce de résistance of tonight's makeover! The ballgown!" Vivi announced.

"Oh, I don't need something as lavish as a ballgown. Just a simple thing like this will do," Rosetta stated, fiddling with the hem of her left sleeve.

"Pish posh! I'm sure you would never let a customer leave this store with anything short of perfection, and I intend to do just the same!" Vivi beamed.

Rosetta felt a warmth bloom in her chest and couldn't resist smiling at Vivi's determination.

Vivi slowly raised her wand.

"Wait, wait, wait!" Rosetta flung her hands out in front of her.

Vivi flinched at her frenzied tone and froze.

"How are you going to do this?" Rosetta asked.

"Well, I already mentioned I can't conjure up clothing out of thin air, so I'm going to transform your dress."

"And you're going to instantly transform my dress, right? You're not going to…" Rosetta leaned in until their faces were inches apart, "have me naked?"

Vivi scrunched her nose, "Why would I do that?"

"You know. Because of them," Rosetta whispered, jerking her head slightly to the left. The girls slowly turned their heads to find the mannequin men staring intently at them. They fiddled about with their clothing and scratched at themselves as they remained rooted to their spots.

Vivi nodded her head. "Right. Yes. Them." She placed a hand on Rosetta's shoulder. "You have my word that I will not disgrace your dignity or image by making you nude."

Rosetta let out a sigh of relief.

"Don't you worry! My magic may not be superb but I would never dare do anything along those lines. At least, not on purpose. Yes, there were a few accidents back when I first started learning clothing transformation, but I haven't made a mistake in a whole year!"

Rosetta held her tongue and took a deep breath.

Vivi once again readied her wand and lifted it above her head. "Ready?"

Rosetta nodded and Vivi pointed the wand towards her, encasing her in sparkles and a bright pink whirlwind. Rosetta had somewhat adjusted to the blinding light, and her hands didn't reach to cover her eyes. She was surprised to find the whirlwind ended much quicker than the previous two transformations.

Once her view was no longer obstructed and she was able to see Vivi again, she felt her body involuntarily slouch. She shuffled over to a mirror behind her and gasped at her reflection.

"What am I wearing?" she cried as she scrambled to gather the skirt of the ballgown in her hands. The ballgown was made with the most garish cyan fabric Rosetta had ever seen. What confused her even more was the black lace adorning the sleeveless bodice under a lattice of white ribbon, as well as the skirt's humorously long train. To top off the odd outfit, hundreds of pearls lined the hems of the gown, sagging the garment and sitting uncomfortably against Rosetta's skin.

"Isn't it gorgeous? You're going to turn so many heads with this look," Vivi squealed in delight.

"Not in a good way! This dress is outrageous!" Rosetta kicked her feet in the air in an effort to not trip over the skirt. "And it weighs a tonne."

"I'm sorry, are you questioning my stylistic integrity?" Vivi placed a hand on her chest. "You should know that fairies are some of the most fashion-forward creatures on the planet."

"I'll believe it when I see it," Rosetta retorted. Her body sagged lower to the floor the longer she stood. "Could you please just change this into something else? We can discuss your stylistic integrity later."

Vivi grumbled and raised her wand, pointing it towards the ballgown and creating another whirlwind and more sparkles. When the magic faded, Rosetta was instantly hit with a tickling sensation on her face. Her nose twitched and she let out a small sneeze.

"What are these?"

"Peacock feathers! All the rage in fairy fashion nowadays." Vivi beamed.

Rosetta grabbed the feathers attached to the neckline of her gown and ripped them out, ignoring Vivi's shocked screech. "Perhaps fairies and humans have different interpretations of high fashion," she said.

She turned to the mirror and grimaced at the sight of bronze fabric trailing down her body. The gown was held together by vibrant purple thread and oval amethyst stones embellished the entire skirt. More peacock feathers lined the back of the gown's collar, standing high above Rosetta's head. They were coloured in a striking hot pink and canary yellow pattern that matched the sleeve's ribbon adornments.

"These don't even look natural." Rosetta waved the feathers in her hand in the air. "No one is going to take me seriously in this."

"Why wouldn't they? If I wore this to a gathering of fairies, I would get everyone's attention."

"That doesn't always mean it's a good thing." Rosetta sighed. Marching over to Vivi, she said, "All right, how about you make me a simple gown? No pearls, no feathers. No knick-knacks or doodahs that might be normal in fairyland. Just a plain, simple, straightforward gown."

Vivi frowned. "Fine. If that's what you really want."

Before Rosetta could utter a thank you, she was hit with yet another shower of magic. As the feathery tickling around her neck disappeared, she relaxed and stretched her neck from one side to the next. This gown felt much more comfortable on her body than the previous two, which elicited a smile. She rushed over to the mirror to take in its design, but a wave of confusion quickly washed her smile away.

Her torso was clothed in a lime green bodice with off-the-shoulder sleeves. The attached skirt ruffled at the waist and continued to do so all the way down; the tiers of outlandish ruffles alternated between off-white, olive green, and orange. Her head pounded at the onslaught of colours and she pressed her hand against her forehead.

"Vivi. Seriously?" Rosetta's mouth hung agape as she turned towards the girl. "I said simple."

"This *is* simple!" Vivi reasoned. "It has no embellishments or accessories. Nothing that would make you stand out where I'm from. What's wrong with it?"

"Vivi. The colours, the skirt. It's hideous," Rosetta said.

"Oh, for heaven's sake!" Vivi exploded, stomping her foot on the ground. "I can't believe this. I have been trying my best this entire night and you've just been so judgemental and rude and hated everything I've done!" She began pacing back and forth just as she had in the storefront earlier on. "What makes you think you're correct? What makes you think everyone would see my gowns and think they're hideous? What do you know about fashion anyways?"

"Well, I am a seamstress," Rosetta replied, wringing her hands as she watched Vivi's face flare up red.

"GOD! Honestly, I've been trying to do you a favour and make you look stunning for the ball but I'm sorry to say this, you've been an absolute hissy brat all night! It's like you don't even want to go!"

Rosetta cocked her head.

"I thought this assignment was going to be fun. I was so excited when I learned my superiors were tasking me with a makeover. And I trusted them! Why wouldn't I? They assign all fairies to their jobs! Saying we're the perfect fit for the people we help. Well, you know what I think? I think my superiors got it wrong this time. Because you and I have not got along tonight at all!"

"Wait, wait, wait," Rosetta interjected. "The ball? Do you mean the queen's coronation ball?"

"Yes, the queen's coronation ball," Vivi snapped.

"The queen's coronation ball…that's next week?"

"What?"

Vivi stopped pacing.

"The ball is next week, Vivi."

Silence shrouded the room. The mannequin men's wide eyes darted back and forth between the girls. The squirrels stopped their squeaking.

"It isn't tonight?" Vivi asked, her voice thin and twangy like the squirrels' squeaks. Milliseconds away from breaking.

Rosetta shook her head.

"Are you sure?" Vivi's glossy eyes bore into Rosetta's, causing the older girl's heart to throb in her chest.

"Vivi, is that what this has all been about?" Rosetta whispered.

A loud whine akin to a kicked puppy emitted from Vivi's throat as she sank to the floor, her grand skirt billowing out around her.

"I'm a failure," she croaked, chucking her wand onto her lap. "I can never do anything right."

Rosetta crouched down next to her. "What are you talking about? I'm sure that's not true."

"But it is!" Vivi wailed. "I'm never going to become a real fairy. I had to retake all of my tests last year because I failed everything. I failed clothing transformation, I failed object teleportation, I failed spell casting. I almost set a superior on fire. Twice! Then I finally passed and got my first real assignment—you! And now I've gone and screwed it all up because—because—because I didn't even read the whole profile sheet! I'm so stupid!"

Vivi buried her head in her hands as her violent sobs wrecked the room. A little voice in Rosetta's brain wondered how Madame Miriam hadn't yet awoken from all the noise, especially considering how the walls of the building were rather thin, but she quickly dismissed the thought and thanked the Lord for making her mentor a heavy sleeper. If Madame Miriam ran into the workroom now, she would be mortified at the physical state of things. The idea of Madame Miriam losing all trust in Rosetta for allowing this to occur sent an icy shiver down her spine.

No, there's no way Rosetta could let that happen. She'd worked too hard to get to where she was now. Her hands turned clammy as she pondered over how to fix this entire situation.

Here she was in the workroom with ten mannequins who'd transformed into bumbling men, a collection of rainbow squirrels trapped in a glass box, and a teenaged fairy-in-training bawling on the floor. This would definitely be the strangest night in Rosetta's life, but she realised how she could possibly fix it all.

Carefully so as not to frighten her, she laid her hand on Vivi's shoulder.

"Vivi, I'm sorry for giving you such a hard time. You did a wonderful job tonight." She paused to gather her thoughts before continuing. "When my mentor Madame Miriam first took me in as her apprentice, I was a blundering mess. I never had any formal training prior to coming here and I didn't have a single clue about sewing or fashion. I was constantly measuring incorrectly, confusing pattern designs, and wasting precious fabric.

"And every time I tried to fix a mistake, things seemed to become even worse. There were so many times when I would run away to this workroom, lock the door, and cry for hours. But luckily, Madame Miriam was ever so patient with me, and she taught me that without making mistakes, I'd never learn. I would never have grown from all the hard work and tedious hours spent trying to correct my mistakes had I not made them in the first place.

"I understand what it's like to try your hardest but still come up short, and perhaps you feel stuck in a rut. You're scared you may never become better. But that's not true. You're going to be a fantastic fairy one day." Vivi's sobs had now reduced to an occasional sniffle, and Rosetta smiled. "I know I reacted rather distastefully to your magic, and I am truly sorry. But I was floored by your skills. You did some amazing things tonight."

"I did?" Vivi detached her hands from her face, revealing puffy eyes and a splotchy, red nose.

"Yes! Your magic was incredible! The mannequins, the squirrels, my gowns! That must've taken a lot of hard work, yet you made it look really easy. You're amazing," Rosetta gushed. "All you need is more practice and you're bound to go far."

"Thank you," Vivi hiccupped, the corners of her lips curling upwards. "I appreciate your apology. And your honesty. It's nice to know someone understands how I feel."

"Yes, well, I don't think I'll ever know what it's like to turn inanimate objects into living beings," Rosetta joked, making them both giggle.

Rising to her feet, she stuck her hand out for Vivi. The redhead's eyes lit up with stars as she grabbed her wand and arose with Rosetta's aid.

"Now, about all of this," Rosetta gestured around the workroom, where the mannequin men were smiling at them and the squirrels bustled about in their box letting out squeaks of cheer.

"Oh yes. Allow me to just…" Vivi raised her wand and circled it above her head three times before pointing it towards the workroom.

The grandest whirlwind of the night soared out of her wand, enveloping the mannequin men and box of squirrels. It whipped through the air at a rapid speed, causing Rosetta and Vivi's hair to fly in the wind. In a flash of pink light, the whirlwind dissipated, and Rosetta found that the workroom had returned to its original state. The men were mannequins again, the spools of thread were arranged neatly on their shelves, and her dress was back to its original state.

"Wow," Rosetta gawked at the workroom's pristine cleanliness. As if none of the night's events had ever occurred.

"All fixed!" Vivi sang. "Now there's nothing more for me to do here."

"Hold on, didn't you say the gown was the second-last step to my makeover? What was the last step going to be?"

"Oh! I was going to create a carriage to take you to the ball. But of course, there's no use for it now since the ball is, as you say, a week away." Vivi twiddled her thumbs and pursed her lips. "But perhaps you need a means of transportation for next week?"

"No, that won't be necessary. Madame Miriam has already prepared every tool needed for our trip to the ball."

Vivi's chest fell but her face remained unwavering. "Oh, okay. That's all right then."

Rosetta eyed the tight expression on Vivi's face.

"But you could still come over. Help me get ready?" Rosetta offered and Vivi's face lit up like a Christmas tree. "Not with my gown, though! I've already picked out what I'm going to wear. You could help with my hair or makeup."

Vivi squealed and bounced on the spot. "I'll find the most fashionable yet human-appropriate hair and makeup looks there are!"

Rosetta laughed, touched by her enthusiasm.

"Well, I'll be taking my leave now. My superiors will be wondering where I am," Vivi said.

"Good luck with everything," Rosetta replied.

From around the workroom, hordes of tiny, pink butterflies began to emerge and swarm Vivi.

"Thank you! And thank you for being so kind and understanding," Vivi rambled as the butterflies surrounded her and began to obstruct the girls' views of each other.

"You're welcome! Goodbye!" Rosetta said.

"Goodbye!" Vivi frantically waved her hand in farewell as the butterflies completely hid her away. They merged into one great pink sphere and in one final blinding ray of light, both they and Vivi were gone.

Rosetta dragged her feet around the workroom to blow out the candles. Shutting the door behind her as she left, she smiled realising that through the craziness and absurdity of the night, she had made a new, unexpected friend.

Too lost in her thoughts, her heart lurched as her feet tripped over something upon reaching the storefront. Her arms instinctively reached out to catch herself and she managed to brace herself against the wall. Gazing around, she found that both she and Vivi had forgotten about its disarrayed state. She groaned and mentally cursed Vivi for not following through on her earlier promise. Pushing aside her annoyance and desperation to go to bed, Rosetta strengthened her resolve and picked up a shirt, her fingers nimbly folding it and placing it on the counter beside her. As her lethargic body cleaned the storefront, she was determined to make it seem that nothing of tonight had ever happened.

Madame Miriam would be none the wiser and Rosetta would remain her talented, golden apprentice.

REMEMBERING HOW TO COOK
Sharmilla Ganesan

Shree was turning forty in a week, and she wished she could stop time. Unfortunately, that wasn't one of her abilities—or anyone else's, as far as she knew.

In fact, "one of her abilities" made it sound like there were other things she could do, when in truth, she didn't even have the ability everyone thought she did.

Which was precisely the problem. In one week, on her fortieth birthday, she would be expected to receive guests, to fulfil the responsibility her family had held for five decades. A role left vacant for nearly eight years, since her grandmother died.

Shree gave herself a mental shake; she had been staring absently out her kitchen window. She looked down at the hot, thick cup of coffee she had made, a few spoonfuls of condensed milk stirred in for good measure. She had tried willing as much magic into it as she could muster but, as usual, nothing happened. The coffee remained just regular coffee. Taking a deep breath, she raised the cup to her lips, sipping gently as she closed her eyes.

It was time to face the truth: her family's gift for food magic had not passed down to her. The mysterious ability her grandmother, her Paati, had brought with her from Trichy to Kuala Lumpur, tracing back hundreds of years in her family, was now at a dead end. It was going to go extinct with Shree.

And she was going to let everyone down. All the people spread around the country—friends, strangers, families, communities—who were eagerly waiting for her to turn forty, to reach that particular threshold of life when she was ready to use her powers on others. Powers she did not have.

Her phone beeped, jolting her from her morose thoughts. It was Leena, texting to say she'd be there in an hour. Shree stared at the message, half wishing she had cancelled instead.

The plan had been to practise her magic for the last month, and then do a trial run on Leena, who was somehow firmly convinced that Shree would suddenly come into her talents just in the nick of time. They'd been friends since primary school, so Leena was no stranger to Shree's family's reputation.

Leena had adored Paati and still talked about her endlessly. She reminisced about the "special" treats Paati made to cheer her up and the wonders she felt while eating them. To Leena, Paati was the eternal storyteller, entertaining them with tales plucked equally from Hindu mythology, her raucous schooldays, or her early years settling into married life in Malaysia.

Shree didn't mind, but found it impossible to lapse into nostalgia with so much ease. Her parents had both died in a car accident when she was thirteen. She then began living with her mother's parents, her Thatha and Paati. Since Thatha's death fifteen years ago, it was just Paati and her.

And now her memories of Paati sat too close to the pain of losing her and, even years later, talking about Paati felt too much like grieving. When Leena brought her up, Shree mostly just listened. As she did when Leena repeatedly told her that there was "totally no way" Shree hadn't inherited the magic. After all, Leena reminded her, Shree's Amma, her mother, could do it too.

Shree flung the cup into the sink in frustration. She had told herself there was more time. Paati had inexhaustible patience with Shree's abilities, or lack thereof. This, despite the fact that Amma's magic had surfaced in her teenage years. By the time Amma turned forty—a few years before the accident—she was more than ready to share her abilities with others.

"Wait and see," Paati used to say to Shree. "You have so much time. No need to start worrying about this now."

That is, until Paati was diagnosed with cancer, and died within a year. Suddenly, there was no one to perform the magic.

Paati had never called it food magic, of course. That was just how Shree began referring to it, and it got stuck as that in her head. Paati simply called it "samaiyal", which meant "cooking" in Tamil. With people who didn't speak Tamil, she resorted to an amalgamation of Malay and English and said "masak special": special cooking.

And when the first tentative phone calls to Shree began a few months ago, it was masak special that many of them enquired about. She wasn't even sure how so many people knew she was turning forty soon, or that she was still living in the same house.

After Paati died, Shree spent a lot of time moving around—Melbourne, Singapore, Phnom Penh, Washington D.C. A few years ago, though, she found herself drawn back to KL: partly a longing for home, and partly the guilt of avoiding her expected role. She moved back into her grandparents' house, slipping back into a space that fit around her as neatly as ever, and yet now felt utterly different in its emptiness.

Her neighbours noticed her return, of course. But she marvelled at the reach of the multiple connected aunty networks across neighbourhoods and derived a bit of amusement thinking about the WhatsApp group chat discussions she must be popping up in.

The calls started coming through the house's landline, the number unchanged for twenty years now. The very first one was a woman asking for "Aunty Rajam's granddaughter". She said her husband used to make a visit to Shree's grandmother each time he went up to KL from Johor for the masak special. They had heard that "the granddaughter" would be taking over soon, and wondered when she would be receiving guests.

"My husband ah," said the lady. "He always talk about your grandma, you know. Says eating her cooking is like medicine for his heart. Not the real heart lah, I mean the heart where got feelings. She take care of his feelings, you know."

Shree dutifully took down each of their numbers, promising to call back when she was ready. She unthinkingly gave her email address to one of the callers, and soon watched with horrified amazement as her inbox began filling up with request after request. Turns out, it wasn't only aunties and uncles passing her contact around; stories of her family's skills had moved down to her generation as well. Eight years, as it turned out, was enough time for a sizeable and very eager waiting list to accumulate.

Shree recalled her earliest memory of learning what her family could do. She had been about five, and was at her grandparents' house. Paati sat with her on the floor in the hall, and fed her a mouthful of rice mixed with steamed lentils.

It likely wasn't the first time Paati laced Shree's food with magic, but before, she had been too young to realise. This time, though, as Shree chewed on the creamy mixture in her mouth, her mind swelled with feelings. She couldn't fully understand them, but it felt like wide lakes ringed with coconut trees, like bare feet on soft grass in muddy earth; like singsong voices reciting rhymes, crushing bear hugs, and heady jasmine flowers plaited through oiled hair.

It was joy and adventure and comfort all wrapped up in a bite, flooding her entire body with a golden glow that kept pulsating within her as she ate. At the last morsel, it slowly receded, leaving Shree feeling warm and safe and loved.

She then understood why all these people who kept coming to visit Paati walked in with sombre faces and weighted shoulders but left after a meal looking years younger. She began noticing how, whenever they went to the temple or for a walk around the taman, people would come up specifically to Paati to say hello, to ask after the family, or to simply smile and clasp her hands for a few seconds.

When Shree went with Paati to the weekly pasar malam, none of the vegetable and fruit vendors would take money from them. It was practically a ritual: Paati would loudly insist, they'd just as loudly refuse, she'd insistently tuck the money into their baskets, and in return they'd pile more produce into her plastic bags.

Shree began paying more attention to Paati's visitors. Some faces she recognised from TV or the newspaper. Some came in large, fancy cars, with burly men who waited outside the house. Others were ordinary people, who came in taxis or got down from the bus at the end of the lorong. No matter who they were, they all had their meals on Paati's small foldable kitchen table, sitting on low wooden stools.

And whenever these visitors came, Shree and Thatha would eat in the hall, perched over the coffee table. He was used to Paati's visitors and rarely interfered or spoke to them except to greet them as they arrived.

When Shree was about eleven or twelve, Paati sat her down to explain how food magic worked and what her family did with it.

"We can cook like everyone else. Normal food, any dish, just depends how well we know how to make," said Paati. "But we can do a different kind of cooking also, where we let a little bit of ourselves flow into the food. Our stories, our feelings, our happiness, our excitement—all of that. And when someone eats that food, well, it makes them feel things, in a way they usually cannot. A little bit of our own feelings, mixed with their own memories."

Shree recalled her own experiences. The bajjis Paati made as a teatime treat, onions and potatoes coated in crisped chickpea batter, every bite setting off symphonies of familiar songs in her head. Amma's bubur pulut hitam, where the richly sweet, black-purple rice porridge made her feel the touch of the bark and leaves of a tree she used to climb all the way to the very top.

Gradually, she understood. When people ate these special dishes, they didn't just taste the ingredients or their flavours. They tasted—or rather, they saw, smelt, heard, felt—pieces of memories, strands of their past. Strands and pieces that were teased out and expanded when Amma or Paati drew on their own pasts, and somehow channelled into the meals they made.

Paati said everyone felt this in a different way, that she couldn't control how these experiences manifested. Some people, she said, heard voices or saw images, fresh and intense as the day they happened. For others, the individual memories were indistinguishable, but coursed through them in waves of joy. Some felt music on their skin, or tasted emotions in their mouths, or heard sound in vibrant colours. And along with these, happiness. A feeling of not being alone.

How her family got this ability, Paati had no idea. All she knew was that it stretched back for as long as she could remember. Her mother could do it, and her grandmother before her, and her great-grandmother before that. Paati recalled her mother and grandmother performing rituals for Annapoorni, the goddess of food, convinced that the family traced its magic back to her.

"But I don't know if that is true. I don't pray much to her at all, and I can still do what," said Paati, with a guilty smile.

Paati also knew it wasn't confined to women; she had had an uncle who could do it. But it passed down through their bloodline, and Paati, Amma, and Shree had each been an only child.

Which is how it came to be that they were the only ones of their kind in Malaysia—at least as far as they knew. People came from all over the country, even flying in from East Malaysia, to see Paati, and later Amma. And no one mentioned others with similar talents.

Occasionally, friends and relatives who travelled to Tamil Nadu came back with stories of people who could do what sounded like food magic. Paati would casually wonder if they might be her distant relations, perhaps branching out from her grandmother.

But Paati never seemed more than mildly curious. Her mother had visited Malaysia just twice, both times before Shree was born. Later, Paati went to Trichy to care for her mother in her last days. Since her mother's death, Paati had never returned to India.

She knew more about Malaysia, Paati said, than India. She never even went outside Trichy until she married Thatha. The India she remembered, that she sailed away from when she was eighteen, was gone, and she didn't recognise this new one. She didn't want to feel like a stranger in the place she had grown up, she said.

But for her guests, it was still Indian food that Paati cooked most often: crispy-thin thosai with coconut chutney; puffy pooris with rich, tangy choley; rice and rasam with spicy potato curry.

Over the years though, Paati did adapt her repertoire, adding recipes she picked up in Malaysia. By the time Shree was old enough to remember, nasi lemak was a staple, with Paati's self-perfected fiery-sweet, onion-heavy sambal elevating the coconut milk-steamed rice. Maggi goreng sometimes made an appearance too, wok-fried instant noodles to which Paati added a dash of garam masala. And there was also her mee rebus, yellow noodles in a piquant sweet potato gravy, where her secret ingredients were liberal pinches of sambar and kurma powders.

Of course, the guests would have eaten practically anything Paati cooked. Shree once asked, what did the masak special actually do for them?

"You know ma, I think many people forget how to keep memories that make them happy, the times when they were most themselves. They don't hold on to how it made them feel, how it sounded, how their body responded; as time goes and goes, all this starts going away also.

"My samaiyal, I think it brings back those old stories and memories. It builds them into something you can feel in so many ways, like you are filled with it, covered in it. And it tells you that this happened, that you were once like this. Most of us need to be reminded, ma."

And these experiences lasted until the dish was licked clean, sensations to be savoured and ingested down to the very last drop or crumb.

Shree, however, didn't miss Paati's food magic. What she longed for was the more prosaic cooking Paati did every day. Those were the foods she would never eat again. Ever. Because they didn't exist anymore and never would. When Paati died, a whole collection of recipes—perfected over years, shaped by habits, made just so—flamed out along with her.

Those were the things Paati made specifically for her—simply, quietly, with a sort of calm and unassuming love that she never verbalised and yet fed Shree mouthfuls of.

There would never be more sauteed bitter gourd, cut into just the right-sized dainty pieces, spattered with turmeric and a tinge of chilli, charred exactly enough for a burnt-black sweetness to emerge.

No more pan-fried green bananas, the hard almost-fruit gently flavoured with spices and left to cook until it became pillowy soft cubes with a slight leathery skin—the only resistance it left being a mild astringence in the mouth.

No spaghetti—which Paati pronounced "SPEH-gati"—a plateful of comfort even once Shree learnt what real pasta dishes were. Still, the tomato puree sauce spiked with chilli powder, filled out liberally with carrots, French beans, and potatoes, felt like the luxuries of childhood.

There would no longer be the only fried mee hoon Shree could ever eat, because Paati knew just when to stop cooking the thin rice noodles to keep their chewy texture.

There was never another large pot of moru sitting in the fridge, made only from fresh cow's milk, brimming with a buttery aftertaste that lingered in the small bits of milk curds coating the tongue.

And there would never again be another ever silver container of badhusha—those round, crunchy-soft sweets frosted with sugar and just enough oil to leave the lips coated in a sticky sweetness—pressed into Shree's hands every birthday, with the annual apology of not being able to give anything more as a "present".

For Shree, these longings began not in her belly, but in her chest. It started with the slow warmth of memory, but expanded too quickly into a seizing heat that clenched at her heart and then her whole body. Amma, Appa, Thatha—thinking of them was soft sadness diffused with smiles and pleasure. Paati, though, brought up a hunger so gnawing that it scared Shree, and she immediately choked it down.

So, Shree focused on fulfilling her role instead. The actual cooking part wasn't much of a mystery. The magic was another story altogether. Even Paati never really knew how it worked. She could control it, the way she controlled the sounds coming out of her mouth, but she could no more explain her food magic than she could the inner workings of her larynx.

Paati did what her mother had taught, which in turn she passed on to Amma and then Shree: think back to something that filled you with emotions you hold close and dear, then dwell on it in your mind as you cook.

"And then, it will just come. You will feel it moving from your body through your hands and into the food," said Paati, certain that someday, it would happen just like that for Shree too.

Of course, by forty, it was supposed to have happened in full force. When Shree asked why forty, Paati again didn't really know; it was how her family practised it, and so it became a custom.

"My Amma told me, by the time we're forty, we're not so busy taking care of children!" said Paati, laughing. "But if you ask me, I think we need time. I think we need the years to collect memories and stories and feelings, enough to think about, so we can share them with others. And with some memories, you need time to look back, isn't it; to separate the difficult parts from the parts you want to remember again and again?"

Leena was now sitting in front of Shree at the kitchen table, watching encouragingly. Shree had settled on her go-to, kung pao chicken. Despite

Leena's seemingly unwavering faith, the failure with the coffee hadn't filled Shree with much confidence. She tentatively reached for an onion to slice, sensing nothing yet.

Was this what forty was supposed to feel like, Shree wondered. Surely, she should have things under control by now, instead of questioning her self-worth over something she didn't actually have to do if she chose not to.

There was no reason she had to receive these guests. She could refuse. Or she could take the easier path, and just move out of Malaysia. But she recalled the hopeful quaver in the voice of the woman who called about her husband, the blissful faces of Paati's guests as they walked out, and she knew she couldn't just give up. She wanted to do this; she really did. She just didn't know how. She had tried so many times to let this magic flow, but however much she reached for it, it seemed like there was nothing there.

Leena had been chattering on in an attempt to cheer her up. Shree focused on her words.

"So I was on TikTok a few days ago, and you know what these kids are making videos of?" said Leena. "That song from the Kamal Hassan movie! You know, the rock and roll one where they're all in those sparkly outfits?

"Remember or not, how we danced around to it in your house? The exact steps from the song! And your Paati would clap along for us? So cute lah she! And I tell you, that song is still damn catchy!"

Shree did remember. The many afternoons after school when Paati came to stay, watching Tamil movies, stuffing themselves with strong, milky tea and digestive biscuits to dip with. Paati sitting in her armchair, clapping and humming along to the songs while Shree and Leena bopped madly about trying to imitate the movie stars' moves. Paati did love watching those songs—Shree had caught her many times, nodding and clapping along on her own to a song on TV.

Shree felt a catch in her throat, that familiar heavy sorrow pressing on her chest. She responded instinctively, like one does to sudden pain, pulling her thoughts back, forcing a blurring over of those moments. She had gotten used to this, letting feelings from the past recede before they got close enough to grab hold of her.

But something was different this time. She could still taste the grainy biscuit in her mouth, soaked in earthy-sweet tea. She could hear Paati's humming voice, rising and falling with the music. She could see her face, widened by a grin. Paati was in her chair, but the clapping made her look like she was dancing too. It made Shree smile.

And suddenly, she felt something give within her, like an exhalation, but not of breath. It flowed from all over her body, a warm, prickling energy, and she felt it move into her hands. The more she recalled the images of those afternoons in her mind, the stronger this sensation began to flow.

She reached over and squeezed Leena's arm affectionately, startling her mid-sentence.

Shree was ready to start cooking now.

Sharmilla Ganesan

THE RIVERS AND LAKES
Collin Yeoh

The old man's house was practically a time machine. The young man stepped out from behind the screen wall of the front gate into a spacious, cobblestoned courtyard enclosed on all sides by high walls. On the left and right were long and slim single-storey buildings. At the end of the courtyard was the double-storied main dwelling, its wide folding doors open welcomingly into the entrance hall. The curved roofs, carved lattice window frames, and lacquered wood furniture all looked like they could have come from hundreds of years ago. Only the ultra-modern steel-and-glass skyscrapers that loomed over the roofs belied the impression.

In the middle of the courtyard stood the old man, looking up at one of those skyscrapers pensively, his old-fashioned outfit of pristine white mandarin shirt and grey loose trousers adding to the illusion of a place out of time. The petite woman who had opened the gate for the young man called to him politely. He turned to his visitor, smiled widely, and strode across the courtyard to greet him. When his guest hesitated just half a second too long to shake his proffered hand, the old man leaned in conspiratorially and said:

"You were going to do that fist-and-palm greeting, weren't you? Like we're in a kung fu movie?"

Both men broke into laughter, the young man's sheepish, the old man's good-naturedly mocking. They shook hands vigorously.

"Master; it is an honour."

"Don't call me that," the old man chided, his good humour unabated. "Come in and have tea. Is Tieguanyin okay with you?"

"Any Chinese tea is fine, thank you."

"Ah! Another appreciator of the real thing. Much better than that cheap Western stuff. No wonder they drown it in milk and sugar, eh?"

They entered the entrance hall and seated themselves at an ornately carved table with four matching stools. The morning sun streamed through the open folding doors from the courtyard outside, bathing the room in bright, cheery light.

"Ah Chun, thank you." The old man nodded to the servant woman as she served them a tea set.

"Will you be needing anything else, sir?" she asked.

"No, all is as we discussed. Please spend the rest of the day with your daughter, and remember to give her my regards," the old man answered. The woman bowed low and left quietly.

As was his hostly duty, the old man poured the tea into the young man's fine porcelain tea cup before his own. He raised his cup, gave a second to the young man to do the same, then inhaled from it deeply before taking a generous sip.

"How do you like it?" he asked when the young man had taken his sip.

"Wonderful bouquet," said the young man sincerely. "And excellent flavour."

"Good, eh?" The old man grinned. "I befriended the man who grows the stuff just so I could get my own personal supply. Benefits of a well-travelled life."

"You also paid off his debt to gangsters and rescued his daughter from a Quanzhou brothel. He owes you more than free tea," the young man said.

The old man's smile turned wry. "You've done your research, I see."

"Having learned of your extraordinary deeds, how could I help but seek out such an exceptional man as yourself?"

"Already with the flattery!" The old man laughed. "It's been an age since I heard it from one so young, however."

The young man bowed his head humbly. "Appreciation for the ancient arts has not entirely disappeared from the world. And now that I've met you, it is my hope that the arts themselves have not either."

"All this before you've even finished your first cup of tea," said the old man, taking another sip from his own cup. "In my day, guests knew how to entertain their hosts with pleasantries before turning to business."

Collin Yeoh

The young man started guiltily. "Begging your par—"

"Oh, think nothing of it," the old man said with a dismissive handwave. "I have always found it amusing that the young, with so many years of life ahead of them, are always so impatient. Whereas I, in the twilight of my life, like to take things slow."

"I'm sure a man of your great health has many more years to look forward to," said the young man, as he took another sip of tea.

"May we both be so blessed." The old man drained his cup, then put it down in a business-like manner. "So, since your patience is being so sorely tested, how shall we proceed? A demonstration, perhaps? To prove I am who you think I am?"

"I would not disrespect you by asking you to prove anything to me," the young man said. "But it would fulfil my lifelong desire to see your skills in the flesh, Master."

"Don't call me that," the old man said again. "What would you like to see, then? I have studied and acquired over two thousand different skills and techniques. Although I've probably gotten rusty at a few." He frowned. "How many decades has it been since I've practiced the deer horn knives…?"

"What about…" A light of pure wonder shone in the young man's eyes as he hesitated. "…qinggong?"

The old man laughed again. "I should've known you'd pick that one." He looked out the door thoughtfully. "You came from the east, didn't you? Did you notice a plum tree with its flowers in bloom, at the corner of this lane?"

"I don't recall," answered the young man.

The old man got up and walked out to the courtyard, followed by the young man. Then, without breaking stride, on a step as effortless as any other, he rose into the air like a leaf caught on the wind, a wind that blew him to the top of the eastern wall where he alighted as gently as the step that took him there was.

"I really love plum blossoms," he said. And then he took another step, one that took him soaring off the roof and out of sight.

The tiny east-to-west lane outside the house had been built centuries ago to allow no more than two rickshaws to pass each other. About a hundred and fifty paces to the east, it ended on a slightly wider lane—built to allow bullock carts—at the corner of which stood the plum tree. The young man ran out of the house in time to see the old man landing on a branch that could not possibly have supported his weight, but did. He stood there, seeming to find no difficulty in balancing on that thin branch, looking at the plum blossoms blooming at his feet in a riot of colour. Then, after a moment, he stepped off the branch, which swayed as lightly as if he were a small bird taking flight, and sailed through the air in a graceful arc that ended precisely back on top of the eastern wall of his house.

Running back into the courtyard, the young man saw the old man float down to the ground with as much seeming effort as descending a single step.

"Forgive me for not bringing back some of those plum blossoms; they were so beautiful that I couldn't bear to pluck them and kill them. Besides," the old man said, "it'd be weird for a guy to give another guy flowers, wouldn't it?"

Awestruck, the young man fell to his knees. With his hands on the ground on either side of his head, he bowed reverently. "Master!"

The old man sighed deeply, in the manner of one for whom the countless times he begged people not to do something did nothing to keep them from doing it. "I said not to call me that."

"Please, Ma—sir," said the young man, rising from his bow but maintaining a deferent posture. "At least allow me to honour you with a toast." He extended an ushering hand towards the house; the old man mirrored the gesture, as a proper Chinese gentleman should, before they reentered the house together.

Seated once more, raising his freshly refilled tea cup towards his host, the young man said, "To a true...*gao shou*."

The old man narrowed his eyes, but since the young man had already drank to the toast, he was obliged to do the same. When his guest had called him Master, he had used the term *da shi*; *gao shou* was a different term, but it meant pretty much the same thing. "That's not something I like to be called either."

"But how can you not accept either title? When you've clearly mastered such awe-inspiring martial skills?"

"Well, for one, because the true masters were those from whom I learned these skills. The man who taught me how to reduce one's own body weight to that of a leaf on the wind took twenty-one years to master it. Do you know how long it took me?" There was a sadness the old man could not hide in his eyes. "Sixteen days."

"That is no surprise," said the young man. "After all, you are the true-born prodigy of legend. You possess a flawless, unrestricted flow of qi throughout your body, the kind that takes ordinary men a lifetime to develop, but that you were fortuitously born with.

Every true martial artist has dreamed of being you, the one in a million."

"One in a *lot* more than a million, my friend! Otherwise there'd be sixteen hundred of me in China alone!" The old man laughed, and continued. "I travelled the length and breadth of the world, learning from every master I found. Each time, I acquired in days skills and techniques that my teachers took years to perfect. This has not always been a blessing." He sighed again. "The patience and dedication needed to study something for so long, the time for contemplation that it affords, and the wisdom that that in turn brings—those were the qualities the old masters possessed. But I? I gained none of them. No, I don't consider myself a master. I don't think I've really mastered anything."

"But…compared to the rest of us…" The young man sputtered incredulously. "How can you say that?"

"I make sounds in my mouth and push air out through my throat," replied the old man dryly. He stood up and walked outside once more, pacing slowly around the courtyard with his hands behind his back like a schoolteacher.

"I didn't earn this qi flow, this ability to harness it so quickly and powerfully. Not like the masters I learned from, who poured years of blood and sweat into their training. For me, it was but an accident of birth." Though he faced the courtyard walls as he spoke, his gaze was into the mists of his memories. "Sometimes I feel like accidents of birth are the source of all injustice in this world. So many people are born with things they do not deserve. For good and ill."

"But it was for good that you used your inborn talent," said the young man, following him out to the courtyard. "Your accident of birth was a blessing to the world. The Tieguanyin farmer is just one of countless people you have helped throughout your life. The eighty people you saved from the mudslide in Sichuan. The serial killer you caught in Kaohsiung. The human trafficking ring you destroyed in Penang. You are a silent, secret hero, fighting for justice and righting wrongs around the globe, and never once seeking fame or fortune for your deeds. You are the last living wuxia—perhaps, even, history's greatest."

The old man laughed. "Wuxia? Now that's a fancy word. The great wuxia, martial heroes who live by the code of jianghu! As seen on TV, and in bookstores and cinemas near you!"

His mocking tone swiftly turned to a scholarly one. "Jianghu. 'Rivers and lakes.' Ever wondered why they call it that?" he asked the young man, who only frowned in confusion. "Because that's where these wuxia live. In the rivers and lakes—and forests, and mountains, and deserts, and swamps. Anywhere but cities and towns. Anywhere where there are no courts, or judges, or police, or laws. Because they live freely, by no law but their own."

"By their honour," said the young man.

"Honour? Oh, that's certainly what they called it." There was no mistaking the cynicism in the old man's grin. "Uphold justice. Right wrongs. Funny how the wrongs they dwelled on the most were the ones done to themselves. Funny how *that* was their idea of honour."

He turned to the young man with that grin. "And as for justice? What 'justice' awaited those who defeated their masters, or seduced their wives, or stole their manuals and learned their secret techniques? These supreme heroes, skilled in the mightiest martial arts, knew only how to hurt, maim, and kill. There were no prisons in jianghu. No monetary compensation. No rehabilitation, and certainly no community service. Only hurt, maim, or kill.

"And what if you were a child, or sworn brother, or pupil of one who was hurt, maimed or killed? Why, it would seem terribly unjust to you, of course—an injustice that you must right. Which you would do so the only way you know how, with the only skills you possess—to hurt, maim, and kill."

The old man shook his head. "I have lost too many friends to this concept of 'honour'. Too many good, kind men and women who should not have died. And who should have known better."

"So you washed your hands in the golden basin? You left jianghu?" asked the young man.

The old man burst out laughing, but whereas before he had laughed in self-amusement, this time it was from genuine surprise. He laughed so long and hard that he covered his face in his hands, making a visible effort to compose himself.

"No, no, I didn't leave. And I didn't wash in any golden basin either. Where would I get one of those? Does Ikea sell them?" He had himself another long and hearty laugh.

"Don't get me wrong; I'm not laughing at the idea of retiring from jianghu. Swearing to never raise a fist in anger again? I'm all for it. I know many who did, and who enjoyed a few precious, well-deserved years of peace at the end of their lives. But I had a reason for not following them, though some pleaded with me to do so. You see, I thought I could reform jianghu."

The old man lifted his gaze upwards, as if looking to what he once thought was a bright future. "The answer seemed as brilliant to me as it was simple. For all that these noble and chivalrous martial artists claimed to respect one another, all they really cared about was who was better. Better at kung fu, better at fighting, better at beating one another up. That's why they guarded their skills so jealously. That's why they valued their precious manuals more than gold. If someone stole your gold, they could just return it. But if someone stole your secret passed-down-through-generations technique, your whole clan had no other choice but to hunt him down and kill him.

"So, I thought, why not expose it all? Teach everything to everyone. Whatever skills I gained, I passed on to anyone who wanted to learn. Stop thinking of martial arts as jealously-guarded secret weapons. Start thinking of them as *art*. Like calligraphy, or poetry, or baking the perfect mantou. Things of beauty whose beauty is their inherent value, and that should therefore be shared with anyone with a desire to appreciate them. After all, is a Hung Gar form lessened because a skilled Baguazhang practitioner can beat it? Is the Bixie Sword style any less beautiful than the Nine Swords of Dugu that was specifically created to defeat it?"

"Ingenious," said the young man.

"You think so?" The old man chuckled. "Nice of you to say. Because *very few* others thought so. Nearly everyone I taught answered 'Yes!' to those two questions I just posed. They only wanted to learn the best, strongest techniques, the ones that could beat all the others. If they found out that I knew a supposedly better style than the one they were learning, they'd abandon it and beg me to teach them the other. Or…" His eyes widened in exasperation. "They'd want to learn the internal arts—qinggong and neigong. The fancy, spectacular techniques, the ones that look so cool in those movies and TV serials. The ones that took decades for the world's greatest martial artists to learn. The ones that they *cannot* master in days like I did, because they're not *me*."

"But your philosophy survived and thrived," argued the young man. "Millions of people now practice Chinese wushu in thousands of schools and clubs all over the world. That only happened because they appreciate the grace and beauty of our art. Because they see the martial arts as art, as you taught."

"Yes, that happened. And I'm glad it did." The old man smiled ruefully. "But that could only happen in an orderly world. A world where one can survive without scrambling for power over others. A world where everyone is subject to a higher authority to whom they could plead when wronged, so that they need not repay that wrong in kind. In other words, a world with courts, judges, police, and laws.

"No, I didn't need to leave jianghu. It no longer exists. Cities lie on the banks of every river, and the lakes are for resort towns and holidaymakers. There's no place left in the world where one is free to live outside the law." His smile turned mocking, but his eyes showed that it was only himself that he mocked. "And it's not like I can even claim that was my doing. Oh no, far greater forces than I created that world. *They* reformed jianghu…by destroying it.

"Now, the only ones who still think themselves part of 'jianghu' are gangsters. Lowlifes. Thugs and bullies, drug dealers and flesh peddlers. Any claim to 'honour' that they make is a sick joke. And how many of them have even taken a single kung fu lesson? Probably couldn't even tell a panther fist from an eagle claw." He sniffed haughtily.

"So there you have it—the sum total of an old man's life." The old man turned back to his young guest. "I sought wisdom, but learned only how to fight. I sought peace, but failed to prevent countless deaths in petty brawls and vendettas. I sought to change the world, but the world changed around me all on its own. Is this the great *da shi* or *gao shou* you seek? Am I still—what did you call me—'history's greatest wuxia'?"

"Of course you are," answered the young man. "For all your humility, you are still a living legend. Your mastery of qinggong proves it, as does all your other long-lost skills."

"What of them?" There was a note of exasperation in the old man's laugh this time. "Haven't you been listening to me telling you how meaningless they are? Criminals terrorise innocents because corrupt authorities allow them to. Mudslides occur because greedy men ravage the land for billions of yuan. Not because there isn't a heroic wuxia there to save the day. Injustice happens because too many are born with too little, and a tiny few are born with too much. No one man—no matter how well he fights, or flies—can change that."

He held his hands before him and looked down on them sadly. "And if he can't...then what good are all these wondrous skills?"

In response, the young man stepped out to the middle of the courtyard and took a position a dozen paces from the eastern wall. He dropped into a stance that the old man recognised as belonging to the Pai Mei style, and took three deep breaths. Suddenly he executed a palm strike accompanied by an ear-splitting shout, and twelve paces away, the wall before him *cratered*, as if struck by an iron battering ram. Yet nothing had touched it that the human eye could see.

The old man raised his eyebrows. "Good neigong. Who taught you?"

The young man stepped out of his stance and stood proudly. "The greatest scientists in China—and the world."

The old man nodded. "So, it is your turn to reveal who you are." He returned his hands behind his back calmly and faced the young man. "You are another true-born prodigy, are you not?"

"I am. And in me, your knowledge will live on. I will master all that you have learned as quickly as you did. In me, the name of jianghu will be reclaimed from the scum of society and restored to honour. In me, the power and glory of the wuxia will flourish once more."

"You alone will do all that?"

"No, not me alone. An army."

Now it was the young man's turn to pace the courtyard, though his steady gaze never left the old man's. "I understood every word you said. I feel their truth in my heart. The wuxia of old were mighty—but fractured, self-centred, purposeless, just as you said. Had they been united, our kingdom would never have fallen to the Manchus, or the Mongols before them. We would never have been the whipping boy of a dozen foreign nations. We would never have endured the Century of Humiliation!"

Amused, the old man said, "I'm older than dirt, but all that's still a little before my time."

"But surely the shame of it boils your blood, as it should all Chinese! The foreign devils plundering our land, carving off islands and territories for their own. Forcing our emperor, as foolish and corrupt as he was, to surrender our dignity to them. Our people starved while they sat in their colonial houses, drinking *our* tea on *our* soil. And then from the east, an invasion of the worst, most barbaric monsters in history. *Millions* raped and murdered!" Any semblance of calm the young man had previously shown was gone now. "Tell me that these injustices do not anger you, that you cannot see its effects till this day!"

"Perhaps I do," said the old man softly. "So how will you right these wrongs?"

"*We* will. You and I." The young man stretched out a pleading hand as he spoke. "Our gifts should not be ours alone. As you said, they are wasted if they belong to but one man in every generation. But now we possess the ability to share those gifts. The scientists who taught me to harness my qi have also been researching how to enable it in others—if you teach me. By studying me as you help me cultivate my power, they can uncover the secret of unlocking any man's qi flow."

His gestures grew more emphatic, more urgent. "We can build an army of martial heroes like ourselves—heroes of invincible skill, unassailable honour, and unwavering loyalty to the nation. With this army, we will avenge our humiliation. We will wrest the title of 'global superpower' from the corrupt and unworthy West. *They* will be humbled before us. And we will once again be what we were always meant to be—the centre of the world."

Suddenly, he dropped to his knees before the old man. "But first, you must agree to teach me. You must accept me as your pupil. You must allow me to call you…Master." He bowed low once again, hands on the ground on either side of his head, as he called the old man by yet another term: *shi fu*.

For a long moment, the old man silently contemplated his would-be student.

Then he said brightly, "Alright. Shall we start with the deer horn knives?"

The young man raised his head. "The…what?"

"I can barely remember the forms now, but I'm pretty sure I know a few that nobody teaches anymore. I better pass them on to you before I forget them completely, don't you think?"

The young man frowned. "Surely it is more important that you teach me to cultivate my internal power. Perhaps others may be interested to—"

"Of course, of course." The old man turned away from the kneeling young man and began a leisurely stroll. "Sorry, about that army you mentioned, I'm a little unclear about its purpose. What would they do exactly?"

"Serve our nation. Restore its glory."

"Yes, but *how*?"

"However our leaders see fit. Our missions will be directed by our highest-ranking generals."

"Wuxia serving the military? Sounds like an oxymoron to me. Jianghu is supposed to mean freedom, remember?"

"We will redefine it then. It will mean something new and greater."

"I see, I see." A hint of mischief played at the corner of the old man's smile, just barely out of the young man's sight. "So this army…it would go to war, yes? Who against?"

"All our enemies. From within and without."

"By 'without', you mean other nations, then? Which ones? The ones responsible for the Century of Humiliation, or others as well?"

"Any that challenge us." The young man grinned wolfishly. "And it would be a war they'll never be prepared for."

"Impressive, impressive." The old man continued to stroll, causing the still-kneeling young man to shift on his knees in order to keep him within sight. "But you said 'within' as well. So…who would that be?"

The young man's eyes narrowed. "Whoever that engages in terrorist activities against the state."

"And what constitutes 'terrorist activities'? Peaceful protest? Criticism of authority?" The old man stopped pacing, and now faced the young man directly. "Or simply having a language, culture, and religion that the state does not approve of?"

"Don't be a fool!" the young man barked. "There's nothing 'peaceful' about separatist rebels and race traitors! They only pave the way for the Western imperialists to conquer us! If they haven't the good sense to be loyal to their ancestral homeland, then we will teach them a lesson—that there is only *one* authority, *one* government, *one* nation that they belong to. And if they won't learn, then yes, we will wipe out their worthless culture. And their deviant religion. And their vulgar peasant's dialects that aren't even fit to be called Chinese."

The old man replied with a stream of Cantonese profanity that graphically described a number of vulgar acts, the young man's mother to whom the acts were directed at, the specific parts of her body they should be performed on, and some adjectives referring to the aforementioned body parts' cleanliness. This gave him the pleasure of seeing the young man startled, but only for a moment.

Regaining his composure, the young man chuckled as he got to his feet, all trace of deference gone. "So, you're nothing but a filthy Southern malcontent after all. Pity. Our scientists could have studied me as you taught me. Now, they will study *you*—on the dissection table. It will make no difference."

"You aim to take me alive?" the old man asked calmly.

"You think I can't? Because of your supreme martial skills?" The young man laughed harshly. "We are well-prepared for you. You see, we have discovered a rare herb that, when distilled and concentrated, produces a singular effect: it blocks the flow of qi."

The old man nodded knowingly. "Xiongcao. Only grows on the peak of Mount Hua."

"You know it? No matter. You've already taken it." He began advancing towards the old man, slowly and menacingly. "I slipped a few drops into your tea cup when you were performing your little flying trick. Oh don't worry, the effect isn't permanent. It'll wear off when you are strapped and secured in our laboratory."

As he neared striking distance, he settled into the same fighting stance as before. "Now, old man, how good is your wushu, now that your superpowers have been stripped from you? I'm looking forward to findi—"

A lightning-quick strike to the chest interrupted him, even as he attempted too late to block it. Suddenly he felt a sharp pain, far greater than the strike should have caused. A wave of dizziness overtook him and his legs collapsed. As he lay on the cobblestones of the courtyard in agony, his eyes widened as he realised what he had been struck with.

"Dian mai!" he gasped.

"Eh. Not really." The old man shrugged. "I do know pressure-point attacks, but they're mostly quite impractical. I'd have to hit six different points on your body, which you're obviously quick enough to block. No, what you're experiencing is called *commotio cordis*—cardiac arrest caused by disruption of the heart rhythm at a precise moment during the cycle of a heartbeat. You don't need qi for that, just really good hearing."

He leaned over the gasping, writhing young man. "I learned it from Wikipedia. And a good VPN."

The last thing the young man saw was the old man's utterly dispassionate face.

The moment the young man breathed his last, the old man's sharp ears heard what he had been expecting to hear. Men, over a dozen of them, pouring out of vehicles parked at discreet distances, barrelling at full speed toward the house. Special Operations Forces troops, most likely. Armed, definitely. Pissed off, quite probably.

The young man had been right. The xiongcao had blocked his qi, rendering his most powerful abilities useless. But he had already known that when he drank that second cup of tea. Besides, he still had all his kung fu. To test that against modern body armour and submachine guns…the fight would be the stuff of such legend as the jianghu has never known.

Fitting, then, if it should be his last. They wanted to take him alive.

He would make sure they didn't.

FLOWER FELL
Syazwani Jefferdin

We weren't sure what started it. The petals took root in our hearts, consuming us from within, growing a rainforest in our lungs. They branched from our stomach acids into the pores on our skin. And there, they bloomed.

A famous ancient myth from the Japanese clan, the *Hanahaki* disease was an illness that one would catch when they experienced unrequited love. The person who caught it would cough out flower petals until they eventually died. The only cure that ever worked was as harsh as the illness: to go through a procedure that would save you but make you forget your love.

But what our ancestors failed to realise was the fact that the disease came about not from a human's unrequited love towards another human. Rather, its true source was nature's unrequited love. Towards us humans. The *Hanahaki* disease is a curse placed on every child of Adam and Eve. That myth, a symptom recorded thousands of years ago, bloomed into the damnation that took uncountable lives. Most of the first generation did not survive the change.

However, humans are adaptable creatures. They began to migrate from the big cities to the countryside, closer to the forests, the greenwoods, plantations, anywhere where they could connect to the trees, and to the earth. To our mother nature. At some point, the change became the norm. We were the lucky ones, birthed thousands of years after the curse first took root. We grew used to sharing our human bodies with nature.

ೃ

Spring was coming.

Looking up at the sky, my right eye squinted against the morning sun while the white moonflower, which bloomed where my left eye should be, reached towards the soft light like a hungry desperate child. It wasn't like it had any fingers or hands, but I could tell that it was pleased to bask in the early morning sunlight. The small white baby's breath flowers along my arms tingled as the sun brushed my skin while the single white Bouvardia on my collarbone hummed with joy at the cool breeze.

For all the white flowers on my skin, my irises and hair were dusky black. The contrast in colours, to some, was startling. In most cases, the floras' pigmentation or the leaves' chlorophyll would seep into the roots of our hair, turning our tresses into a bicolour or, sometimes, tricolour combination. Some would even have differing skin tones if the pigmentation had stronger effects.

As I stroked the Bouvardia gently with my fingertips, I wondered whether mom and grandma were going to photosynthesise too. I wondered what it was like to not have to sit under the sun every other day…to not be surrounded by foliage…to not be consumed by foliage…

"Maybe they'll skip today for big sis," I mused to my flowers. "She's due anytime soon so she's going to need all the care."

"Talking to yourself again? Or are you conversing with your flowers?"

My attention shifted to the blonde boy who had taken a seat on the boulder beside mine. "Good morning to you too, Haku."

He smiled at the greeting, the carnations around the side of his head glowing a beautiful red under the morning light just like the red highlights on the tips of his hair. "Here you go, lil dudes." Pulling both his pants legs up to his knees, he thrust his legs out into the sun, revealing tiny red daisies that poked out from around his ankles and below his thighs.

"So, have you considered my proposal?"

I blushed, averting my gaze. "I–I don't have the time to think about that! I'm busy with the new baby's arrival and all. Big sis really needs me now more than ever. Especially after…"

Haku's grin faltered slightly. "Must've been hard for her to lose Abel like that."

I took my time agreeing. "Yeah, it was."

We were the lucky ones? Well, not all of us, I guess. Sometimes, the effects of the curse continued through a particular bloodline and someone would become a sacrifice. Unfortunately, it had taken my older sister's husband and soulmate, the kindest and softest man she had ever dated. When Abel began to vomit out a mixture of petals and roots and leaves and blood, the glimmer of hope had immediately left my sister's eyes. Her bright pink bougainvillea wilted. He lasted three days before he took his own life by consuming the colourful Oleanders that ran down his back. The curse was a far greater pain than the flowers' poison.

What a joke.

"Ahh, keep frowning like that and they'll turn grey, your flowers."

"Oh, shut up!" I turned away to stare absent-mindedly at the little stream flowing gently by our bare feet. Of all the memories, my mind *had* to wander to the one that had caused us so much suffering and heartache.

"Are you afraid?" Haku tried to get a glimpse of my face.

"What of?"

"That if we marry, I'll get the disease and die."

I gulped, crossing my arms around my chest as if to hide the anxiety sprouting from the roots of my heart. Delicate fingers reached to pull them apart. I turned to face him, my left hand in his.

His blue eyes crinkled at the sides as they tenderly gazed at my baby's breaths. "White is precious and all, but don't you think pink would be better?"

I felt the blush creeping back onto my face. "Huh?" I scoffed. "If you want pink, go find pink."

Syazwani Jefferdin

He tilted his gaze towards me, a mischievous glint in his blue orbs. "You know that red and white makes pink, right?"

I couldn't even react when he leaned down to brush his lips against the single baby's breath on my ring finger. My body shivered involuntarily as he looked back up at me with a teasing chuckle.

"Oh my, your white petals are turning pink, Sa-ku-ra. They're finally living up to your name."

I snatched my hand away, resting them atop my chest so they could feel the thunderous thumping of my heart. "You—you're a hundred years too early for me!"

"Aww, I'm only two years younger than you. And to wait a hundred years!" Haku sighed dramatically. "Not that it isn't possible, but that's still such a long wait."

"Hmph!"

"You are a cruel woman." He smiled. "I don't dislike it."

Yes, it isn't impossible for the current generation of humans to live far, *far* longer than their predecessors. Nature, the first living thing on earth after the microorganisms, lived the longest. So, we did too, after the change. Our human lifespan increased considerably from an average seventy-five years to at least three hundred and fifty years. We, who have disrespected our elders, now live in their mercy, aging slowly and forever uncertain of the future.

"I won't die, that I can promise you." Haku's sudden declaration halted my train of thought and I gave him a sideways glance. My one eye widened at the sincerity written on his features. "I won't let some disease take me away from you." He replied to my expression with a boyish smile. "Ok?"

I blinked at him before a smile tugged at my lips. "Ok."

"Sakura! Are you here—Sakura!" My neighbour was out of breath as she ran to where we sat. "Misaki!! She's—"

Before she finished, Haku and I were running out of the woods and towards the cottages. He stayed outside while I rushed inside mine to see my sister, Misaki, sitting up, arms wrapped around a white bundle. My sister was messy, but she was glowing. The pink bougainvillea on the right side of her neck that had slowly withered over the years from grief seemed to glisten alongside the beads of sweat on her skin.

The baby was early! "What's wrong? What is it?"

The midwife turned to me in a daze, her eyes wide. "Nothing," she said simply. "Nothing is wrong. She's normal. Look."

Carefully, Misaki lifted the white cloth and I looked down at the human baby in my sister's arms. A human and nothing more; no flowers, no leaves, no twigs, nothing.

For a second, I thought I had stopped breathing. But the intense pounding of my heart brought me back to Misaki's eyes and Abel's smile on my niece's tiny face.

"What does it mean?" I slowly held her hand, not even noticing the tears cascading down my right eye.

My sister looked like she was about to both cry and laugh but she simply said, "It means we're forgiven. Mother nature has forgiven us. The curse is broken."

UP IN FLAMES
Stuart Danker

There were three truths when it came to wizardry. First, was that copper was an irreplaceable conduit for the Neesha people. Second, was that wand gestures had to *always* match the chants. Lastly—and perhaps the most pressing one—was that if you were tasked with conjuring a flame but ended up summoning two stalks of basil instead, you'd pretty much fail your audition for magic school.

Liam didn't know why his magic always turned out wrong. He'd uttered the chant '*marapi*' and practised his gestures a thousand times over, yet he never seemed to ever get it right.

The easiest diagnosis would be Liam not being of Neesha ethnicity. It's believed that only the Neesha people had the talents required for wizardry, but Liam didn't believe any of that nonsense. He did summon *something* after all, didn't he?

Unfortunately, his lack of magical prowess would betray his Xing heritage, and Xings typically worked in skilled labour rather than dabbled in the mystic arts.

"That was…quite unique," said Kazim. "I've sat on the panel for seven years now, and I've never seen anyone summon spices."

"Now, now," said Ketua Wanchi. "At least the boy has *some* magic in him. And he isn't even one of us."

"Yes, ketua," Kazim said. "Which is *exactly* why he's not going to join us. Ever."

"No need for that," said Wanchi. "Nowhere in the scriptures does it say that only one race is allowed into the school."

Kazim snorted. "The scriptures are ancient history. I can't see any use for it other than posterity."

"The *scriptures*," said Wanchi, "are what our art is founded upon."

"That doesn't change the fact that no other race has ever made it through magic auditions, and for good reason." Kazim jutted his chin towards the stalks of basil on Liam's desk, as if to prove his point.

All Liam could do was stare back and watch this argument unfold. Not that it mattered anyway. He had already failed his audition. He gave the copper ring on his finger a little twist. A reminder of his dad.

"Don't let anyone tell you what you can or can't do," his dad had told him, back when the ring still belonged to the old man. Back when his dad was still alive. "I may not be a Neesha, son, but that doesn't stop me from chasing my dreams of wizardry. One day, you'll need to make a similar decision, and whatever it is, I hope it's one you'll be happy with."

I'm sorry, dad, he thought. *It's another loss today.*

Behind the long table of judges was a plaque that read: 'Copper for the enlightened, silver for the lost ones.'

It stood to reason that all of the judges—and practising wizards—wore at least one copper implement on their body. It went without saying that you couldn't find silver in the school, let alone in the entire Maub.

"So what's it going to be?" Kazim said, his four copper rings clinking as he drummed his fingers on the table.

"You show promise, boy," said Wanchi, "but I'm afraid you didn't make the cut."

"Okay," said Liam. There was always next year.

☙

"It's only one copper, but I hope it helps," Liam said. "You sure you don't want any bread? My mum always throws the ugly ones out."

"You always ask that," said the beggar, pocketing the copper coin he'd been given, "but you've already been kind enough. I don't want to trouble you."

"I'll see you next week, then. And I'm bringing the bread regardless."

Helping those in need always gave Liam a sense of joy and purpose, which proved to be invaluable during times like these, when he had nothing else going on for him except failing magic auditions every year. It was time to pick a career now, and his mother would seethe at the thought of him waiting another year to try again.

Not that she hadn't seethed enough already since Liam was following in his father's footsteps. "All your father ever did was play with his juvenile magic," she'd said. "We'd have been better off had he gotten a real job. And now you want to waste your time like him? I can't always be the one who feeds the family, you know!"

Sure, he'd felt bad chasing his dreams. There were no Xing magicians after all. But he *could* conjure, couldn't he? Even though his products belonged more on the spice rack than in magic school? If he could do that, didn't it mean there was a chance?

"That was a pretty kind of you," said a voice, yanking Liam back to the present. It was Ketua Wanchi. "You have enough for yourself?"

"Ah, sir! I uh, yeah, I'll be fine. That guy needs the money more than me."

"So you have talent *and* character. Good, good. But you're nineteen now, if I remember correctly? Isn't that two years past your choice of rites?"

"Yes," said Liam. "But I know what I want to be."

"I know you know," said the ketua. "I saw your attempt at the *marapi* spell. You did everything perfectly." He had a long grey beard which he now stroked, as if milking it for his next words. Copper rings of various shapes adorned all of his fingers. "Maybe your gifts lie elsewhere."

"I'm not going to give up."

"Well," more milking, "you *do* work harder than most students I've seen. Or wizards, even."

"Then maybe you can help me? You can tell me what I'm doing wrong, because I don't get why it doesn't work for me."

"You know I can't be seen helping you, boy," said Wanchi. "That's just the way it goes. The descendants of Neesha have priority."

Liam let out a long breath through his nose. "But I've worked hard. And I've memorised the two hundred uncommon gestures, *on top* of the five hundred common ones."

"You have, have you?"

"Ask for any and I'll show you."

"*Muda draga*."

Liam held out his right hand, as if he were holding a cup, his left fist resting below. Then he moved both hands in a figure eight.

"Good, good," said the ketua. "How about *raja linga*?"

Liam demonstrated the proper gesture without a second thought.

"Not bad, especially seeing how you know more than our graduates. But I'm afraid that's still not enough to pass the auditions."

"But why? I know more than the average student, I'm sure of that. I watch the entire audition every year and the people that you let in haven't even read the scriptures!"

"I wish things were different, boy, I really do. But there's nothing much else I can do." Then, as if trying to make up for the disappointment he'd caused, Wanchi added, "But I tell you what. I'll read through the scriptures and see if there are any loopholes that could warrant your admission. Just don't get your hopes up."

"All right," Liam said. Despite the ketua's words, he didn't even plan on hoping. All he knew was that he was going to try his darndest to get selected next year.

☙

"Damn it!" exclaimed Liam. "Ma, you want more thyme?"

"What, to make up for the time I lost from taking care of a career-less child?"

"Not time, Ma. Thyme! For your bread."

They shared the tiny kitchen, which also functioned as their dining room and bedroom, so Liam knew his mother was just playing dumb. The sprigs of thyme were just an arm's length away from her, after all.

Liam's mother tipped her head, staring at her son from above her eyeglasses. "You need to let that go."

"Let what go?"

She raised an eyebrow at the thyme. "That. It's time you considered picking a career. I hear butchery has some good benefits."

"But I don't want to be a butcher, Ma!"

His mother picked the dough she was kneading and slammed it back on the table. It felt like she'd put her whole back into it. "I want you to follow your dreams as much as the next mother, but you weren't born for this, okay?"

"You're saying I can't be a wizard because of my *race*?"

His mother shrugged. "Hey, you said it. Not me."

"I've studied the scriptures, Ma. Nowhere does it say that only Neesha are allowed to be wizards. Anyone can!" Liam was standing now. He didn't even remember doing that. And his fists were balled too.

His mother, not to be outdone, squared up to him. She'd taken off her glasses, fingers staining the lenses with flour. Now she used it as a pointer, aiming the frame towards Liam. "If that were true, wouldn't other people have made it in already? Explain to me then, why there aren't more of us in wizardry."

"Why can't I be the first?"

"Come on, son. Listen to yourself."

Liam held up the fresh thyme, the stems bending in his grip. "Well, if Xings can't be wizards, then how come I'm able to conjure *this* out of thin air?"

His mother let out a long sigh. Was it Liam's imagination, or was she kneading the dough that much harder? "If you're going to conjure spice," she said, "at least make it a usable amount so we can sell it. Face it, son. You just weren't born for it."

Liam crushed the thyme harder, copper ring biting into the neighbouring fingers. "Dad was a Xing, but at least he showed support."

"Your dad was a fan of magic, but did he ever make something useful out of it? No! Because he *wasn't born for it.*"

"You too, mum?"

"What?"

"Everyone thinks I'm stupid. Nobody encourages me. In fact, they go out of their way to discourage me. And that's all fine because I don't care about them. But you?"

His mother slapped the dough into a bowl and walked out their tiny shack. She uttered her next words without looking back. "The bills still need to be paid, son, and I can't hold on to my career forever." She left Liam alone to stew in his thoughts.

Can't be a wizard my ass, he thought. *I'll show her. I'll show the world.* Then he gave his wand a twirl with the intent to vaporise his mother's dough. Instead, two cloves of garlic materialised out of thin air and fell into the bowl.

"Damn it!" he said.

☙

Liam didn't want to have to do this, but what choice did he have? It was worth a shot. People change, right? So when he saw Kazim leaving the school gate at the end of the day, he quickly ran up to the teacher. "Sir? If I could have a second?"

Kazim snorted. "What is it, *Liam*?" Somehow, Kazim managed to make Liam's name sound like an insult.

"I've been working hard these past few months, and I'm hoping you had some pointers for next year's auditions?"

Kazim stopped walking and rounded on the boy. "You want my advice? Don't try. Your kind will never be wizards. So stop wasting your time and, most importantly, ours."

"With all due respect, sir, I've read the scriptures from front to back, and the other way round, and I see no mention of race—"

"You presume to question me?"

"No, sir, I just—"

"If you want to be a wizard so much, you can always pay for it. Head off to the kingdom across the sea. I heard they take all kinds of people in and teach them mediocre magic."

"But I don't have any money—"

"Then you have no business being in the industry." Kazim resumed walking, prompting Liam to give chase. "We don't run a charity here, boy. We need merit. If we were to admit people based on their *aspirations*, then we wouldn't be much of a school now, would we?"

"But I know almost every word from the scriptures. And I've memorised all two hundred uncommon gestures. Even your graduates don't even know—"

"Now you presume to question our syllabus? I think you've overstayed your welcome, *Liam*." That insult again. "It's time to think hard about your choice of rites, because it certainly isn't going to be wizardry."

And just as Liam's mother did not too long ago, Kazim left him there to stew in his thoughts. Liam rolled the copper ring on his finger.

What would you do, dad? But there was no reply.

༅

Liam had braved his mother's disapproval for this. He'd sacrificed sleep. He'd even reread the scriptures despite having memorised the entire tome. It was the least he could do. This year's audition was going to be his last attempt. He'd done as much as he could, and if that wasn't enough, then perhaps butchery was what he was meant to do.

It wasn't that he didn't want to be a wizard anymore. He just couldn't afford it. It was already three years past his choice of rites, and if he didn't pass today, then it was probably for the best that he quit. At least mum would be proud then.

The same panel of judges sat across Liam. He turned the copper ring on his finger.

"Just make it quick," Kazim said.

Liam channelled his energy, chanting the words by heart before speaking them aloud. He flicked his wand the same way he'd practised thousands of times before. Something caressed his face. That was a draft, wasn't it? The loose sheets of paper that were his notes began to riffle. Maybe this was it. Maybe this was the day he'd enrol in magic school.

And then the wind died, and the flapping sheets of paper fell lifelessly on the table. Wisps of smoke trailed from the corners of the page. *Wait a minute. Smoke?* Hopeful, Liam spread his notes open only to find a tiny scorch on the edges, dots of orange eating away at the paper. He let out a sigh.

"Another year, another waste of our time," said Kazim. "I hope you spare us next year." The other teachers flanking Kazim nodded their heads. At least Wanchi didn't join in.

Liam stacked his notes, ready to leave the school for the last time. *Stupid*, he thought, *maybe I just wasn't born for it after all.*

"Is that a copper ring on your finger, boy?" said Wanchi.

Liam looked up. "Um, yeah."

"Would you try again, but without the ring, please?"

"With all due respect, ketua," said Kazim, "we have tons of other *talented* applicants waiting. Perhaps we could move things along?"

"Let's just give the poor boy one last try. He's not coming back next year, after all. I'm sure of that."

Kazim snorted. "Fine. Be quick, boy."

"What a waste of time," another wizard said, prompting a glare from Wanchi. Kazim chortled in reply.

Liam twisted the ring from his finger and laid it on his stack of notes. With a half-hearted chant, Liam went through the motions of conjuring a flame. *This is stupid.* Maybe the ketua just wanted to see him fail.

But this time, with the flourish of his wand, Liam felt a gush of wind whip up from under his feet. A *gush* this time, so obvious that his shirt billowed like a hot-air balloon.

"What's this?" Kazim's voice barely carried through the wind.

"Haven't you read the fourth mark in the scriptures, Kazim?" Wanchi said, voice equally muted from the draft.

"Of course not," Kazim said. "Nobody has time to read through the entire thing."

This conversation could've very well been a dream at this point, because Liam was more preoccupied with the growing tickle in his chest. Surely, this was a placebo?

"The fourth mark states," Wanchi said, "that the people of Neesha should favour copper as a conduit. It also states that silver is for the lost."

"I know what copper does," Kazim said, his hair now twirling in the wind.

"Then it might interest you that these conduits only affect the Neesha people," Wanchi said, his beard now joining Kazim's hair in dance, whipping away at his squinted eyes. "We've yet to discover what conduits other races use, but apparently, copper tamps the Xings' reservoir."

The wind reached a crescendo and Liam completed the chant in his heart. He took a look at the copper ring on the table, and with one final thought of his father, whipped his wand in a figure-eight.

This one's for you, dad.

A crimson blast reached out to the heavens, sending the ring, paper, and chunks of wood into the air. The pillar of fire stretched upwards, through the brick ceiling, where the blue sky now peered through. The mortar surrounding the hole was still gooey from the heat.

"What," began Kazim, his mouth changing shapes without actual words coming out. Then finally: "What just happened?"

"It turns out," Wanchi said, "that this boy here was training much harder than any of us. He was just terribly handicapping himself while doing it. I wonder if he'd be stronger had he worn a silver ring instead."

"So," Liam mumbled, "I…I can join you guys now?"

"Certainly not!" Kazim said. He shot up, sending his chair screeching backwards, as if to physically assert himself over the magic he could not match. "Your kind shouldn't be allowed to use magic, especially of that strength!"

"But I—"

"I'm afraid the man is right," said Wanchi. "This isn't the place for you."

Liam's heart dropped. Once more, they were going to deny his entry because of who he was. There was no winning this. Kazim's mouth stretched into a satisfied smirk.

"But," Wanchi continued, "seeing as to how this was the best display of magic I've seen—and knowing that you understand the scriptures better than some of our experienced wizards—I'd say you're better off running your own school."

"I can't," Liam said. "How would I even start?" He sidestepped to dodge a drop of molten mortar. He'd barely had time to process his magical powers, and now the ketua was asking him to open a new school? The world was moving too quickly. Just as it had when he got the sudden news of his dad's passing, many years ago.

"Oh, don't worry," Wanchi said. "I think the market will go wherever there's talent, and you, my boy, may have outdone even myself."

Kazim turned slowly towards Wanchi, like a weathervane in a light draft. "Surely, you can't be serious? It's blasphemous to even think that more than one magic school can exist in Maub!"

"And what are you going to do about it?" Wanchi said. "I suggest you start brushing up your own skills before your students decide to switch schools."

"You...you can't..."

"Now, boy. I actually wonder if that was a fluke— "

"You can't do this!" Kazim yelled.

But Wanchi just carried on as if there wasn't a grown man throwing a tantrum beside him. "If you'd be so kind, could you try that again? Just for marketing, you see. And please, mind the ceiling this time."

Liam felt the smile grow on his face. He looked at Kazim's wide eyes, face glued in a look of horror and disbelief. The wind buffeted Liam's shirt once more. And with a flourish of his wand, he chanted, "*Marapi.*"

TAXATION
Rowan C

There is smoke, there is heat, there is *fire*.

Ban blindly reaches for a support, any support at all, a metallic taste in her mouth. Something is streaking down her face and dripping onto her teeth. Finding purchase (that must be the cabinets, she thinks deliriously), she pulls herself to stand. She coughs as she wipes her eyes, finally opening them to scan her surroundings.

The explosion has set Seresthia's town hall aflame. The open door betrays another ring of fire outside the building, and the shouts and cries of people outside are muffled over the roar of the flames. The sound of shifting rubble catches Ban's ears, and she wipes her face again (she's bleeding from her forehead, it's getting in her eyes) before stumbling over to the pile.

She pulls the wood away to reveal the face of Leres, groaning and coughing.

"What…what was that?" he asks.

"A Fireball," Ban replies.

In the smoke and the orange glow of the flames, she sees Leres's eyes widen as he inhales sharply. This starts a coughing fit from the man as Ban keeps moving the rubble, freeing him. Thankfully, his arms and legs still seem to work fine, evidenced by his getting up on his own.

"There's no time," she calls out over the deafening roar of flames as he opens his mouth, "we have to get out now."

"The man, in the forest, that Nancy saw," he tries to explain anyway as they head for the door, avoiding fallen debris and keeping an eye on the roof. "We followed him to a bunch of crates, we found crates of it in there. They planned it for Tax Day, all of it, we should've seen this coming…"

Kicking the door wide open, Ban escapes into the cooler night air, a muttering Leres in tow. Beyond the ring of fire, people are screaming and yelling, fleeing from the town hall.

As her people abandon her, she stands her full height, facing the person who orchestrated all of this through the flames. By her side, Leres does the same, both of them not betraying the fear and panic within them, shared by the tenuous arcane bond between their minds. Her last thought to him before she opens her mouth to speak is merely of love.

"Of course," she says, voice ringing over the chaos. "It all makes sense now."

Taxation

And it really did, considering the circumstances of yesterday...

☙

Ban's eyes started drooping halfway through the document. When a blink started lasting beyond two seconds, she leaned back in her chair with a sigh, rubbing her eyes.

Corcam's Tax Day always drained Ban and her people in more ways than one. Every month, tax representatives came along in their empty carts, checking the accounting records in the town hall before going door to door for collection: one round in the morning and one round in the afternoon.

The Morning Taxes were derived from each home's income, based on the amount of gold earned in a month. The higher the income, the higher the percentage of their income was taxed, but officials working for the Crown (like Ban) had minor exemptions to allow them to pay less. Those who worked in the fields were taxed less gold in general, but provided a fixed rate of produce from their silos as well, based on prior agreements. The town of Seresthia had to collectively fulfil a certain amount of agricultural produce (grains, vegetables, fruits, potion supplies and the like) which would be consumed by the inhabitants of the Royal Palace. The rates at which they're taxed typically left them with sufficient supplies, but sometimes barely so—they would have just enough to last them through the month as long as they all ate conservatively.

Afternoon Taxes were a different matter altogether. It's not just the matter of a different system—everyone above the age of three was taxed individually at a fixed amount—the subject of taxation was different as well. Ban dimly remembered the first time her parents sat her down to explain that she should limit making her toys walk around and speak things, how she should save her energy. She did remember the first time she felt *drained*—a bone-deep exhaustion that she'd never felt before, a wrong sort of emptiness within her. She had been sapped of energy for days, just like every child's first time, but her body quickly adapted to the monthly Afternoon Taxes just like everyone else. She remembered learning how the kingdom taxed their biological reservoir of magical energy (also known as mana) and how the tax affected said reservoir—it limited its development, her teacher had proclaimed with an almost patriotic zeal, for the safety and harmony of Corcam, for who knows what one can do with too much power?

If not for Ban assigning each Tax Day and the days after as rest days, there would definitely be a drop in productivity for the week. As it were, she sometimes had to deliberate how many rest days they could take. It wouldn't do much harm currently as it wasn't harvest season yet, so today (the second day after Tax Day) was a good day of rest for most people. Paperwork was not the same as carrying bags of fertiliser and clearing weeds, and in her high station, she could afford to work harder on such days.

Stifling a yawn that betrayed her mana drain (still the most lenient one yet, Ban thought to herself), the brunette picked up her stylus again and attempted to go through the document, reading it aloud this time. For all the good it usually did her to speak, listen, and read at the same time, this time the words came out meaninglessly, a garbled chunk of percentages and hops supplies.

Taxation

This wasn't working. Ban shook her head and set both items back down, rubbing her eyes. She stared at her reflection in her coffee, wondering if it would last her through the day. Her reflection stared back up at her: Brown curly locks fell down to her shoulders, framing her square face. Desk work had made her softer and she'd always been a little stocky, so she'd always looked pudgy (though people would typically describe her face as pleasantly plump), her cheekbones framing it well. Frown lines were coming in over her brown eyes and eyebrows, but so were her smile lines. If it weren't for the ache starting to set in her fingers, she'd say that she looked older than she felt. Streaks of white even lined her hair, just noticeable from a distance.

Having enough of deskwork, she got off her chair to take a walk. Her cloak was bundled in the corner of the office, a small wooden affair offsetting stone walls that were plain and blank with the exception of a framed certificate of her appointment. She peered out of the big window situated right behind her chair, the southern direction allowing the light of day to shine in without the oppressive heat and light. Today, the sun seemed bright enough that she decided not to take her cloak.

Taking one last look at her desk and making a mental note to clean it up, she stepped out of her office.

൛

Waving the guards outside the town hall to be at ease, Ban took a deep breath of fresh air as the double doors closed behind her. As the sun beat down on her from the blue, cloudless sky, she made her way through the streets.

The other administrative buildings and the guards' barracks greeted her sight, the usual brick and wooden aspects of the scenery. The clacking of her shoes upon the cracked stone roads echoed in the sparsely populated town centre, the atmosphere subdued after Tax Day. Just above the eastern buildings, treetops were visible, the top of the forest farm peeking above the rooftops. They could probably do with less of these niche non-timber products, Ban had always thought; make room for more fields for grain and vegetables. However, with the high-quality mushrooms and herbs bringing in revenue and providing for much-needed potions and tinctures, she never spoke up against it.

Beyond the walls of the town centre, in all other directions, lay their fields of…currently, green, with paths leading to farm estates within a day's walk. Ban idly wondered if it would be too irresponsible of her to take the rest of the day off, but quickly dismissed it as the echoing sound of distant hooves and heavy footsteps reached her ears. She navigated through alleys and streets with ease, arriving at a street which directly led to the gates of the town.

A tiny retinue of cavalry and infantry had just been waved through the gates, which were now being closed behind them. A messenger nearly ran into her, skidding to a halt right before his chief.

"Ah—Chief Wister. Tax Minister C'leirio is here to pay us a visit," said the blond, lithe man, hardly out of breath. The man with his blue eyes and aerodynamic cheekbones was named Bester, nicknamed Pester in their youth. His quick words, faster legs, and inquisitive nature was what earned him the nickname in the first place, and he had found his place as a messenger, even as a Device Operator. "Says it's regarding, ah, current political affairs."

And as he said that, she noticed the enchanted verdant robes of a Minister amongst a sea of red tunics and steel. Her eyebrows shot upwards as she processed the information. Strange. "We usually receive royal missives from the transmission tower."

"Yes, chief," he said respectfully. "The minister did also bring news regarding our transmission tower; we were due a major update. Some renewal of equipment, changes to the runic script and power capacity."

"I see. I must admit, the town mage did not inform me of anything of the sort." She frowned. "Did you receive word of this beforehand?"

"I would've informed you if I did, chief. And I'm sure Krant would have too."

It must be a discreet visit, thought Ban. There was something going on, some deal Tax Minister C'leirio must be willing to strike with their town. Ban's instincts told her to not like this situation. Certainly, some caution was needed, but if she could lower their tax rates, the town would appreciate it.

"Very well. I'll meet them here, P—Bester," she amended.

Having caught the slip, Bester gave her a quick grin before sprinting back to the cavalry.

After an exchange, the front-line parted to fully reveal a man on horseback, wearing simple travel clothing underneath the enchanted robes with a badge to further mark his distinguished position as the Tax Minister. From afar, the man with salt and pepper hair (mostly salt) waved with a polite smile, and she returned a set of her own. She stood comfortably at attention until the group was within five feet: a bit close for conversing distance, but city folk never needed much space.

"Well met, Chief Wister," called the minister in a geriatric's croaky voice, his crow's feet wrinkling with his smile.

"Well met, Tax Minister C'leirio," she returned, bowing. "It is an honour. To what does Seresthia owe the pleasure of your presence?"

"Well," Minister C'leirio started with a small chuckle, "the time for taxing the kingdom has come and gone, the first since the death of King Glaron IV, may he rest in peace." The last phrase was echoed by his guards and Ban herself. "I was thinking, how fare our lands in this time? And so, I took it upon myself to visit the states and settlements, inquiring about their general wellbeing and production output, among other things."

"Well, Minister C'leirio," she said politely, "we are honoured to receive your care, and we look forward to providing our hospitality in return." A few people had started peeking out of the buildings in interest at the commotion. A tavern owner, capped and aproned, was frantically sweeping the steps of the tavern entrance and lighting candles. "You and your men must be tired. Come, rest your horses at the stables and join me for some tea. It would seem Lawton's is open at this time of day."

"Very good, very good indeed."

The group dismounted, and a few local stable hands came to take the reins of the horses, leading them away. With a bow (and the beginnings of a headache), Ban escorted the Minister and his guards into Lawton's, the afore-mentioned man giving an even lower bow.

Taxation

They exchanged pleasantries over a good soothing cup of Lawton's Best Leaves (Lawton was, if not resourceful, straightforward), talking about the climate, yield, and the tax representatives' professionalism.

The Minister chuckled at hearing about one representative's friendliness with Ban's children, before saying: "I appreciate that she has an eye for the attitude required in service. We are, of course, servants to the people, and it behoves us to work well with the people we serve."

"Of course."

Minister C'leirio put his cup of tea down with care before speaking again. "In fact, on the matter of service, I was hoping to speak to you regarding current politics. I'm sure you have received news from Corcam'liq."

"Indeed, Minister C'leirio." Ban nodded with a polite and attentive smile, curious to see where this is going. "I hear that King Glaron IV is succeeded by his daughter, Queen London?"

"Oh, not quite so soon queen, no," laughed the Minister loudly, before continuing with a tone that was conspicuously lacking in condescension. "She is not yet of age, and she is still considered a princess. For now, the kingdom's decision-making responsibilities fall on the shoulders of formerly Vizier, now Regent, Faren Apotros. It will be, of course, *Princess* London's will and intentions, but Regent Apotros will, ah, refine her plans and give inputs on her new policies. It will not do for the Princess to be in charge so quickly while her education is still lacking and her experience so sparse."

"In running a kingdom, yes." She hesitated, wondering how to approach this conversation before she carefully reached out with an assumption. "Forgive me, Minister C'leirio, but it sounds like you do not approve of this current arrangement."

He laughed with a practiced humour. "Very funny, Chief Wister. Whatever arrangements the kingdom makes, you will find no disapproval from me. Whatever opinions I have regarding the matter is inconsequential; after all, I'm sure the High Ministers, with their broad range of views and deep understanding of the kingdom's machinations, know what to do best for Corcam."

"I'm sure," Ban backtracked quickly, giving a small chuckle of her own. "But I have heard…that many prefer the late king's direction, his leadership."

"Oh, our beloved, late king!" At this, Minister C'leirio sat up slightly straighter, smiling into the distance. "Yes, I do find myself as part of this group. The former king had a good head on his shoulders, in my opinion, old and outdated as it may be," he joked. "A fine sense of logic, a reliable understanding of foreign matters, and even a good show of compassion towards the citizens of Corcam."

"I see," Ban said neutrally. "And the Regent and Princess do not possess those qualities?"

"Well, there is no denying Princess London's compassion," Minister C'leirio returned a smile that hinted at reluctance, "yet I have heard, though loathe am I to quote such heresy, that her young mind is rather unchecked. These, ah, speakers have even gone on to say that Regent Apotros has found his place, not as someone who necessarily makes things happen, but as someone who gives the facts as they are and carries out the 'monarch's' decisions to the best of his abilities.

"It's interesting," continued Minister C'leirio, confiding, "to see how the common citizen views the situation."

She thought of how their tax rates had seemed more lenient in the month since the old king's passing. "Some of these common citizens would say that the kingdom has been adapting to the new changes in administration quite well."

"Oh, no doubt, no doubt. But…" The older man seemed hesitant to continue, closing his mouth and opening it again while tapping his wispy beard, but he did so quietly. "In your confidence, I must admit that the decision was made to provide some reprieve for those who still mourn King Glaron IV. In another month or so, everything is slated to return to normalcy, as advised and decided by the Regent himself. It does seem a little troubling, with what these people have said, and how it all seems, if we are to…well, somehow *believe* them, to add up, to line up. What this says about the kingdom."

She struggled to choose if she should give him the benefit of doubt: these could very well be his own words that he was pinning on some faceless scapegoat. However, he might've been genuine—and wasn't that a whole new ballgame? Not having been close to the man at all prior to this, she decided to move for a safer approach: "I see. If I may…"

"Oh yes, of course," he chuckled. "There was a point in my having this conversation with you, and it was to listen to your opinion. Seresthia has been a great contributor to Corcam's resources in many ways, and a word from the people here does mean something."

For all her skill in politics, Seresthia was merely a farming settlement (big as it may be). There's something here in the minister's questioning that made his curious visit shift into a more suspicious light, but Ban didn't dare step over that line yet.

"Respectfully, sir," she slowly began under Minister C'leirio's encouraging eye, "I am rather concerned with Princess London's age and how things are being handled. I must admit, however, that she has yet to prove herself on the throne. I do not like Regent Apotros's long-term plan as it has been presented, less so the baiting, as you have said."

"Right." He gestured at her kindly, aware that she had not finished.

"However, it is only a matter of years before Regent Apotros is once again Vizier, is it not? This…temporary period before Princess London's coronation may be trending the same way it was during the old king's reign," she slowed down slightly, emphasising her mention of King Glaron IV. "But I do believe in giving the Princess a chance to show that she has control over the Regent and make her mark first before we make more decisions."

He nodded as she finished. "Well said, well said. It does…pique my interest," he said after a pause, smile slightly faded, "that Apotros would go back to being a Vizier." She made no reaction to the loss of titular formality as he continues. "I mean no disrespect to the man, but…after having his influence on her for so long, she may be tempted to defer to Apotros's judgement even after her coronation. Her potential may be clouded with, ah, his interesting lessons on kingdom administration."

"Even so," she said, standing her ground, "I think I would like to see her on the throne and judge with my own eyes. What if she's Guardian-blessed?" Protectors of humanity, shapers of nations, the Guardians had been there since the dawn of time, eternal beings displaced from their home (a world called Gaea) to guide their world. Even King Glaron

IV wasn't Guardian-blessed; no one has been for centuries. Still… "We can trust nothing but only what we see."

"Hm. We can trust nothing but only what we see," he repeated in quiet wonder. "You have a way with words, Chief Wister! I quite admire it," he added with a chuckle, "and you've given me much to think about. I'm afraid I've kept you for rather long, I didn't mean to distract you from your tasks."

"Not at all," she assured him, thinking behind her smile. "Mana drains always make me drowsy anyway, I wasn't making much headway."

He laughed at that. "Indeed, they can be a hassle. I think we shall be staying at Lawton's, it's a very nice place."

Lawton himself bowed low next to the counter, ready to meet the minister's needs on a skeleton crew.

"Please," continued Minister C'leirio. "No need to attend to us, we will be on our way soon enough to further towns. Thank you for that conversation, it was quite enlightening."

"I hope you enjoy your stay, minister." Recognising the dismissal, she bowed to him and walked out of the tavern.

☙

"Ma!" Three high-pitched voices rang in the tiny hall.

Ban looked up from her shoes to her children, half-wincing from the noise, half-grinning.

"Children!" And that was their cue to come rushing forwards to tackle her in a big hug.

From her position on the floor, she looked up at the approaching figure of Nancy, one of her oldest friends. Ban and Nancy were almost sisters, joined at the hip in all ventures. They grew up together, never losing touch even though Ban travelled to Corcam'liq, the kingdom's capital, to advance her studies. When she came back, they reunited as if they were never apart, and even though they pursued different things in life, they had their nightly family dinners.

"I hope they weren't too much trouble today," chuckled Ban as her children giggled on her.

"Aren't they always?" laughed the shorter woman.

The head of Darrol, Ban's oldest, flew up, his black hair (like his father's, but a mirror of Ban in everything else) mussing up from the motion as he glared at the woman in mock affront.

"No, no, they were still tired when they got up today. But we did some chores and got a good nap today, didn't we?" Nancy's blue eyes flashed with amusement as the children sang a chorus of yeses. "I think their mana's nearly fully replenished."

"Oh, I miss those days. Alright, darlings, Ma needs to walk." They dutifully got off her and helped her up, before Yves, still a toddler and the youngest of them all, raised her pudgy arms to be picked up. "It's been a while since a drain has taken me out, but replenishing always takes so long now," she went on as she hoisted Yves onto her shoulders.

"Right?" Nancy held Mori's hand as they emerged into the living area. "Ugh, I feel like I need a good twenty hours of sleep just to be able to think anymore. And these lil' tykes…" She wrapped an arm around Mori's shoulders and pressed a kiss onto the second's brown locks (just like her mother's, but a tiny version of her father in everything else), resulting in a giggling girl. Nancy sighed, her joking demeanour falling away. "Just a good sleep and a nap, and these angels are flying again."

"Hopping bunnies, more like." Ban grinned, her heart softening as she watched Nancy and bounced Yves in her arms. It had always warmed her heart to see Nancy treat her children like her own, that she'd remained a part of Ban's life even until now. "What's for dinner?"

"Stew!" cheered Darrol and Mori, echoed a second later by Yves.

Mori launched into a full explanation: "There's meat an' potato an' carrots an' we added a teensy bit of honey an' we got bread—"

"Honey, you say?" Ban did her best to keep up with the conversation as Nancy headed into the kitchen area to bring out dinner. Footsteps thumped down the stairs to reveal the town mage, Nancy's husband. "Hey there, Krant."

"Big Chief Ban," the tall, heavy-set man boomed with a twinkle in both eyes, closing a book gently. "Back from herding a flock to herd another, ay?"

"Is that my crook or are you just happy to see me?" she joked, and he threw his head back in laughter. "How's your day been?" she asked as Darrol and Mori bounced over to Krant's side.

"Oh, the children were a delight as always. Go on, darlings, see if Nance needs help."

The grin faded into a weary smile as Darrol and Mori did so, and he held up a book he'd taken from the Wister home library. A thick tome boasting a leathered hard cover presented a faintly glowing title that had been inscribed with mana-infused ink a long time ago: *Menna Devyces: Advanced Theoreticks and Mechanismes of Long-Distance Informasyone Transmissyone*. "Sometime during their nap, Bester came up to the house. Said Tax Minister C'leirio came for a visit?"

"Yeah, yeah he did." She frowned, not at Yves holding her hands out for Krant, but at this piece of news. "Bester said something about a major update, that we needed one. He mentioned that he didn't receive any word of it, and if you did, you would've told me," she said as she handed over the flailing toddler to her favourite uncle.

"And Nancy would have if I had forgotten," assured Krant, adjusting his hold on Yves so that she wasn't sitting on the book. "But both of us remember no messages regarding the update, so I think it's safe to assume they didn't send word ahead. Many updates about that mana theft guerrilla group, though. Anyways, that Minister…Cleric?"

"C'leirio."

"That guy." He smiled as Yves lightly clapped his forehead with her palm. "Quite right, Yves, thank you. He brought a few technicians with him to perform the update. And if you could stop now, m'dear," he added to Yves, who was now giggling violently while clapping away at his strong jawline, "I'd thank you again."

"Hm," Ban said, taking Yves off Krant as Nancy carried out a huge pot with two mitted hands. "They must have been in armour. I didn't see any of the typical technician wear."

"No more business talk, now," instructed Nancy as Darrol came out with the cutlery and Mori with the basket of bread. Waving the ladle at her husband and her best friend, she continued in a manner not unlike their mothers: "Whatever you both have to say, save it till the kids finish dessert."

"Ah, so they've earned it, then?" a silvery voice came from the front door.

The children ran shrieking to their father. Krant gently put down a wriggling Yves, and the toddler joined her mother to greet Leres, security head of the town and Ban's husband.

"I have it on good authority." Ban hung back as the shorter, lean man picked up both Darrol and Mori, before she leaned forward for to peck him on the lips. "Word of the aunt and uncle, in fact, Sergeant Orwell."

He gave a soft smile as the children fake gagged, with none of the cynicism that he wore on a regular basis. "Well, who am I to question Chief Wister?"

൜

After the children had finished their fruits and gone on upstairs to play, the adults remained seated in the dining area, discussing the events of the day.

"I don't know what to tell you, Ban." Krant shrugged his broad shoulders. "No message came from the throne or otherwise, except for the one about the old king's death. And that came through Pester."

"No, no, I believe you." Ban sighed, slumping in her chair. "This just seems very odd, that's all."

"The entourage themselves seemed pretty above the board," piped up Leres, setting down his cup of tea. "Standard equipment and gear, no sense of hidden communication that I could see. I've got men posted near Lawton's and some of the other guards are in the extra barracks, so if anything happens, the night shift will let me know in the morning."

She gave him a grateful look that he reciprocated with an easy nod. Leres had always trusted Ban's instincts and caution, even if they turned out to be for nothing. His vigilance was a testament to his capabilities as the town's Head Guard. However, while he'd always analysed and filtered everyone else's feelings and theories, even for officials of higher authority than Ban's, he always took hers seriously and erred on the side of caution for her.

"And, if you're still unsure about them, I can take a look too." Nancy took the teapot and started pouring more tea into everyone's cups. "I think I'll have enough mana tomorrow to send out a *SiaoDi*, take a look around Seresthia and even in the woods. Lawton's kids even came out today, their sister said he wanted 'em out of their hair. Can't hurt to ask if they've got anything."

She set the teapot back down as Krant grinned and took her hand fondly, thumb rubbing over the runes inscribed on her wedding ring.

Ban remembered the wedding well. Eight years ago, Nancy and Krant had a loud, joyous, fun affair, quite unlike the one she and Leres had. Ban couldn't miss it for the world, so she had sucked it up and partook in the celebration with her best friend.

It was during the dinner that Krant had pulled Nancy's hand gently, showing and explaining to her the runes he kept hidden during the ceremony. It was a magical artifact to summon familiars, a little "sibling" (called *SiaoDis* and *SiaoMeis*, based on the Guardians' language) to keep her company or to protect her when he couldn't be around.

She had merely kissed him and booped his nose with a soft "thank you", and Ban had recognised the dangerous smile her friend occasionally wore. Weeks after the wedding, Nancy caught the Marck boys sneaking moonshine in the fields with her "little brother" and tipped off their parents. Ban had wordlessly assigned more of the budget to Krant's artifact purchases and gear development after that.

"That's a plan all right, Nance, Leres," sighed Ban in relief. "Thanks."

They nodded as Krant grinned. "This is literally the safest room in the whole town. Anyways, tomorrow I'll join Pester to look at the tower. I need to understand the updates they make to it, check it out…maybe even send word and, ah, request an explanation regarding the lack of notifications," he sniffed with a sophisticated voice before he smiled with less humour compared to the Krant's Signature™. "You're right, something's going on. But we'll see what we can do about it."

൦ൈ

Nothing happened in the night that Leres's men knew about, and by the time Ban got to the office, she was mostly convinced that it would be a normal day. Except that it wasn't.

What had been foretold to be a sunny day turned grey and overcast by noon. Just as she finished yesterday's report, Pester came in with another one from the responsible technicians that informed of technical difficulties, delays, and time extensions, possibly until the next morning. And during teatime, when Nancy came in with the kids for an impromptu "bring your kids to work" day, Ban knew something had to be up.

"Spotted a sneaker, not two minutes away from the walls," Nancy muttered over the heads of the children in their colouring session. "Camouflaged in greenery. Almost had a headache trying to keep up, even with *SiaoDi*."

Ban nodded once. "I'll send Leres to investigate. Maybe he can rally the scouts in time. What of Lawton's?"

"Not much. The kids say Minister C'leirio's staying until tomorrow and leaving at dawn, and he's planning to take a walk in the evening out to the fields."

"Out and back," mumbled Mori and Darrol, still concentrating on their artworks, and after a brief pause, Nancy nodded.

"Well done, children," Ban said to them warmly, before continuing in a quieter voice. "Any word about the transmission tower?"

This time Nancy shook her head, and Ban looked away to stare into the distance as the other woman explained.

"Seems to be on schedule, up to tonight at the latest according to the extensions." Watching Yves fist another colour-marker to make yet another swirl, Nancy crossed her arms and frowned up at Ban worriedly. "We're left isolated from Corcam and the other cities, towns. I don't like it; I know they mean well but if mana thieves come into our city…"

"I get that." She nodded tersely. "Thanks, Nance. I'll get Leres in here; we'll figure out some arrangement. Just don't let the tykes hog him for too long."

And they didn't. He came in in record time, the family sharing a swift hug with all five members ("Ah, come on, budge over," Nancy mock-grumbled, joining in as the children giggled) before he closed the door, and it's just him and Ban. It's quickly arranged: as he's the best scout without armour, he'd track down the sneaker with a small team, and the rest of the guards would guard the walls of the town.

Towards the end of the meeting, they privately re-established their empathy bond: with their mana still recovering after Tax Day, they produced the most tenuous of bonds, capable of merely confirming each other's life status and strong emotions. She sighed as she felt the warmth of his love envelop her heart, and his eyes closed briefly as he felt hers. They looked up at each other in sync before regathering themselves: her the organisational charts, and him the maps.

"The children were hoping to hear a story for bedtime. From you." She nudged over a scroll to him which he picked up without looking. *Be safe. Come home to us.*

"Tell them to choose a book when you see them later." He stepped around her carefully, knocking a filled desk drawer shut. *I will.*

"May your mission go well, Sergeant." She had missed it, for the short amount of time that they didn't have their bond: they moved so in-sync when they had it, needed no words to feel the security and warmth (and sometimes passion) they both felt for each other. *I love you.*

"Thank you. Clear skies, Chief." They'd never needed to say the words themselves, but even just hearing their inside joke like that made her heart melt. *I love you too.*

And he was gone.

၀၃

Ban had to read to the children instead, but they didn't mind. Her children were angels, and she didn't deserve them.

Well, she thought that only sometimes. This would be one of the times, she reflected as Krant and Nancy joined in on the story-telling fun, providing good voices and hypnotising visual effects. Without too much of a fuss, they accepted their dad's absence and climbed into bed for their mother to tell them a story. Ten minutes of a full-blown performance later, they had started nodding off to sleep, and within the next five, they were all out.

She couldn't help but feel the worry grow for her husband. She'd never needed to choose before, but if it came down to it, she didn't know if she'd be able to sacrifice Leres for Seresthia. She couldn't imagine a world where he wasn't there with her, watching her back as she led the city; where he wasn't there to turn to the sunrise to greet their children with her, nor bow to the sunset where the fallen walk towards.

Ban had no illusions about what Leres's job entailed, and she'd prepared herself the best that she could. But sometimes, the worry overcame her, and she couldn't help but fear the worst, regrets resurfacing with a vengeance. She should've shut up that one time, she should've taken his surname regardless of her professional position as Chief, she should've—

The worry became suffocating in a house full of reminders of the fragile peace they cradled in their arms. She stepped out of the front door, quietly telling Krant to let Nancy know, and was greeted by the sight of the streets at night. Fireless torches lined the walls and thresholds of the homes around hers, flickering their warm brilliance until the dawn came. The streets were empty of people, save one person in a cloak having a stroll. The figure unhooded and Ban saw who it was.

"Minister," she said, surprised. "Couldn't sleep?"

"Oh my, Chief Wister?" He chuckled as he walked up to her, raising a metal flask in greeting. "Oh, I'm afraid so. Travel doesn't much agree with me, I had a hard time sleeping yesterday too."

"I'm sorry to hear that," she replied with a frown, stepping away from her door. "I don't suppose you'd like some company on your walk, would you, sir? I was about to go take a lap or two as well, clear my mind of things." *Including asking you some questions*, she thought.

"Oh, but I insist," he beamed, waving her over before offering her the flask. "Something to warm you up this chilly night? Hot chocolate always works for me."

She hesitated before nodding. "Much thanks, Minister. Very kind of you." He passed her the flask, uncapped, and she took a few sips of the sweet, warm drink. Almost immediately her body flooded with warmth, a welcome shield against the cool night air. "Oh, this is a nice drink."

The old man looked pleased with himself. "The secret is some honey. You take a small bit and mix with the chocolate, then heat it up again. Works every time." He accepted the flask back as she made a sound of acknowledgement. "So, what troubles you, young Wister?"

She snickered at the term as they continued down the path, feeling lighter already. His companionship was surprisingly agreeable. "Oh, if I were truly young again," she was tempted to put a dramatic hand out for flair, "then maybe my mana would regenerate faster and I would be able to keep up with my children's antics."

"Well, when you get to my age, child, talk to me again," he grumbled back to her laughter. The walk continued, but in more companionable silence. Albeit a vacuum of silence.

"It's just...my family, I suppose," she finally answered his question. "What with the big changes in administration, those mana thieves out there, and similar issues—I'm just worried for them, is all."

He hummed in understanding as they slowly made their way to the centre of the town. "It cannot be easy, being a person of position and a family person. Having to juggle that balance, making sacrifices here and there. I have children of my own," he added, "all of whom have left the nest. I know how that feels, back when I was working my way up to my current position."

She nodded, acknowledging his relation to the situation and his knowledge of it. "I don't know, I think I'm just naturally anxious," she confessed with an embarrassed laugh. "Seresthia is a peaceful place, not a big city or port town like the mana thieves have targeted, and the kingdom respects our contributions. But…but I keep expecting the worst at times. I've always been quite cynical. And I can't imagine what I'd do if I had to choose between Seresthia and my family, my husband, my children…"

They arrived at the town hall as the minister patted her on the shoulder, nodding with understanding. "Well, firstly, you have my word that you will not get a black mark on your record for heresy. In case you were worried about that."

She snorted. "I appreciate that."

"Secondly, I don't think your situation is unfamiliar to many of us in positions of power," he continued quietly. "Once, I would have died for Corcam, and yet here I am living for my family. I've been lucky enough that nothing bad has happened in my life, that nothing has threatened everyone's safety. But I understand wanting reassurances and having none. The white hairs came early," he joked again.

"Got a few on the way," she smiled as they stopped right by the entrance of the hall. "Thank you, Minister. For your understanding. I think I needed to hear that."

Taxation

"Well, I'm going to stop you there, actually. Far be it for me to deny my own contributions, but…" And he hesitated. "I think I can do better than that. More than just listening and providing an ear and such. If—and pardon an old man's social missteps—but if you want solutions, I do have one."

ൣ

"I don't understand," Ban managed to say.

Within Ban's office in the town hall, in the minister's hand, where he had previously held a hip flask to offer to Ban, there now sat a mana crystal.

A flat, rectangular tablet, glowing an iridescent blue (almost like the sea on a sunny day. Ban had been once; she dimly remembered the day, but the crystals always remind her of the sea now) that she'd seen all her life. This one was missing the contraptions typically attached to it: the handgrip for the contributor, where it absorbs their mana; the crystal holder with its built-in gauge, to show the levels of mana collected. Just the crystal itself, with runes inscribed upon it. It had the standard runes: protection from overcharging and exploding, physical theft, general destruction, and such. Ban barely recognised them, only from her fundamental magic lessons taken during her political training and Krant's occasional teachings.

Tax Minister C'leirio had just offered it to her.

"Don't you?" Even now, his tone was kindly, understanding, just as croaky as it ever was. "We both have people to protect, goals to achieve. But for all my position in the kingdom, all the security the kingdom can offer to me, the guards can only do so much. I could—can only do so much."

Rowan C

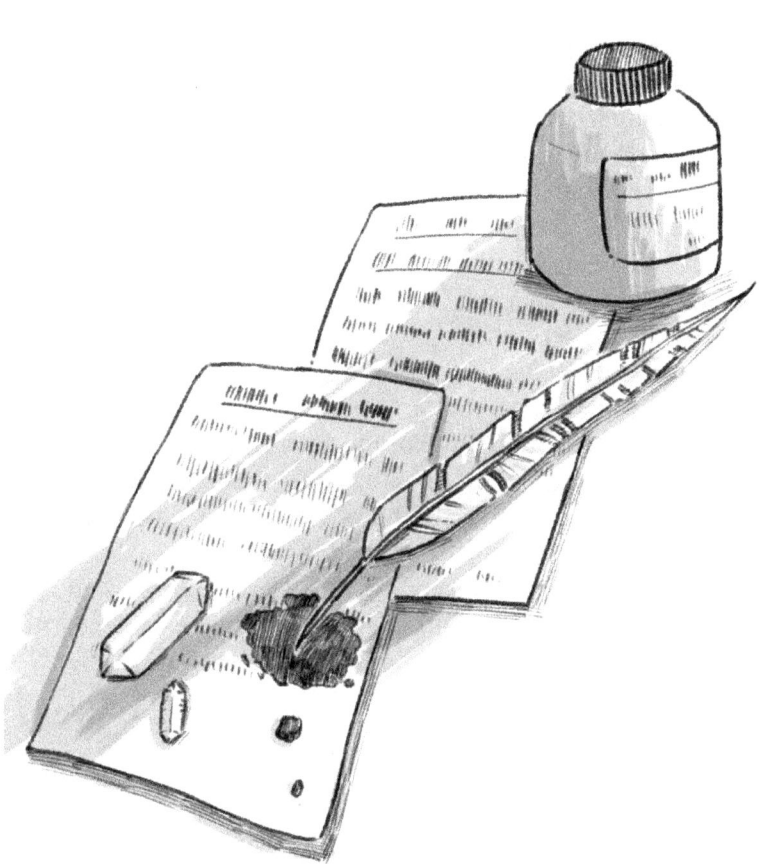

"Right," she said, struggling to follow. Her brain felt slow, almost as if trying to go two different ways as she scrambled to catch up. "So, uh, you used the crystals...?"

"Perks of the job," he grinned almost modestly. Almost. "The crystals first come under the Chancellor's scope of responsibilities, the finance sector, to be documented by the tax department before we hand it over to the Arcanist. We usually collect such high amounts of mana anyways, who will miss one or two units here and there, hm? Usually, during times of chaos, too. So much happens every year, a couple of crystals being misplaced? Not uncommon."

"I can't imagine." I can take it *I can't take it* he's offering help *he's part of the mana thieves* imagine keeping it all *imagine losing it all*, screamed her brain.

"Chief Wister—*Ban*," he whispered, staring into her eyes. His gaze burned into hers with a desperate, fervent, fiery fever. "I saw your children running around without a care in the world. Who do you have watching over them? Just a random maid?"

She finally blinked, breaking eye contact and looking back at the crystal. "She...she's my best friend, Nancy," she said, nearly managing to summon the indignance, but instead sounding like a stubborn drunkard. "She does good."

"But can she do better?" He stepped in closer, and she let him, unable to back away. They were of the same height; they stared eye-to-eye. "Someone—no, everything needs to be better for your children, your family. My only regret," he added, still speaking with fervour, "is that I could never do right by my family. I had to hide them at the time, keep them safe from those who found King Glaron IV unpopular. He eventually brought order to the kingdom, but the times

I have risked my family for my own duty towards the Crown, I have regretted all of them."

She was paralysed by his words. Could this be it? Could he be right? This was a solution, wasn't it? All those sleepless nights and heavy days where she had to send her husband out on patrol for actions against local ruffians and special missions to deal with mishandling of magic by their own people. All those prayers to the Guardians for her children to grow up safe and happy, that time they nearly burnt themselves out with fever.

She shouldn't have to deal with risks anymore. Her station had promised her financial stability, safety from attempts against her life and family, but C'leirio was right. It was not enough. Never enough.

She reached down for the crystal…just as Leres burst into the office.

"Ban!" he yelled, a wild look in his eyes. "They've oiled the fields!"

Her heart stopped, leapt to her mouth. In a moment of panic, she could only gape at Leres, then at the minister, whose eyes had widened with shock.

"Chief Wister, you have to take it, this is the time for it. It's happening, the mana thieves have come, you have to do this!" C'leirio said frantically.

"No," she whispered. Slowly, her mind returned. "No. I won't take it," she said louder, stronger. "We'll find a way to deal with them without it, we'll—we'll gather our forces—"

"What forces can withstand power like this? You only have one town mage, he can't go up against a whole guerrilla army!" He urgently pushed the crystal towards Ban, face in a desperate grimace of begging. "Please, Ban! Don't make the same mistake I paid dearly for!"

Taxation

"*Don't listen to him!*" shouted Leres, as a sense of apprehension and distrust of the old man flooded in from him to her. She stumbled back. "The man in the forest—" images of a man dressed in camouflage clothing, snarling and running "—he said—" and as clear as day, she heard the man's confession ring in her ears, Leres's words lost in the echo of the memory.

Feeling her own heart skip a beat, she looked at the minister.

His face turned blank and he only murmured "shame" as he closed his hand around the crystal. It glowed as his body folded into a tiny pinprick with a sucking sound and disappeared.

A glowing orange ball crashed through the window and into Ban's office. She narrowly reacted in time, flipping her desk to try and dampen what was it come, or even bat the ball back out.

It didn't work. With a resounding boom and a bright flash, she was thrown back.

ღ

And now he stands before them. Tax Minister C'leirio, flanked by his guards, stares at them across the ring of fire, the dancing flames obscuring his face yet exposing him.

"I warned you, Chief Wister," calls C'leirio in that croaky voice of his, but this time with a teasing tone. "Your family was in danger this whole time, and you had the means of protecting them. Too bad you declined to take it."

"You put them in danger in the first place," Ban shoots back.

Leres doesn't add anything, but he keeps thinking *hurry up hurry up hurry up*.

She can keep the old man distracted, sure. "Lured me in with safety and understanding when you really sabotaged the towers, oiled the fields. What was in that hot chocolate, eh?"

"I wasn't lying, my dear. It really was honey," he says, shrugging. "And a drop or two of affability essence. I was very eager to get to know you."

"I can see that." A chill runs down her spine, causing her to shiver in the heat. "Understandable, all things considered."

"In any case, Chief, look at the situation now. Your town hall is burnt, your tower is compromised, and your fields are filled with oil. Dangerous combination with sparks, that."

A bit more time! begs Leres.

"You disloyal, blasted betrayer," she says with a tremble to her voice. Not hard to fabricate. "The Crown…the Crown will hear of this, and they will find you, and—and they will save us, they will, it's not too late for them—"

"Ban, please." The kindness returns to C'leirio's face. "Don't do this to yourself. Join us—we need your resources; we need to feed ourselves and we don't want you fuelling this failing kingdom. And I promise you, other than that, we'll leave your town alone. We'll never harm you again. We'll make sure you have protection under us, safe from Corcam's armies. We could even swear an oath on it," he adds with hope. "A magical oath, a binding. My soul to yours, and to damnation I head if I can't keep it, for your peace of mind."

She doesn't need to pretend to not know what to say. Leres has seen what he was waiting for, and his relief is palpable. She has not, however, and a small part of her mind whispers cruel possibilities to her, raises her anxiety, and her worries threaten to overwhelm her again.

"You...you mean it? An oath?"

"Ban, oh sweet child, of course I do. It shouldn't be hard to find the ingredients for it, no? A piece of metal for bond longevity, make sure it stays until my dying breath; some of my blood, to tie it to me, makes me the subject; a blessing from my mother, to show that I have thought this through—"

"Have you?"

C'leirio pauses as his guards react quickly, turning around confront the source of the booming voice. There are many sounds of impact as arrows bounce off a conjured shield of pure force.

"About time, you dramatic idiot," sighs Leres at Krant, who's floating in the air a full foot off the ground.

Krant's short hair is standing up entirely, his clothes flapping in an invisible wind as he holds his arms outstretched from his body, grasping two glowing crystals filled with mana. His pockets are full of many more crystals, and he stares down at the scene with two crackling eyes of purplish light.

"Clearly, you have not thought this through," he says, before waving a hand over the scene. Above him, there's movement, and a fine drizzle starts falling. With a start, Ban realises that Krant has brought forward the storm that had been estimated to happen tomorrow.

"And you have, have you?" C'leirio forms a small shield against the rain: a clear, blue-tinted window of force. Drops of rain slide down it, keeping him and the men by his side dry. People start trickling out to the once-empty streets—armoured people, each carrying their own mana crystals. "You, going against all of us. We've all wielded powers you've only dreamt of using.

We create miracles daily, subvert terrible fates, and induce magnificent catastrophes. With our will alone, we shape the world to suit us."

The rain has now become a downpour and thunder rumbles ominously in the distance, both drowning out the flames. Soaked to the bone, Ban can only squint up at the sky, unable to perceive Krant's expression in the rain, the dying light proving to be hardly any help at all.

"You'd think that that's what I want, don't you?" asks the floating mage.

"Why wouldn't you want it?" laughs C'leirio, and it does not feel like he's bluffing. "The power over the world at your fingertips, my boy. Just a thought and a word—" Suddenly, his hand glows with light, vibrant violet spilling out of from where he holds his crystal.

Ban barely sees similarly coloured light tracing Krant's fingers as he gestures in the air, chanting loudly over the rain to hear himself. A few of the guards react quickly and throw bolts of energy at him, but a twitch of his head strengthens the shield around him. Where the guards had made enduring windows of protection, a compact sphere of indigo surrounds Krant, hiding him entirely behind its opaque walls. With a final pulse, the light in C'leirio's hand fades away.

"Something about a thought and a word?" Krant's voice booms from inside the sphere as the men nervously take a step back. C'leirio is still looking at his empty hands in shock—the crystal has just disappeared in less than a second. "Oh, joy. Guess we don't need the proper techniques and rituals anymore, do we?" He gives a booming laugh, one Ban privately describes as "laughs in twelve years of formal arcane education".

"You can try to stop me," continues Krant, voice emanating loudly from the ball. Violet flashes of light appear where every mana crystal was hiding in the guards' uniforms and hands. Cries of shock fill the air, and some even start running. "Magic isn't perfect, and there are weaknesses in each spell taught in case any of us go rogue. But I don't think I'll be put down before—"

"They're here!" Nancy's shout, impossibly loud, originates from the direction of the gates. Ban wipes her face again as a brilliant blue glow surrounds the perimeter of the town and fades just as quickly. Over the rain, she hears faint sounds of shouts and clanking, more blue-indigo energy pulsing and fading closer and closer to the centre of the town.

Expecting C'leirio to run, she's surprised to look back and see that he hasn't. Until she notices lavender energy running in his veins and on his skin—Krant's unique magical signature holding the minister in place. The old man grits his teeth, his flexing muscles the only indication he's struggling to get out of his bonds.

"May the Crown have mercy on you," says Krant, visible now that his shield has faded, the rain causing his robes to cling to his form. His eyes are still glowing, but barely, as he stares down the mana thieves. "All of you."

ೞ

The Margrave's men soon arrive.

Amidst the arrests, a makeshift tent is erected for the Inquisitors as a base for their on-site investigations. Having been most in contact with the former Tax Minister C'leirio, Ban is tested for magical influences and effects, in case he planted any sort of control over her or cursed her. When she mentions the affability essence, the diagnostic shifts to account for potions and other chemical mixtures. She is quickly diagnosed to have ingested, and subsequently given an antidote for, only the essence, something that would lower her inhibitions and mental faculties to the point where she was very suggestive and willing to share her secrets.

Their questioning continues on towards the morning, the Margrave personally overseeing some of it regarding C'leirio's interactions with Ban and her knowledge of his complicity with mana thieves.

"The power the mana crystals hold…" the Margrave says at one point, her voice clear yet gentle over the lightening rain. "It's not part of the security sector to deal with the crystals, but I can only imagine. You would've had the power to protect Seresthia from further threats. It would have been easy to hide C'leirio's body with the power you have gained, to erase the town from Corcam's mind."

"I…I haven't considered that, ma'am," she says, feeling a little lost in the late hour, before her mind catches up. "Are you suggesting—"

The Margrave holds her hands up. "I do not mean to accuse you of anything. But if Mage Krant Thelmyst, Nancy Thelmyst, or Operator Bester Swift, all of whom have handled these crystals, were to be influenced by this power and tried to persuade you onto that course of action, what would you have done?"

"I…" Nancy, that makes sense, but Pester? "I would have gotten my hands on a crystal and alerted your office, and the Arcanist's office." The wrong thing to say would be persuading them to give up the power, which she would try in the first place, but she could be charged with treason if she said that.

The Margrave fixes her with a piercing stare but doesn't continue on that line of inquiry.

Taxation

It's sunrise when they find themselves in the tent by the town centre, mages having been deployed by the Arcanist to rebuild the hall just outside the tent as they were being debriefed by the Margrave, and Ban learns what happened to her companions. Leres gained a confession from the man in the woods: having worked with C'leirio, one of the mana thief's responsibilities was to hide three crates of mana crystals. Leres had sent an arcane message with his own mana to Krant and Nancy, informing them of the situation.

Krant had used his mana to teleport him and Nancy there, and with the mana crystals, they had decided to send Leres to Ban's location while Nancy messaged the Royal Transmission Centre. Gathering as many crystals as he could take, Krant helped to coordinate the Crown's men's teleportation with Pester's help (whom he woke and teleported to their location outside the town centre) before heading over to aid Leres and Ban. Nancy, in the meantime, had used a crystal to clear the fields of oil, a long and arduous task in which she was subsequently assisted by the Arcanist's mages, some of whom are still at it.

Ban can only sit there, her mouth agape internally as she listens to the lengths her friends have gone to save her and the town. In any other circumstance, they would have been tried for treason for misappropriation of the kingdom's resources. However…

"Regent Apotros has sent an imperial missive regarding the decree on misappropriation," says the Margrave, and Ban hears the implicit "as if I need reminding." "You have used the kingdom's resources in times of emergency to protect Seresthia, the kingdom's agricultural supplies, and subdue the mana thieves. For that, the Crown thanks your contributions, and sees fit to reward your town…"

☙

Relieved that the official letter will be sent within a day or two (she missed some of what was discussed due to exhaustion), Ban staggers home with the others. Hardly any words are exchanged except for looks of processing and disorientation, all in the vein of "what just happened?"

The children! thinks Leres, and the two of them start sprinting home. Behind them, Nancy calls out, stumbling alongside Krant, but they are ignored.

Ban and Leres burst through the door and rush up the stairs, not caring how loud they are as they call for their children. The house was unharmed in the conflict, the town hall being the only building touched in the whole event, but that hardly soothes them as they run to their children's room. Stuck in a feedback loop of anxiety and panic, they don't notice the runes across the floor until Ban bumps into a wall of force and is thrown against the opposite wall.

Groaning, she takes Leres's hand as she gets up. "What...what was that?"

"Krant's doing," he says, pointing at the purple runes that line the door and disappear into the room under the gap. "Probably made them a protection circle before he came to get us," he says in relief as Nancy and Krant burst in to the house, huffing and puffing.

"Yes—protection," pants Krant, climbing the stairs slowly, his stamina low, "nothing—touches them—keyed to—deactivate—when any—wake." He finally makes it upstairs and sets his hands on his knees. "I can take it off now, if—ok," he concludes as he sees the look on their faces. He gets on his knees to rub off a rune with a glowing finger.

As soon as he gives a "go ahead" gesture, Ban and Leres both rush into the room in a clatter. They crowd the beds, and the children slowly wake up in the embrace of their parents.

"Mama? Papa?" Mori rubs her eyes with a groan and props herself up on Leres's shoulders. "G'morning?"

"Yes, baby," sighs Leres in relief. "Good morning, darlings. Good morning."

As Yves and Mori echo their father, Darrol scans their faces and asks quietly: "Is everything ok?"

The family comes together in a group hug, Krant and Nancy included, and Ban finally feels peace. "Yes, darling. Everything is all right."

THE FIERY TALE OF EMBUN AND THE PRINCE
Julia Alba

Ever since I was old enough to remember, I have always wanted to see beyond the mountains.

My parents' house was on the outskirts of a small village deep inland, near the foot of the long chain of mountains called Banjaran Titiwangsa. My father was a farmer. My mother weaved baskets and mended sarongs for the neighbours. Whenever I told them about my dream, they said it was too dangerous because of the demons living in the mountains. Demons ate humans. They fed on our bodies and drank our blood.

According to Mother, the only way to kill demons was by using magic, which only the Maharaja and his family had the power to wield. The Ketua Kampung always assured us that the royal guards would protect us. I never had any reason to doubt him. My parents trusted the Ketua, so he must have been right.

At the pondok, I learnt sewing and cooking with the other girls. I shared my dream with them, too, but was only met with scepticism.

"Why would you want to leave?" one of my classmates asked. "We have everything here."

I glanced out the window, where the outline of the mountains was visible. "Do we? How do we know? We've never even left the village."

The girls were horrified. "Demons," one of them muttered. "There are demons out there. The village is safe."

I kept quiet. I couldn't argue with that.

That night, my father shook me awake while it was still dark out. As I blinked drowsily, he picked me up and carried me out of my room. The next thing I knew, he was shoving me into a kitchen cabinet.

"Don't leave," he ordered, slamming the doors shut.

The cabinet was dark and cramped, a tight squeeze for my fourteen-year-old body. I tried to make myself more comfortable, but a scream made me freeze.

It was Mother. Mother was screaming.

I pressed my palm against the door but didn't push it open. Father was screaming, too, and I remembered him ordering me not to leave. My blood ran cold. I couldn't move.

I didn't leave, not even when their screams stopped and were replaced with horrifying squelching, gnawing, and gulping sounds.

Suddenly, a loud crash erupted from the front of the house, followed by heavy footfalls, things being knocked down, and angry yells. The air turned hot, burning my nostrils. I couldn't breathe. I was being roasted alive.

But I stayed put. I wrapped my arms around my legs and gasped as torrents of scorching air clawed down my windpipe.

I couldn't make out what was happening. I heard agonised roars, barked orders and the crackling of flames. I smelled burnt flesh—the odour so rancid, it brought tears to my eyes. My head was spinning. My body was numb. I was grasping the ends of my life.

Then, light hit my face, bringing with it another wave of heat. I flinched back.

I blinked, my eyes adjusting to the brightness. I knew of sunlight and warmth, but what assaulted my senses that night was a completely different beast.

Right outside of the cabinet stood a boy I'd never seen before.

He was taller than me, with high cheekbones and unblemished skin. His short black hair gleamed under the flickering light. A crown shaped like golden leaves sat around his temples. An intricate songket was draped over one shoulder and tied at his opposite hip. Smoke wafted from his bare hands.

He was staring at me, looking as shocked as I felt.

"Tuanku?" a male voice said from further into the house.

A man with shoulder-length hair appeared behind the boy, his hand holding a spear. His eyes widened when he saw me crouching inside the cabinet. He lifted a hand to his mouth and yelled, "We have a survivor!"

After that, everything was a blur.

I was coaxed out. The kitchen was alight in flames, but I wasn't given time to take in the scene or grab anything. I glimpsed a pile of scarred remains on the floor before the man hauled me out of the house and handed me to someone else. The person who accepted me wore a thick moustache and didn't carry any weapon.

"Get inside," he said gently, ushering me into a carriage. "There might still be demons around, so let's be safe rather than sorry."

My mind was still in shock, but at the mention of demons, my legs moved of their own accord. The carriage was dark, so I felt around for a place to sit. As I collapsed on a bench, I stared out the window at my house. A big cloud of smoke rose from the roof. They must have put the fire out.

I jumped when the carriage opened again. The boy with the crown of golden leaves climbed in, carrying an oil lantern. He snapped his fingers and instantly, a small flame danced inside it. He hung the lantern from the ceiling and sat next to me.

"Send a pigeon to my father," he told the man with the moustache through the open window. "Tell him the situation."

After the man left, the boy turned to look at me. "What's your name?"

It took me a moment to find my voice. "Embun."

"Do you have anywhere to go?"

I immediately thought of my parents, the back of my eyes burning. "Are my parents really…?"

For a moment, the carriage was silent aside from the sound of our breathing.

"I'm sorry," he said, avoiding my eyes.

My heart clenched. "What about my neighbours?"

"None are left. We suspect most fled when the demons attacked the first few houses."

"There's no one in the village? Not even the Ketua?"

The boy nodded. "He must have escaped as soon as he sent a message to us. I don't think it's a good idea to wait around. The demons might come back."

I tried to think, but my head throbbed. I held my head in my hands and closed my eyes. Maybe if I didn't look at this mysterious boy, I could forget what happened tonight.

The boy, however, kept talking. "Would you like to stay with me?"

"What?" I clutched my head even tighter, my eyes still shut.

"Bonda said I need to find friends," he explained, sounding morose. "I thought she'd help me with that, but she's…not here anymore."

I dropped my hands and looked at him. I caught him looking sad, but the expression vanished when he noticed my gaze.

Knowing that this boy had also lost someone close to him made me feel an odd kinship with him. I didn't know his name, but he seemed to know about the void in my chest. He had probably felt it himself. And that made me less frightened of him.

"What do you want from me?" I asked.

"I don't know." He sighed wearily. "You haven't answered my question. Would you like to stay with me?"

"But I'm a girl," I pointed out helplessly. "And you're…"

"Ah." He made a disgruntled sound, his eyebrows furrowed. "Do your teachers teach you that boys and girls can't be friends?"

The Fiery Tale of Embun and the Prince

My mind raced. Of course, they can't! Even at the pondok, girls and boys were separated into different classrooms, never allowed to mix. The adults must have good reasons to do that; they wouldn't have done it otherwise.

Despite all these thoughts, I couldn't utter them aloud. My chest felt hollow. I felt aimless. All this while, I had counted on my parents to give me direction. Now, I had lost them. And the other villagers had left me behind.

The boy scratched his wrist, an impatient frown on his face. "I'm sorry. I rarely talk to people my age. I'm not familiar with…what's common."

I'd been indecisive for long enough. With my parents gone, I had to look for my own direction. I had to make decisions for my own well-being. If I made the wrong choice, then so be it.

"Alright," I said. "I'll stay with you."

His eyes widened. Then he relaxed, a small smile on his lips. "I'm Zahid," he said, tilting his head toward me. Then he leaned forwards and tapped a finger against the wooden panel separating us from the driver. "Take us home."

Somehow, I fell asleep during the journey. When I woke up again, the carriage had stopped. Zahid opened the door, jumped out, and beckoned me to follow him. I poked my upper body out, took in my surroundings and promptly fell out of the carriage.

Zahid couldn't catch me in time. I barely felt the impact of hitting the ground, too shocked by what I saw.

I was in a compound surrounded by buildings that were taller than any house I'd ever seen. The wooden panels were gleaming, almost shining. There was a beautiful garden near where the carriage was parked.

The sun had just risen, the light casting a soft glow on the flowers. It was like nothing I had ever seen.

In a daze, I followed Zahid and the guards to one of the buildings. There were so many doors. The corridors looked so long, they felt endless.

We eventually stopped at a pair of open doors. Zahid confidently strode inside. I only moved after being urged by the guards.

The teachers at the pondok taught us to worship kings because they were the shadows of God on earth. We learnt about the Maharaja and how he protected all villages from demons with his destructive Fire magic. My teacher hung the royal emblem on the classroom wall for protection.

Now, I stood in a royal address chamber, a small, shaking orphan in tattered clothes standing inside a large room filled with nicely-dressed guards and maids. The Maharaja was a large man with a thick beard, sitting on his tall and majestic throne.

Zahid was on one knee and bowing, somehow keeping his crown on his head. When I first saw him, he had smoke coming out of his hands. He lit a lantern with a snap of his fingers. I remembered the fire in my kitchen and realised *he* had caused it. It was no surprise that the son of the Maharaja would inherit his magic.

If I hadn't just had a devastating night, I probably would have made the connection sooner.

"Who's this?" the Maharaja asked, nodding at me. "Have you finally found a friend?"

"Yes, Ayahanda."

"Very well." He waved a hand at the group of maids huddled near the sidewall. "Please take care of her for the prince."

☙

The maids didn't know what to do with me at first. The Maharaja's command was clear and vague at the same time. Initially, they tried dressing me like a princess, but I hated it. I hated having people dress me in strange clothes or hold my hair as if they had any right to. No, only my mother had ever washed and tied my hair. Only my father had ever brought home clothes for me.

Tired of my protests, the maids tossed me old uniforms that had gotten too small for them. The sleeves were too long, but I cut them with a pair of scissors I borrowed from the kitchen. After I was done with them, the clothes resembled the dresses and sarongs my father would have gotten after bartering some crops. I convinced myself that that was what they were, and I wore the clothes gratefully.

Even though the palace had thousands of rooms, I shared one with Head Maid Orked. She was a middle-aged woman with wrinkles across her forehead and around her mouth. Despite her stern demeanour, she was kind to me. She was delighted when I told her I did most of the housework back home. She listened quietly when I recounted my encounter with Zahid.

"The prince never had any friends," said Orked. "After the Ratu passed away three years ago, the Maharaja promised he'd accept anyone the prince brought home."

I wasn't surprised that Orked knew the royal family well. She must have been working at the palace for ages. "Why aren't there any children here?" I asked her.

"Workers aren't allowed to bring families into the palace. They have their own compound outside."

"What about you?"

Orked smiled. "I'm unmarried. I have no family. Like you, I lost my parents to demons."

Orked showed me what she and the maids did daily. She took the maids' duties and responsibilities seriously and ensured the other maids and I did, too.

I fell into the role she offered me easily. Cleaning and house chores were familiar to me. I used to do them at home. I learnt them at the pondok. I used to race with the other village girls to see who could sew the fastest; I always lost, but my skills were good enough for Orked.

Almost a year passed before I met Zahid again.

I was helping Orked clean a bedroom. It was bigger than any of the rooms I had entered before. When I asked why none of the other maids helped us, Orked put a finger to her lips and continued dusting the tables.

Suddenly, the doors opened, and a smell of smoke irritated my throat. I gave a violent cough.

"Ya Tuhan," Orked gasped.

I wheeled around and gasped, too.

Zahid was covered from head to toe in soot. His clothes were torn and singed at the edges, and his hair was messy. His crown lay askew on his head. Slamming the doors behind him, he didn't look surprised to see Orked, but his eyes widened when he saw me.

"You—!" He squeaked before glaring at Orked. "You're bringing her into this?"

"You're the one who brought her here," Orked said sternly. "You need help. I won't be here forever."

Zahid looked indignant at first, but his expression turned resigned when he looked at me. He seemed defeated. "Please don't hate me."

"Why would I hate you?" I asked, confused.

Zahid furrowed his eyebrows, looking unhappy. Instead of answering me, he turned away with a grunt, pulled up his sleeves and started scratching his arm. His blackened fingernails left angry red lines on his skin.

Orked carried over a basin filled with water and made Zahid sit on the floor next to it. Then she called me over and asked me to sit next to him. She knelt behind me and took my hands.

"I'm going to show you how to take care of the prince," Orked said gently but loudly enough for both Zahid and me to hear. "This is a duty the Ratu bestowed upon me and now upon you."

"I've never met the Ratu." I watched Zahid closely when I said it. I saw that same glimpse of sadness on his face when I mentioned his mother.

"The prince has chosen you, so the duty falls on you, too," Orked replied. "If you have any more questions, you may ask me later. Right now, your friend needs us."

She showed me how to scrape out the soot under Zahid's fingernails using a blunt metal tool. When we washed his hands, I felt warmth radiate from them. They reminded me of when I used to hold my hands over a flame to keep myself warm on cold nights.

Orked kept reminding me to be gentle. I focused hard on her instructions. That was how I noticed the scars and rough patches of skin on Zahid's fingers. His palms felt raw compared to my own.

I heard a sniffle. When I glanced up, my breath caught at the sight of tears falling from Zahid's eyes. He quickly stooped forward and dropped his head until I couldn't see his face.

"Are you all right?" I asked, but nobody answered me.

We washed his face and hair next. After that, we left him to bathe alone. Orked brought me to Zahid's massive cupboard and showed me where his clothes were kept, quickly pointing out what attire was for what occasion. I learnt which type of fabric was flame resistant and which was not. Then, Orked made me observe her apply medicinal ointment to Zahid's palms. We left him again to fetch his dinner. Orked fed him because he couldn't use his hands.

The entire time the three of us were together, Zahid cried silently.

༓

"It hurts him, you know," Orked said when she and I were alone in her room, "the more he uses his powers."

I gaped at her. "Then he should stop using them!"

"If he stops using his powers, who will fight the demons?"

"The Maharaja, of course. And the royal army!" I cried. The image of Zahid crying was still stuck in my head. "He's just a boy!"

Orked raised an eyebrow. "He is sixteen. Old enough to fight in wars."

I didn't have a comeback for that. I didn't know what was expected of boys, let alone a prince. "Why can't the Maharaja fight? Why leave everything to his son?"

Orked glanced at the door and paused before lowering her voice into a whisper. "The Maharaja has no magic."

My jaw dropped. "But…the teachers said…the Maharaja is—"

"The shadow of God on earth?" Orked spat. "The Maharaja is just a man. No God speaks through him. If anyone is special, it's Zahid."

This didn't make any sense. "But the Maharaja has been king for a long time, and he is known for his magic. Does that mean…"

Orked nodded. "Zahid has been fighting demons since he was four years old."

My hands fell to my sides. I couldn't imagine being made to face demons at that age. No wonder he didn't act or talk like the boys from my village.

"Listen, Embun," said Orked solemnly, demanding my attention. "Soon, Zahid will start changing. You will know when. When he does, I ask you to stay by his side. Assure him that he's doing the right thing. Get him to accept himself for what he is."

"*What he is?*" I echoed in horror. "What's wrong with him?"

Orked's face drained of colour. "Nothing! Remember that, Embun. There is *nothing* wrong with him!"

I suddenly felt protective of Zahid, which was stupid. He was a magical prince, while I was…what was I, exactly?

But my role didn't matter. As soon as Zahid asked me not to hate him, I remembered that I still owed him for saving my life. I had to repay him somehow, even if I'd be repaying him for the rest of my life.

I'd be anything he needed me to be.

౦౩

Whenever there was a call for help from any of the villages in the Maharaja's domain, Zahid would go with the royal army to drive away the demons. The attacks were unpredictable. Sometimes they occurred as frequently as every week. Sometimes, two months went by between attacks. Orked and I would wait in his room for his return.

The longer this went on, the more worried I became. What if he had to stay after a battle to help the villagers? Why must he endure the pain all the way home?

Zahid always had a scowl on his face when he returned from a battle. Lately, his injuries had gotten worse. His raw skin now extended beyond his palms and reached his shoulders. I noticed how he often clawed at his limbs, as though he hated being inside his own skin.

No matter how much pain I knew he was in, he never cried in front of me again.

His mood would improve after the hand wash. After a bath, he'd be open to talking. Orked rarely spoke to him, but I did. I never left the palace, so I was always curious about where he went. I asked him whatever I wanted to know, and Zahid indulged me. He told me about the village next to a big lake, the nomadic tribe who made houses on trees, and the demon clan who kidnapped children.

I couldn't help finding his stories impressive. Zahid never painted himself as the protagonist in his stories, but I saw him for what he was.

A hero.

He saved people and expected nothing back. He did it continuously and selflessly despite its toll on his body.

When I turned sixteen, I got a room of my own in the maids' quarters but continued to help Orked take care of Zahid.

One day, Orked had to stay behind because she was feeling unwell. This was my first time tending to Zahid alone.

The Fiery Tale of Embun and the Prince

While he bathed, I sat next to a window that overlooked Banjaran Titiwangsa, my elbows on the windowsill. It was already dark, but I could see a faint outline of the mountains, the peaks so high that they disappeared behind white clouds. I still longed to travel, to see the world, but the image of a pile of burnt remains in my kitchen lingered in my memory.

How could I wish to go away when Zahid was stuck here, fighting? My dreams were trivial compared to his duties.

I was staring at the view when Zahid suddenly spoke.

"Looking at the mountains?"

I jumped away from the window, bumping into him. Wincing, he stepped back from me. He wore a vest that exposed his arms, the skin pink and raw. It looked painful.

I hastily led him to the small table where I had placed jars of Orked's medicine. "I'm sorry for getting distracted."

Zahid stayed quiet while I began putting medicine on his shoulder. Being so close to him always made me feel warm. Even when he wasn't lighting lanterns with his fingers, he was still as hot as flames.

Since Orked wasn't around, I had to focus on the task, so I didn't ask him anything.

Instead, he had questions for me. "Why were you looking at the mountains?"

I considered my answer as I scooped out more of the ointment from Orked's jar. "Have you ever wondered what's beyond?"

"No. Ayahanda said crossing the terrains would be too troublesome and risky. Besides, it's not necessary. We have all the resources we need on this side of the land."

I shot him a bewildered look. "I don't intend to go there to look for *resources*. Honestly, that's no fun."

Zahid chuckled. "What would be your reason for going there?"

"No reason," I replied. "Just…for an adventure, I guess."

"An adventure? I've never thought of that." For a second, Zahid looked like he was going to laugh, but he caught himself. "I'm sorry I never looked for you after bringing you here. I wanted to show you around the castle and get to know you, but I couldn't find the time. The demon attacks grew frequent and, well, I'm sorry."

"I don't mind," I said. "You gave me a new home. I'm very grateful."

"I brought you here to be my friend, but all I've made you do is tend to me as if I were a child." Zahid turned his face away. "It's bad enough with the Head Maid, but with you, it's embarrassing."

I withdrew my hands and sat back. "Do you hate me?"

Zahid snapped his gaze at me, looking stricken. "Of course not!"

"Then stop thinking this is embarrassing," I said. "I want to help you. Friends help each other. You've done so much to protect the people against the demons. If something happens to you, I can't imagine—"

I couldn't bring myself to finish the sentence. I resumed rubbing medicine on his arm, purposely avoiding his eyes.

When I got to the inside of his left forearm, I touched something cold and sharp. It didn't hurt, but I was startled enough to gasp and yank my hand back.

Zahid tensed. He scratched the part I had touched. It was quick, but I saw shiny blue bits coming off his skin. One of them fell on my sarong. It looked like a scale but much larger than the ones I had scraped off of fish. This single scale was as big as my fingernail.

As fast as lightning, Zahid grabbed the scale off my sarong, his hand leaving a trail of heat on my knee.

"What's that?" I asked.

Zahid had gone pale. He turned his whole body away from me. When he spoke again, he sounded distant. "Could you please get my dinner now?"

"But your other arm—"

"I can do it myself." He clumsily curled his fingers around the medicine jar, his whole arm trembling. "Please hurry. I'm hungry."

I went to the kitchen to pick up his dinner and carried the tray back to his room. Zahid was dozing off on the floor, his head on a cushion. He was still wearing his crown. Orked's medicinal jar was empty; he had somehow succeeded in applying it onto his other arm by himself, albeit very sloppily. Half of the medicine had ended up on the floor.

He jolted awake when I set the tray on the table.

"Why do you sleep with your crown on?" I asked, wiping the spilt medicine with a rag. "It must be uncomfortable."

He adjusted his crown self-consciously, ignoring my question. "Thank you. You can go now."

I bristled. "The skin on your hands is still healing. It hurts you when you touch anything. How are you going to feed yourself?"

He sighed. "Please, Embun. Let me maintain some dignity in front of you."

"Fine. I'll leave," I huffed. "But only if you agree to my request."

He inhaled deeply. "What is it?"

"The next time you go, bring me with you."

"It's dangerous," he protested, narrowing his eyes.

Even if it were, I'd be by his side. As long as he was fine, I didn't care what happened to me. I also trusted him to keep me from harm, but I didn't tell him this.

"It'll be fine," I said instead.

Zahid looked down at his hands. "If I agree, will you go?"

I squared my shoulders. "Yes."

"Very well," he said stiffly, sounding awfully like his father. "Now, please leave me alone."

I practically stomped my way to the maids' quarters. As I got nearer to my room, my steps slowed. I thought of the strange blue scale I had seen. I couldn't help but remember what Orked had told me long ago.

Soon, Zahid will start changing. You will know when.

I still didn't know what this meant, but I was determined to find out.

ೞ

We set out after sunset.

Before we left, Zahid made me promise not to leave the carriage. Then he climbed onto a horse and hurried to the front of the line to lead his army.

The carriage was meant for Zahid. I could tell because it was more spacious and nicer than the others. I had packed a few bags containing supplies: his medicine, water, food, and even a couple of sets of clothes for both of us. I didn't know how long we would be on the road, after all. I rarely travelled so I couldn't estimate how long the journey would take. There were several other carriages, mostly to carry

The Fiery Tale of Embun and the Prince

weapons and supplies. The generals were on horseback while the majority of the soldiers were on foot.

After what felt like a long time, I opened the slot on the wooden panel separating the driver and me. "Excuse me, sir?"

When the driver turned to look at me, I instantly recognised him and his moustache.

"I know you!" I exclaimed. "You were the driver who first brought me to the palace!"

The man laughed. "Indeed. I'm honoured you remember me, Lady Embun."

"Where are we headed, sir?"

"You can call me Tandang," he said. "We received a message that a demon was sighted at a village in the east. We're heading there now."

I glanced at our surroundings. In the dark, all the trees we passed looked identical.

"Does the prince have to go every time a village calls for help?" I asked. "Why can't the royal army handle them themselves? I know they can fight demons too."

"Yes, the royal army is armed with special, magical weapons that can damage demons," Tandang affirmed. "But the Maharaja has ordered the prince to answer every call."

I crossed my arms. "Why? That's too much work for one person."

"This is just my theory," said Tandang, "but I believe the Maharaja wants the demons to be defeated by Fire magic. It is his brand, after all."

I knew that the Maharaja had no magic and that his Fire "brand" was just him exploiting Zahid's power, but I didn't know how much Tandang knew about it. Orked had warned me not to talk about it openly.

"You mean the Maharaja wants the people to remember that he holds power over them?"

Tandang nodded. "Would this be your first time watching the prince fight?"

I realised with a start that, indeed, it would be.

Tandang smiled. "You must see it for yourself. Then you will understand why the Maharaja wants his son to fight every time. It's good for his image."

I grimaced. What was good about taking advantage of your own son for the sake of your reputation?

We were at the back of Zahid's retinue, so when I heard people screaming, I knew Zahid and his army had already started fighting the demons. Tandang steered us behind a barricade made of several soldiers, shields and wooden barriers.

"We're here, Lady Embun," Tandang called as I opened the wooden slot again. "Please stay inside the carriage."

I didn't see any villagers; they must have escaped or had been evacuated. Several houses had gaping holes in the walls, and a few had been reduced to piles of rubble.

My blood ran cold at the sight of the demons. There were dozens of them clawing, biting, and clashing with the soldiers. Most were out in the open, but there were also noises coming from the houses and stables.

Demons looked similar to humans, aside from their abnormally pallid skin and red eyes. They had unnatural hair colours, ranging from sunflower yellow to orchid purple. They had indestructible claws and sharp fangs. They could burrow and hide underground. The worst thing was their odour; they smelled of rotten meat.

An explosion sounded from one of the houses. A large ball of fire shot out of the front door and landed in a heap of ashes on the ground.

Zahid walked out of the house, looking enraged.

Demons rushed towards him in a big group, their claws out.

I was inside my carriage, a good distance from Zahid and the ongoing fight, but I could feel the air becoming hot.

Zahid's hands were glowing. As the demons approached him, fire engulfed his hands and licked up his arms. He emitted pulses of magic so strong, I could almost taste it. With every swing of his arms, fire swept forward like waves, leaving trails of bright gold in their wake. He moved so fast that it looked like he was dancing while surrounded by golden light. His crown shone like fireflies. His black hair gleamed. His face was bathed in flickering yellow and golden light.

Anyone who witnessed him like this would be enchanted.

People saw Zahid as an extension of his father, so his marvellous display of power only strengthened the Maharaja's image. If people blindly believed in the Maharaja's power, they would respect and be devoted to him.

But in reality, the Maharaja had no magic. Orked had said: *If anyone is special, it's Zahid.*

Zahid was, without a doubt, very special.

Demons bellowed in anguish as flames enveloped them and turned them into ash. The rancid stench of carcasses mixed with smoke and burnt flesh made me sick. I pinched my nose and breathed through my mouth. Tandang must have taken pity on me; he closed the wooden panel, preventing the smoke from entering the carriage.

The back of my throat felt itchy and uncomfortable, so I gulped down some water and wiped my face. How could Zahid stand doing this so often?

The noise had quietened down. The carriage door opened and Zahid rolled himself onboard, which I found very strange until I noticed how badly his hands were burnt.

Zahid collapsed on the cushions, cradling his hands to his chest as I went straight for the medicine. I almost dropped the jar when the carriage lurched into motion.

"We're done, right?" I hastily coated his hands with Orked's ointment. "Let's go home now."

He shook his head. "No, we can't go yet. Several demons escaped and fled to Timah Village. We need to go there."

"To another village?" I almost shrieked. "Look at your hands! You're in no condition to keep using your magic."

"I can't sit around and do nothing when the other village could be attacked. We can reach there before the demons kill anyone." He tried to take my hands, but flexing his fingers made him flinch. "I'll be fine. You're here to treat me. People need me, Embun. Please."

I dropped my gaze. The skin of Zahid's hands was peeling, exposing the pink, shiny flesh beneath. Even after sloshing medicine all over them, I knew his hands were far from healed.

I was torn between insisting that we drive back to the palace and letting Zahid have his way. It killed me to see him like this. His body couldn't withstand the intensity of his own powers.

But he had a duty.

And I wasn't getting in the way of that.

Zahid told Tandang to update his father about the detour. A messenger pigeon flapped its way to the palace as we headed to Timah Village, Zahid fidgeting restlessly the whole way.

When we arrived, we didn't see anybody. All the doors and windows were closed. No torch was lit. There were no signs of an attack or a hasty evacuation. It was unclear whether there was anyone in any of the houses.

I followed Zahid out of the carriage, ignoring his weak protests. I sniffed the air for that tell-tale stench of carcasses, but I couldn't smell anything.

"Should we check each house, Tuanku?" asked a soldier.

Zahid narrowed his eyes. I tried to imagine what he could be thinking, but I had no clue. All I could think of was returning to the palace and making Zahid rest. He could use more medicine and a bath.

Suddenly, something grabbed my ankle and yanked me off my feet.

Yelping, I hit the ground hard. The strange grip around my ankle tightened and pulled me away, dragging me across the dirt. Zahid called my name, but he sounded far away.

I looked down, and panic seized my throat. Around my ankle was a pale hand with long claws. The hand was connected to an arm that burst out of the ground, pulling me away from Zahid and the army.

I couldn't remember whether I screamed. I tried to kick the hand, but it held on. I clawed at the ground but found no purchase.

I heard someone yell my name again. I had trouble seeing past the tears in my eyes, but I thought I saw a fireball zipping through the air. It struck the wrist of the hand that held me.

The grip around my ankle loosened, and I quickly pulled my leg out of its grasp. Once free, I rolled onto my hands and knees, pushing myself up. I heard a noise behind me, and I stupidly glanced back, only to be frozen in fear when I saw a demon—with large fangs and red eyes—lunge at me.

Zahid pushed me out of the way, sending both of us rolling to the side. When we stopped, he had his arms around me, his body above mine, shielding me. He pushed himself up, his hair dropping to his forehead. His crown had fallen off.

Neither of us had time to say anything because more demons rushed towards us. My eyes widened in horror when I saw the anger burning in Zahid's eyes.

"No, Zahid, don't!" I reached for him, but he had jumped to his feet, flames engulfing his fists.

The first wave of fire disintegrated several demons. The next vanquished a couple more. I could hear the royal army fighting clusters of demons around us, but all I saw was Zahid slowly crumbling. After the third wave, he collapsed to his knees and clutched his head. I crawled towards him but halted when his body started shifting.

The horns appeared first. They grew from his temples, bending and tapering until they were as long as my forearms. Meanwhile, his body grew and elongated. I heard the horrible sounds of bones crushing and grating against one another. His clothes ripped as he outgrew them, revealing green-and-blue scales instead of skin. His hands and feet transformed into talons.

At the end of the transformation, Zahid was a long serpent-like creature with scales the colour of the

The Fiery Tale of Embun and the Prince

ocean, horns as dark as granite, and four eagle-like limbs.

He was something I had only heard of from stories, only seen pictures on tapestries at the palace.

A dragon.

I couldn't breathe.

Zahid created another wave of fire with a quick flick of his tail. This blast was much stronger than before. He glided in the air around me and attacked any demons that dared to approach. He opened his maw and shot a column of fire into a group of demons.

I sat dumbfounded on the ground, images flashing behind my eyes.

Orked warning me: *Soon, Zahid will start changing. You will know when.*

Zahid scratching his arms and legs.

The lonely blue scale on my sarong.

Zahid adjusting his crown.

Looking around, I spotted Zahid's crown lying in the dirt. He had worn it when we first met and never took it off. He even slept with it.

When I picked it up, I sensed a strange energy emanating from it.

The battle ended quickly. When I stood up, I noticed the windows and doors opening one by one. Villagers filed out, whispering amongst themselves. It took me a short moment to realise that they were muttering, staring and pointing at the dragon.

Zahid twirled around and flew towards our carriage. I saw Tandang with his mouth open, but he remained on his seat, hands clutching the horses' reins as Zahid slipped inside. Even though he was long—he could easily wrap around the carriage twice—his whole body disappeared into the carriage.

I ran towards the carriage. When I got in, Zahid was back to his human self, hiding his body beneath an extra sarong I had brought along. I tossed his crown at his feet and quickly turned to close the door. When I turned back around, the crown was back on his head.

We stared at each other, speechless.

"I can explain," Zahid said, while I asked, "Can we go home now?"

He nodded. I relayed the message to Tandang, who obediently drove us back home.

I gave him a moment to get dressed. We drank some water and shared some fruit. After we ate, I took a new jar of medicine and scooted over to him. I thought we could talk while I tended to his injuries.

Imagine my astonishment when I saw that his hands were perfectly fine.

"How?" I gaped at him. Just an hour ago, his hands were peeling. "How have you healed so fast?"

Zahid looked just as surprised, though he appeared too tired to ponder it. "I don't know. Maybe because I transformed?" He winced. "I...I don't do it often."

"You're not hurt? At all?"

I checked his palms, his knuckles, his wrists, his arms, and even his shoulders. With the amount of magic he had used, he should be a raw piece of meat. But his skin was fine.

He was fine.

I was incredibly relieved, but this only gave birth to more questions. I wanted to hear answers from Zahid himself.

"Since you're all right, could you explain to me now? How long have you known that you're," I paused, shaking my head in disbelief, "a dragon?"

"I've known all my life. Using magic makes me want to transform. It's an instinct thing. I'm still me, just in a different form. Bonda made me this crown to stop me from transforming."

"To stop you from transforming?" I recalled his beautiful blue scales. "Why?"

Zahid grimaced, looking affronted. "Because it's not normal! The people wouldn't trust me to protect them if they knew I was a monster."

"You're *not* a monster!" I insisted. "You've saved these people hundreds of times! It shouldn't matter how you look doing it."

He leaned back and closed his eyes. "If only Ayahanda thought the way you do."

"What did your father do?"

"He said the people would hate me if they found out. People are bound to fear or hate things that look different from them. They might look at me and think I'm a demon."

"Is that why there are no children at the palace?" I asked, finally seeing it. "And why you never mix with people your age? So that this secret doesn't get out?"

He nodded. "Most of the palace staff know, especially those who have served for a long time. They're not allowed to talk about it, not even to each other."

Since he had his eyes closed, I took the opportunity to observe his face. It was nice not to see him scowling and gritting his teeth in pain. Watching him fight, both in human and dragon form, was an experience I would never forget.

Finally, I asked, "How does it feel? Becoming a dragon?"

He took a deep breath. "Like freedom. I'm stronger. Faster. I can fly. Magic comes easier, like second nature, and I…" He trailed off. "But it doesn't matter. I can still use magic when in human form."

I stared at him incredulously. "Are you dumb?"

He cracked open an eye. "Excuse me?"

"You always get hurt when you use magic because you use it while in human form!" I exclaimed. "Think about it. A normal person doesn't go up in flames; our bodies can't stand that much heat. But you know what can? A dragon! When you used magic as a dragon, your human body was fine. The transformation even healed your injuries."

Zahid was staring at me with both eyes now. "You think so?"

I refrained from smacking his head. "Yes! Don't you see? You can use your powers without hurting yourself if you transform into a dragon before you use them. Easy!"

I truly believed I had found a brilliant solution to his problem, but he didn't look convinced.

"Didn't you see the way those people looked at me? They were scared of me."

"Because they don't know you. If you explain to them, they'll see that you're still their beloved prince."

Zahid was quiet for a moment, studying me. "What about you?"

I blinked. "What do you mean?"

"Now that you know what I am," he said, "what do you think of me?"

My face suddenly felt warmer than usual. "Well, you saved my life again. You were really amazing. You *are* amazing."

Smiling, he took my hand and brought it to his lips. He kissed my knuckles, his hot breath lingering on my skin as he muttered, "Thank you."

☙

As soon as we arrived at the palace at dawn, Zahid was summoned to the Maharaja's chamber. Even though I wasn't invited, I tagged along. As we walked, Zahid slid his palm against mine and weaved our fingers together. When I sent him a quizzical look, he returned a smile.

We arrived at the same chamber we had entered when I first came to the palace. Everything looked similar, but I felt different this time. I was no longer a lost orphan with no friends. Now I knew where my loyalties lay, and it wasn't with the man sitting languidly on the throne.

As Zahid went to kneel before his father, I slipped inside and hid behind two guards near the entrance.

"I received a letter from the Timah Village," the Maharaja said, waving a piece of parchment. "The Ketua Kampung asked me whether it is true that the Prince has the ability to turn himself into a beast."

Zahid stiffened and kept his head bowed. The whole room fell silent; no one dared to make a sound.

"Well?" said the Maharaja.

"My crown fell off," said Zahid. "Then I was attacked. I...changed then. I'm not sure how the villagers could have seen me. I apologise for my mistake."

"Mistake," the Maharaja echoed. "You could have tarnished the image of our kingdom. You could have destroyed the people's faith in us."

"I'm sorry, Ayahanda."

"Guards. Bring the prince to the dungeons."

Zahid's head snapped up. I gasped in horror. The maids near me whispered, aghast, "The dungeons?"

"You will be released the next time a village calls for your help," the Maharaja continued.

This was unfair. Ridiculous. I felt anger rising in my throat, but then I realised that none of the guards were carrying out the Maharaja's orders. They were all glancing nervously at Zahid and then at each other.

Zahid had said that all the palace staff knew his secret. Did they know how he had been used by the Maharaja since he was a little boy? Did they know how he was forced to fight demons throughout his childhood? Did they know how he was denied being his true self?

"What are you waiting for?" the Maharaja hissed at the guards. "Take him away!"

"Please forgive them, Ayahanda," said Zahid calmly, standing up to his full height. "Your problem isn't with them. It's with me."

The room fell silent again. I held my breath.

"You know, all my life," Zahid continued, "I did everything you ordered. I fought demons for you. I never took off this crown Bonda made to stop me from changing. You've never once asked me how I was. Or how I felt."

The Maharaja's face turned red.

"Until someone asked me today," Zahid continued, "I never realised what it felt like being a dragon. Now, I'm telling everyone here. The feeling is pure delight. Happiness." He smiled sadly. "Like nothing you've ever made me feel."

The Maharaja stood up, looking like he was ready to shout, but Zahid was faster.

He shoved his crown off his head and turned on his heels. The transformation was faster this time because he wasn't fighting it. It was over in a blink of an eye.

There was a collective gasp. I couldn't help but be enraptured again by the sight of Zahid in his dragon glory.

He twirled towards one of the windows and jumped out.

I, along with everyone else, rushed to the window. We all watched in awe as Zahid's blue figure flew towards the sky and disappeared in the distance.

ଓଃ

The guards outside the Maharaja's private chambers eyed me suspiciously, making me fidget.

"I'd like to speak with the Maharaja, please," I politely requested, balancing a tray of water and some fruits.

"Are you the prince's friend?" one of them asked. "You look familiar."

"Yes," I squeaked. "I, um, we want to bring him back, but I think I need to talk to the Maharaja first."

Seemingly satisfied, the guards pulled aside their spears and allowed me entry.

It had been three days since Zahid's unexpected exit. As much as I wondered how he was doing, I trusted him. He was a dragon, after all. From his display, I had the impression that he was ready to accept himself.

I'd like to see if I could convince his father to accept him, too.

The Maharaja was on the floor, reclining against large cushions and staring into space. He fiddled with Zahid's crown, his fingers idly tracing the leaf patterns.

I knelt next to the door, put my tray down, and knocked against the wooden doorframe. I placed my hands together above my head and bowed, waiting for his grunt before approaching him. I put my tray on the small table by his side. He hadn't looked at me yet, so I waited.

When he noticed I hadn't left, he swiftly turned towards me, his face red with fury. But then his face slowly fell as he recognised me.

"You." He didn't know my name, of course. "Do you know where he is?"

I shook my head.

He slumped back against the cushions. "Then why are you here?"

"To talk, Tuanku Maharaja," I answered, trying hard to keep my voice from trembling. This was my first time speaking to the Maharaja. "I think something needs to happen if you want the prince to come back."

The Maharaja put Zahid's crown down and rubbed a hand down his face. "What do you expect me to do?"

"Apologise to him. Let him know that he doesn't need to hide who he is and that you will love him no matter what."

He scoffed. "He knows that."

"No," I said. "No, he doesn't. And you're bad at showing it. You told him people would hate him if his real nature got out, but that's not true at all. You're just scared of what people will think of you."

"What makes you think you can talk to me this way?" he snapped. "I should throw you in the dungeons."

My hands shook, but I replied, "If you do anything to me, your son will hate you forever."

That shut him up. He studied me closely. "Do you know how he became what he is?"

I didn't. I'd heard rumours and speculations among the palace staff, but I refused to believe any story about Zahid that didn't come from Zahid himself.

The Maharaja was gazing expectantly at me, impatient for an answer. I shook my head again.

"I had magic when I was younger, but it was very weak," the Maharaja said. "The more I aged, the weaker my magic became. I knew if I didn't do anything, I would end up powerless and my younger brothers would usurp my throne."

I gulped, forcing myself to stay silent.

"During one of our travels, my wife and I captured a dragon. In exchange for its freedom, I bargained for power, but all it did was put a curse on my son. He was only two years old at the time." His expression darkened. "Needless to say, we didn't take too kindly to that."

My stomach turned when I imagined what they could have done to the dragon in retaliation. "And then you saw what Zahid could do and decided to take advantage of him?"

I winced as soon as the words were out of my mouth. I expected the Maharaja to scold me again, but he simply gazed at me forlornly in response. He didn't even deny it.

"It was my wife's idea," he admitted with a sigh. "I thought I was protecting him. If people knew what was wrong with him—"

"There's nothing wrong with your son," I interjected. "In fact, he is quite extraordinary. A prince unlike any other."

He paused for a moment, seemingly in thought. "It has been many years since my wife passed. I have...begun to see the error of my ways," he said, glancing at Zahid's crown. "What do you propose?"

"With all due respect, Tuanku Maharaja, I've already shared my humble opinion," I said with a bow. "But there are people other than me who want to tell you something."

The door opened and two men walked in. One was Tandang. The other had greying hair and a square jaw. They both pressed their palms together, raised them to their foreheads and bowed their heads.

The Maharaja frowned at them. "Fuad? Tandang? What are you two doing here?"

The grey-haired man stepped forward and dropped to one knee. "Tuanku Maharaja, I've had the honour of serving as your Head of the Royal Army for years. Today, my advisor Tandang and I would like to discuss a battle strategy we've devised."

The Maharaja scratched his bearded chin. "A battle strategy?"

"We believe our forces are strong enough to defeat the demons without the prince. The prince doesn't need to join every single fight. He can…" Fuad faltered for a second, but he inhaled and said, "He can be free, Tuanku."

The Maharaja leaned towards me. "Is this your doing?"

"Oh no, Tuanku, I don't know anything about fighting demons." I shot Tandang an appreciative grin. He smiled back. "This is all them. We want our prince to be happy. With your infinite wisdom, we hope you'll let it happen."

"Very well." The Maharaja nodded at the two gentlemen. "I'd like to proceed with this meeting immediately."

I backed out of the room and walked until I reached the corner where Orked was waiting for me.

She took one look at my face and sighed in relief. "I suppose we can move on to our next plan. I should get packed."

"Yes, I should, too," I agreed, still smiling. "We'll wait for Tandang, and then we'll go."

༄

We had no idea where Zahid was, but we knew where to look. We started at Timah Village and asked the villagers if they'd seen the prince.

As I had predicted, the Maharaja tagged along with us. His carriage was the most massive and majestic one of all. All the villagers, even the children, marvelled at the Maharaja and his impressive entourage.

The only one who approached us with answers was the Ketua Kampung, who trembled in the Maharaja's presence. He collapsed onto his hands and knees in front of him.

"My deepest apologies, Tuanku!" he cried, his forehead on the ground. "It was never my intention to offend the prince. I just asked because my villagers were curious, you see. But when the prince came to explain the truth to us, we accepted him openly! We are honoured to have a powerful dragon protecting us!"

The Maharaja's eyes widened. "You truly accept him?"

The villagers chorused an enthusiastic "Yes!"

The Maharaja wiped his eyes and cleared his throat. He asked the Ketua to stand. "Do you know where he is?"

The Ketua said that Zahid had gone north, so we headed in that direction. We passed by two villages before we reached our destination.

We were sure we were at the correct village because Zahid was waiting for us at the entrance.

He wore a plain, short-sleeved shirt and a pair of trousers that stopped at his calves. A checkered *samping* was tied around his waist. He seemed excited to see us.

My heart skipped a beat. I grabbed my bag, ready to leap out of my carriage, but Orked stopped me with a hand on my shoulder. She gestured out the window.

The Maharaja exited his carriage and approached Zahid. In his hand was Zahid's old crown.

Zahid raised an eyebrow at it, his smile vanishing.

Once he was close enough, the Maharaja tossed the crown on the ground between them.

"Your Bonda made this using powerful *sihr*. Only your magic can destroy it. So, please," he said, his chin quivering, "forgive me for everything I've done to you, for everything I've made you do. You're free to be yourself. I need my son back."

I could sense the tension in the air, as if the entire royal entourage was holding its breath. It was rare, perhaps unthinkable, to hear a king apologise to another person in public.

Zahid chuckled dryly. "I've been looking forward to this."

He held his palms out and shot a beam of fire at the crown, reducing it to a pile of ashes. Once he was done, smoke rose from his hands.

A wave of stunned silence washed over everyone.

The crunch of twigs beneath shoes broke the silence as the Maharaja strode forward and seized Zahid into a hug.

The royal guards clapped tentatively while the rest of the palace staff simply watched in amazement as the king and the prince held each other.

Eventually, the Ketua Kampung arrived and invited all of us to enter the village. After the Maharaja went away, I flung my bag over my shoulder, jumped out of my carriage and ran towards Zahid, who spread his arms wide. I threw my arms around his shoulders, my breath almost leaving me when he embraced me tightly.

As soon as he released me, I grabbed his hands and looked them over. "Do they hurt?"

"A bit," he admitted, eyes twinkling. "I feel much better now, though."

Thankfully, I didn't see any bad burns. "Why didn't you transform?"

He snorted. "I didn't want to get my clothes torn off in front of everyone."

I blushed. "I didn't think of that. Well, that's inconvenient, isn't it?"

Zahid's laughter rang like music to my ears. "There's something I want to show you. Follow me."

He took my hand and led me down a short path between the trees. Our fingers linked together as we walked until we reached a clearing.

"Look up there." He pointed at the sky.

I looked up and saw the peaks of familiar mountains. "Banjaran Titiwangsa looks so close from here."

Zahid murmured in agreement. "Do you want to go?"

I gaped at him. "Go up there?"

"Go up, go around, go over. Whatever you want." He grinned. "Let's go on that adventure you always wanted."

I had so many questions for him. I wanted to know what he had been doing these past few days, what he wanted to do now, what his plans were. How many times had he transformed already? Where did he get that shirt and that samping? How had he been sleeping?

But it was hard to think with Zahid smiling at me like that.

"How?" I asked.

"In case you forgot, I can fly," he boasted with a laugh. "You have extra clothes for me in that bag, don't you?"

I nodded. I was already smiling, incredibly intrigued by his offer. "Everyone else will be looking for us."

"I promise we'll be back before it gets dark." He reached towards me and tucked a strand of hair behind my ear. "Do you trust me?"

Absolutely. With my life. "Yes," I said.

"Then get up," he said, before transforming before my eyes.

He twirled around me a few times, showing off his lithe, muscular body and shiny scales. I couldn't help but laugh at his antics. I carefully straddled him and wrapped my arms around his neck, which was the same width as his human shoulders.

As I gazed at the mountains, I recalled a time when I thought my dreams were trivial compared to Zahid's duty. I thought my purpose was only to take care of him after he brought me to the palace to be his friend.

But here he was, indulging me and my far-fetched fantasy.

As he launched us into the sky, I wondered if Zahid had actually wanted to take care of me all along.

The Fiery Tale of Embun and the Prince

THE DAHLIA OF HUTAN KILAT
Hamizah Adzmi

The seventh of seven always listens well.
He's the favourite, the rare bloom of the seven,
His elder brothers know they will continue to be shadows
unless they put out the sun.

The seventh of seven always follows the rules.
The most important one: never meddle with humans
for they are meant to be looked down on, figuratively, literally.
"Never cross the boundaries, adik kesayangan," they tell him,
"Unless you want to be bound to an unwanted earth."

The Dahlia of Hutan Kilat

The seventh of seven listens well to his brothers,
so when they invite him to join their adventure,
a harmless one, they promise,
he follows them.

"Adik kesayangan, let's play a game, a harmless game
   where we hide from you."

The seventh of seven searches until the sky is bruised,
and in the middle of searching, he hears screams from
   the river.
A mortal child, being pulled by a monster current,
help me, help me, she calls out to no one.

The seventh of seven always listens well
this time, to his heart—
if his brothers were drowning,
he would want them rescued.
And so he saves the girl,
forgetting that he was meant to follow the rules.

When the seventh of seven tries to return home,
he finds himself chained to the ground.
The trees shield him from the skies,
yet he can hear his brothers' laughter in the winds.
The forest's voice is louder,
You are bound to us now.
The guardian of the forest turns his golden eyes away
   from home,
claws digging into an unwanted earth,
breathing out fire as he cries for home.

   *– A Record of Discovered Monsters and Other Beings:
   Last Updated: 2008,* **found in Seri's family library.**

2020

"You want to do *what?*" There was a storm in her mother's eyes.

Seri Dahlia didn't flinch, sitting still on the oak chair in the library of their home. "I will be serving the dragon of Hutan Kilat," she repeated, keeping her voice level, "as well as the residents of the forest—"

"The *residents.*" Her mother's mouth twisted in disgust. "Those beasts—"

She was brought up not to cut off the elderly, but at that moment, Seri forgot all about it. "Mak, they're my *friends.*"

Mak retreated, sinking back against the rattan chair. Next to her, Seri's father glanced back and forth between them, looking like he wanted to say something, but he wasn't a huntress, he wasn't a part of the family legacy. He wasn't a part of this conversation.

"*This* is your reality, Seri." Mak gestured around. Bookshelves that reached up to the ceiling lined up against the wall, along with glass cabinets where their family proudly exhibited parts they'd taken from the monsters they killed—a strand of a pontianak's hair; the cloth of a pocong; a severed, mummified head of a weretiger; and many others. "You're a huntress, yes, but you're also a 25-year-old woman. You should be *working* in the city, not escaping to a forest! Have you thought of what would happen to your career?"

"I don't have a career plan." Seri shrugged. "Jobs are scarce nowadays for people with my degree."

"And what about the future?" There was an edge to her mother's tone, a metaphorical flail. She was grasping at straws. "One day you will have to get married, have a family of your own. You cannot possibly do that in Hutan Kilat, surrounded by those creatures." Her mother inhaled sharply. "Be realistic, Seri."

Seri almost laughed. She was a huntress of supernatural creatures, who wielded a powerful keris, and yet, at the end of the day, her mother still wanted her to hold a steady job, to have children of her own.

The option to run away had always been there. Respect and the love she had for them prevented her from doing so. Seri levelled her gaze with her mother's—an act of defiance that could result in her being thrown out of the family. Still, she held her ground. No one could change the path she was going to take.

"This is what I want."

ଓ
2011

Usually, Seri's mother would be with her when she was hunting away from the city. But since she turned sixteen, she was allowed to use the heirloom keris she'd inherited from her grandmother—who used to be a huntress herself—to carve out portals that would take her to faraway places.

No, it couldn't take her to a different continent. She tried. Even with magic, Seri couldn't run away from having to pay for flight tickets.

The other downside was that the keris wouldn't let her decide *where* she'd end up—something she needed to work on. There was one time when she accidentally ported herself right in the middle of a group of pontianak out for a hunt, and another time, she'd stepped into a mound of tiger poop. She wasn't sure which was worse.

Today, she came prepared. Her track pants were rolled up to her knees, she even cut her hair because a pontianak had pulled on it the last time, and she was armed, of course, with the keris. She adjusted the utility belt around her waist, where she kept colourful vials of potions.

Most importantly, Seri had her phone with her. She was surprised when she found out that there was actually a network signal this deep in the forest. Those advertisements weren't lying when they said you could make a call anywhere.

Her mother's instructions were simple enough: *Capture a toyol. Avoid the Guardian of Hutan Kilat.*

It was dark here in the forest, and the only things guiding her path were her sense of hearing, the stars above, and her own flashlight. It'd be a lie to say she wasn't scared; in one way or another, everyone was scared of what the darkness could give you.

She had been here before, many years ago, with her cousins. The memory of that day was hazy, but she was sure there was supposed to be a river. She must be far from it, considering there was no sound of water running. Good. The last thing she needed was to jump into the water to capture a toyol when she couldn't swim.

She trudged on, sweat trickling down her neck as she strained her ears to discern any suspicious noises. Toyols were small and fast; if she got distracted, they could easily escape. Fortunately, they were also noisy beings with no sense of strategy. They were found mostly in the city, where they would often steal from humans, or be used by humans to steal from other humans. Sometimes, they would end up straying away from their usual urban dwelling, ending up in a forest such as this one. It was better for Seri to capture it before another human did.

And then it came: a churlish giggle that sounded like a baby's. Seri whipped her head towards the direction of the sound, hearing leaves rustling, small footsteps tapping fast against the ground. Well, she didn't win those gold medals for her school as a sprinter for nothing.

The darkness loomed ahead, but Seri was accustomed to it by now—with the keris in her hand she had something to protect herself with. She dove into the darkness, her flashlight swinging with her hand, showing glimpses of a small creature running in front of her. Just as she got closer, she threw one of the vials her mentor had prepared at it—a gassy substance concocted to entrap creatures.

Her aim was perfect. She heard a gasp, followed by a morose whine as the toyol was pulled in by smoky tendrils from the broken vial. *Yes!* She smiled to herself, pleased that she wouldn't be returning empty-handed that night.

She was about to retrieve the toyol, when a gust of wind blew out the vial's magic. A tall figure emerged from the darkness—definitely *not* a toyol. A pair of golden eyes met hers. A djinn? Another pontianak? Another hunter? Or a bomoh practicing in the forest, maybe? Either way, Seri unsheathed her keris, ready to defend herself.

"Human, why are you hunting for Nia?" the figure spoke, his voice lighter than what she'd imagined. It was deep, but gentle like a breeze.

Shining the flashlight at the figure, she saw that it was a man, or at least it *looked* like one anyway. His hair was short and dark, his skin tanned. He was wearing some kind of loose tunic shirt and trousers. What kept Seri from believing he was human, though, were his eyes.

And of course, how he called her 'human'. No actual person would do that.

The being spoke in a language Seri wasn't familiar with, but all hunters were gifted with the ability to understand and be understood in tongues that were out of this world.

"To take it back to my mother." She cleared her throat. "My mentor, I mean."

His gaze fell onto the wavy blade in her hands. "You're Mak Cik Yana's daughter?" Now he was speaking in Malay, though heavily accented, like he wasn't completely used to it.

"How did you know—"

"You look alike." He clicked his tongue. "She seems to have forgotten that hunting is prohibited in my forest."

"You're the Guardian of Hutan Kilat," she said in realisation. "Terjah." She had read about him in her family's *A Record of Discovered Monsters and Other Beings*. Most Guardians were centuries old, and were well known enough to be spoken about in folklore. Terjah, apparently, was new.

"I am. What's your name?"

"Seri," she replied, silently squirming as he bent down to pick up the toyol.

As he moved, a string of gold shimmered from his arm to the ground. Magic, tethering him to the earth. It was like a chain.

He cradled the small being in his arm like he was holding a cat. "Well, it's nice to meet you."

"My mother said toyols are like pests. We'd be doing you a favour, getting rid of it."

When he scrunched up his face, she doubted he was much older than her. "Don't you think I'd know better than her?"

"She said you're new to this place."

"What do *you* think?"

Seri chewed on her bottom lip. "She's going to nag me if I come home with nothing."

"Ah. She did that to me too, when she came to visit."

"To *you*? But you're a forest guardian."

He shrugged. "She seems to think I'm too young and have no idea what I'm doing."

"You're a gazillion years old, probably." Seri brought down her weapon to her side, shoulders feeling less tense.

"I'm seventeen."

She scrunched up her nose. "Are you going to say 'I've been seventeen for a long time'?"

The very human pop culture reference completely escaped him. "You're only seventeen once."

"Never mind. Why're you attached to a toyol?"

"I'm not attached." Terjah placed the small creature on the ground. Instead of running away, it clung onto his leg instead.

"You gave it a name," she pointed out.

"It got separated from its clan. Nia was weak when I first found it. I don't think it can even do any magic."

Seri let out a non-committal hum while the toyol whimpered, trying to hide behind the forest guardian's leg.

"Anyone who comes here looking for a shelter shouldn't be harmed," Terjah added, and there was a firmness in his gentle voice.

They were in an unusual deadlock. Even if Seri brought the toyol home, somehow, in the end it wouldn't make much of a difference except to show her mother that she *could* handle this on her own. On the other hand, if she didn't…

"Ugh," she sheathed her keris. "My mother's going to scold me and this is going to be all your fault."

"What if you told her you made a friend?"

"A friend?" She looked around, frowning.

"I meant myself," the guardian actually sounded a little nervous. "We could be friends."

"Oh." She scratched her cheek. What did her mother say about befriending a forest guardian? Nothing, right? "All right. But friends need to get to know each other first…is this a trick?" She waved her flashlight at his face, making him squint.

"I'd do no such thing!"

It was basic knowledge that, in order to be taken seriously as a huntress, you weren't supposed to befriend beings that came from the forest. But Seri was sixteen, and at that age, there were few things she took seriously.

The corners of her mouth twitched upwards. "Then we can be friends."

༄
2012

Seri flopped down on the cool floor of the family living room, covered in sweat after an extensive silat lesson with her mother.

"You were very distracted today," Mak commented with a disapproving *tsk* as Seri took a long swig from a bottle of water.

"I was wondering, Mak—what do forest guardians eat?"

"They don't have to eat," she replied dryly. "They only do it for pleasure. Why are you curious?"

Seri sat up, nodding. "Do you think Terjah would eat me?"

"Why would you think that?"

"Because he showed me his dragon form," a pause, "he has very sharp teeth, you know."

Ever since Terjah revealed to her that he was able to shift into a dragon, Seri had practically hounded him about it during her visits. When he finally turned into a dragon in front of her, she wasn't able to speak. She was a huntress, she was supposed to have seen many different beings by now, but never a dragon.

He was huge, his size almost covering the ceiling of the cave where he resided. His scales looked like they were made out of jewels; they were a blend of different hues of pink, aquamarine, and purple, which sparkled in the dim light. Terjah's eyes were more golden when he was a dragon, though they never lost their softness.

He left her speechless. Her brain could not process the beauty she was witnessing with her very human eyes.

"No, I don't think he'd eat you," Mak said dryly, dragging Seri away from the memory.

She palmed her chin. "Yeah, I didn't think so either."

"Were you scared?"

"No, I thought he was beautiful."

There was an even longer pause this time, and she could *feel* her mother's worried gaze on her. "You do know that he can never leave Hutan Kilat, don't you?"

Seri folded her legs, crossing her arms over them. "I know."

☙

2013

"You look miserable, Terjah," Nia said bluntly. "Or as Seri would say, very 'moody'."

Terjah, in his true dragon form, let out a sigh. He was curled up on his mound of precious jewels—magical ones he was meant to protect from humans and other beings alike. That was, first and foremost, his duty as a forest guardian, and one of the reasons he wasn't allowed to leave.

Smoke came out from his snout, and Nia, being too close to him, coughed.

"She's been teaching you inappropriate words!" he gruffed. Almost a year ago, Seri had wanted to hunt Nia down and now, she spent her visits teaching the toyol how to communicate like a human. As a result, the toyol had been mimicking her blunt way of talking. Terjah thought it was funny, but not when it was directed at him like this.

"Stop moping and go talk to her," Nia chided, arranging a row of jewels on the ground. It wasn't even looking at him, completely immersed in the beauty of the precious stones. Sometimes, Terjah had a feeling it never wanted to leave simply because it was surrounded by treasures.

"How? She hasn't come here in weeks."

"Can't you text her? With that square thing?"

The dragon glanced down at the phone resting on one of the rocks. Seri had given it to him because she'd gotten a new one and thought it'd be a convenient way to communicate when they were apart.

"She didn't reply to my last text!" He lifted his chin, sulking. Terjah's last message to her was, 'When are you coming again?' It was sent *two hours* ago. Surely she'd have time to decide when she'd carve out a portal to visit him—*them*.

"Then send her another one," Nia suggested.

"Fine," the forest guardian reached out for the phone and, forgetting that he was still in his dragon form, accidentally crushed it with his paw. He groaned.

Nia laughed. "Silly dragon."

Terjah hid his face with his tail. It was unconventional to have a human friend, he knew this. He was sure that his celestial family was laughing at him from above, especially since they would also know that Seri was the human he saved from drowning many years ago, and the reason he was bound to the forest.

It wasn't something he wanted to bring up. He had no experience in friendship, but he knew that 'hey, remember when I rescued you from the river?' would be awkward to bring up in a conversation. What if Seri felt like she owed him? He didn't want that. He liked their friendship too much. It gave him a glimpse into a life that was beyond the cave walls, beyond the forest.

He liked it when Seri came over with books. Conveniently, human languages came naturally to beings like him, and he enjoyed poring over them with her, though he wasn't sure why some genres were called 'fantasy', as if they weren't real. Seri gave him a peek into her life, too—she would complain about how tough monster hunting was, school, her parents wanting her to be a doctor or an engineer (he was still unsure as to what these were).

In return, he showed her around the forest, explaining to her the herbs he was growing, the jewels he was protecting, and introducing her to the other supernatural beings who used it as a temporary shelter…well, the ones who were willing to meet her, anyway. Terjah found that the beings didn't trust her and she didn't trust them.

Seri was his first friend. Terjah had no one else. His six brothers, he realised when he was first bound to this earth, always had something to hide. They were often jealous of him. It was why they tricked him into going down to earth. They knew he would have a soft spot for humans. Terjah never felt like Seri was hiding anything from him. She was very transparent about her emotions.

So it came as no surprise that she looked absolutely livid when she stepped out of the portal she'd carved with the Taming Sari a couple of days later. Terjah, who was in the middle of entertaining Nia by flinging jewels for it to catch, immediately stopped when he saw her.

Seri's long ponytail swung behind her as she strode up to him, hands on her hips, fixing him with a defiant glare. "Oh, so you *are* alive," her tone was sarcastic. "You must've been too *busy* to reply to my texts, hm?" She shot Nia a glare, and the toyol immediately hid behind Terjah.

"Did she change her mind about hunting me?" it quaked, and at least that got Seri to soften just slightly.

"No, no, she's just angry with me." Terjah gave it a pat on the head before turning his attention back to his angry friend. "Uh…so…I broke the phone you gave me."

"He crushed it while he was in his dragon form!" Nia tattled.

"I didn't *mean* to—it was an accident!"

Seri stared at both of them before a smile cracked on her face. "Where's the phone now?"

When he showed the broken pieces of the device to her, she broke into fits of laughter. Terjah could feel his cheeks heating up and it wasn't because he was trying to breathe out fire—not that he could, when he shifted into a human.

"This isn't funny!" he insisted. "I'm sorry for breaking your gift."

Catching her breath, Seri wiped a tear from her eye. "It isn't? You broke a phone with your mighty dragon paw! What were you trying to do, type with your cl–claw?" And she started laughing again, clutching her side.

Terjah had no idea that laughter could be so infectious. He started joining her until his cheeks no longer felt like they were on fire. Instead, they were just aching from smiling too much. Only Seri had this effect on him.

"Why didn't you reply to me?" he asked, when their laughter died down. "You stopped coming to visit us too. I thought…you didn't want to be friends anymore."

Seri's eyebrows furrowed. "Of course I still want to be friends with you." She heaved out a long-suffering sigh. "I had to prepare for my SPM exam. I have to do well if I want to get into a university."

"Oh." Terjah pursed his lips. "You talk a lot about exams! I can't keep track!"

Seri chuckled. "You're right. But exams are my life right now! I'm in my last year of high school."

"Does that mean you will never return to it?"

Seri nodded.

"How do you feel about that?"

Her hands fidgeted over her jeans. "Weird. It's like I'm about to enter 'adulthood' but I still don't know who I am, or who I want to be. I don't even know what course to study in university!" She rolled her eyes. "My father's still holding out hope that I'll become a doctor, but my grades aren't great."

"It must be nice."

Seri blinked. "It is?"

"I...may not know what you mean much by university or grades," Terjah began carefully, "but uncertainty means that there's a chance for you to explore, right? Trying to figure out who you are and what you like is an adventure in itself. That's what I think anyway." He crossed his arms over his chest. "I kind of wish I had that."

Terjah already knew what he was meant to do for the rest of his life. He was a forest guardian, bound to this earth. Whether it was a curse or a blessing, he had made a choice when he rescued Seri from the river.

"But being here *is* an adventure."

Now it was time for him to throw her a confused stare. "What?"

"I'd rather be here with you, discovering everything about the forest, about the jewels, about the beings that come here, than out there with humans!" She gestured at the cave entrance.

Terjah reached out for her cheek, pinching it. "Don't be a silly human."

She batted his hand away, pouting. "Speak for yourself, phone-crushing dragon!"

☙

The Dahlia of Hutan Kilat

2014

me
third week of uni
i'm bored
do something

my favourite dragon
I can't control your mood

me
maybe that's a skill you should work on!!
do you like ur new phone?

my favourite dragon
Yes, but i'm trying not to use it too much.
Can't expect you to come here and help me charge
it every time.

me
lol you know i don't mind :)
i'm still bored

my favourite dragon
You're always welcome here

me
are you telling me to skip class???

my favourite dragon
Seri you can literally create a portal
It takes you less than a minute to come here 😑

me
excellent emoji use
see you!

Hamizah Adzmi

Seri sat down on the river bank next to Terjah, their legs dipped in the water to help them cool down. She tilted her head up, admiring the canopy of trees, which shielded them from the sun. Seri was still in her long-sleeved purple blouse and blue jeans, her backpack leaning against a tree bark where she'd thrown it. She had rushed over the moment she got his text.

"How many friends have you made so far?" Terjah asked.

"I'm not sure! But I do have a lot of Instagram followers now." Seri displayed her phone for him to see. She'd explained to him once what Instagram was—some kind of gallery where humans display pictures and wait for other people to react.

"Do you talk to them?"

"My followers? Not really."

"So not all of them are your friends?" Sometimes, Terjah would wonder if she ever got tired of answering his questions. But she never showed it. In fact, she seemed to like that he was always curious.

"Right," she admitted. "Sometimes they just follow you just to find out what you're doing, through pictures."

"How bizarre." He kicked the water. "I'd rather ask you myself and have you tell me everything."

She smiled. "Me too."

On the other side of the river, a tigress prowled from behind the trees. Seri immediately recognised her. She waved and the tigress nodded in acknowledgement. The being was a weretigress, and Seri had found her while she was out patrolling in a newly-developed suburban neighbourhood a couple of months ago. There were plenty of those now, replacing small patches of forests. The weretigress was cursed by some kind of enchantment that prevented her from turning back into a human. Seri brought her here where she could be safe while she and Terjah tried to figure out how to break the curse.

"It feels like you've been helping out supernatural beings more than doing any 'hunting' recently," Terjah teased her. "Is your mother fine with this?"

Seri covered her mouth with a hand, stifling a laugh. "You know she's not! But I like doing this. It's better than hunting. My ancestors are probably rolling in their graves, cursing me."

"Well, *I* think it's admirable," he said fervently, and it made her turn a little pink in the cheeks. She looked away.

"Seri?"

She turned to him. "Yeah?"

"Why don't you swim?" he asked, a little nervously. "This forest is…your second home, but I've never seen you try to swim in the river."

Seri stared ahead, her eyes distant. "I'm scared of the water."

"Even now?"

"Not right now. I feel safe here with you. But if I was alone, I'd probably stay away."

"Why?"

"You're going to think it's silly. I almost drowned once, when I was a kid. I don't remember much anymore, but whenever I'm near a river or the sea, I get queasy, like something bad is about to happen."

"I…see." There was a careful edge to Terjah's tone, one that didn't come out often. Seri fixed her gaze on him while he stared ahead, golden eyes filled with conflict. "Have you tried learning how to swim?" He was switching to forced casualness now.

She shook her head. "Between classes, hunting, and hanging out with you? No." Seri pressed her hands

The Dahlia of Hutan Kilat

against the damp ground. "Are you trying to avoid telling me something?"

Terjah exhaled. "Nothing escapes you, does it?"

She grinned at her friend of almost three years. "Not when it comes to you."

"It was me," he said softly. "I saved you from drowning."

It was you? Seri's heart hammered against her chest, her stomach churning with guilt. He wouldn't lie to her. "Was I—does that mean you're stuck here because of me?"

Terjah winced. "It wasn't you. My brothers tricked me into following them down to earth and they—I'm not sure which one of them—made the currents strong. They knew I couldn't help saving you."

"I'm sorry," Seri whispered. "If it wasn't for me— "

"Stop." Terjah raised his palm. "It wasn't your fault. I made my choice to rescue you and I don't regret it."

"But what about your family? What about home?"

"Home is here," Terjah gestured at their surroundings. "Family is where you're around those you trust. My brothers would've come up with a different plan to get rid of me."

"Why would they do that?" Seri had no siblings, but she couldn't imagine her own family betraying her.

"It's…complicated." Terjah gave her a rueful smile. "The short version of it is that they were jealous."

Seri folded her arms. "How long have you known it was me?"

"From the moment we met."

She groaned. "And you didn't want to tell me because?"

"I didn't want you to blame yourself."

"But I do." She rubbed her eyes. "How do I make this up to you?"

Without warning, Terjah bent down and started splashing water at her, breaking the thread of tension between them almost instantly.

Seri let out an indignant shriek. "What was that for?!"

"Keep being my friend," he said with an easy smile.

You were cursed because of me. And yet, Terjah didn't look like someone who was cursed. Under the sunlight, his eyes sparkled, his face filled with warmth. Years ago, he could've told her to go away. He could've even plotted for revenge.

Instead, Terjah let her stay and shared a piece of his home with her. The magnitude of his trust rendered her quiet. For a minute or two, she could only stare at him as he shut his eyes, lifting his chin as if content to just be there. He was beautiful, for reasons beyond his golden eyes, beyond his dragon form.

Daringly, she touched the shimmering, golden chain that kept him tethered to the forest. "I will keep being your friend, then."

ෆ
2018

Seri chugged down a mug of coffee she had ordered while her friend from university, Kamal, stared at her in awe over his plate of roti canai. They were in the middle of Kuala Lumpur, surrounded by office workers having breakfast.

The Dahlia of Hutan Kilat

"I heard coffee can make you nervous," Kamal raised his voice over the sound of people chatting and vehicles outside.

"Being nervous is better than sleepy when you're being interviewed," Seri replied tersely. She wasn't a morning person, and last night's hunting session at an abandoned factory had left her exhausted, even though her mother was there helping.

Helping. Thinking about it made her let out a small sound of disbelief. Seri had wanted to take the beings they found—a wayward toyol and langsuir who were more confused than dangerous—to Hutan Kilat, but her mother had imprisoned them with her magic before she could do anything.

"What is the point of inheriting a powerful keris when you do nothing with it?" her mother had demanded when they got home.

Seri couldn't answer her. That would require a long explanation on how she had actually been avoiding using it, because a couple of swipes from the keris and the beings would be extinguished. Seri didn't want that, and she couldn't possibly tell her mother the truth because it would be against a very fundamental belief their family has held for generations.

"Thanks for passing my CV to your company, by the way." Seri gave Kamal a smile. They became friends when he was possessed by a spirit when they were second years. He was an overachiever who landed a job barely a month after they finished university. Seri wouldn't have asked him for this kind of favour, but after three months of trying and getting rejected, she had to try.

Kamal waved a dismissive hand. "What are friends for?"

This was going to be her fourth interview in two weeks. Seri had been warned that after graduation, she would be spending most of the time sending out job applications. She had no idea how tiring it would be and how many times she would be rejected.

"I hate job interviews," she groused. "I don't want to work in an office."

Kamal smiled wryly. "There are bills to pay."

And with those five words, Seri could picture her future. She could see herself in the woman in the driver's seat, looking despondently ahead at the red traffic light; in the man scrolling through his mobile phone as he half-heartedly ate his breakfast. This was adulting: working forever and making just enough to survive.

She blocked these images out with the memory of the wind playing with thousands of leaves. Moonlight and stars guiding a path in the dark. Warm, golden eyes. Joyful, unnatural laughter that could only be found in Hutan Kilat.

"So how're you celebrating your birthday tonight? Going out with Evelyn?" Kamal and Evelyn were both her classmates back in university.

"No, I already have plans." A bright smile blossomed on Seri's lips as she remembered that she would be seeing Terjah. "And can you please stop using me to meet up with Evelyn?"

"Hey! I only asked because it's your birthday—"

She grinned. "How long are you going to keep wasting time, huh? Pining's going to get you nowhere."

"Speak for yourself," Kamal huffed. "I bet you're meeting the *same* guy you've been sneaking out to see at night."

Normally, Seri's knee jerk reaction when Kamal tried to provoke her was to tell him that she was only meeting a *friend*, that it was none of his business, but this time, she sat there in silence, her cheeks coloured.

"Wow, not even one rebuttal?" Kamal placed a hand under his chin. "Is there progress, then?"

She'd rather deal with a hundred orang minyak than talk about this. Seri glanced at her watch. "Come on, we're going to be late."

The interview ended up being just like every other interview, where Seri was forced to put on a mask and pretend to care. But when she stepped out of the portal into Hutan Kilat, she forgot about it all, immediately engulfed by Nia.

She made her way into Terjah's cave, where he was seated on his throne-like chair, a pensive expression on his face. Seri had told him of her plans a couple of weeks ago and it looked like he was still unwilling to relent.

Still, when he saw her, that expression melted away into a softer one. "Happy twenty-third birthday," he said.

"Thank you," she said, approaching him. "Have you given more thought about…my idea?"

Terjah's mouth formed a hard line before he asked, "Are you *sure* you want to do this?"

"It's only for a couple of hours."

He crossed his arms over his chest. "You could get hurt."

Seri rolled her eyes. "I'm not a delicate human."

"And you underestimate my powers."

"I don't." Seri let out a sigh. "I know you care about my safety. You'd stop if it gets too dangerous."

"You're doing this for me," Terjah looked at her face, as if searching for the truth. "It's your birthday, not mine."

"Yes, and on my birthday, I want to spend time with the most important person to me." Seri's voice thickened when she saw Terjah's eyes widening. Could it be that no one had ever told him this? "I want you to know what it's like to be away from here. You deserve that." It wasn't enough to give him books to read, to tell him stories of her day, to show him videos and pictures on a phone. She wanted him to be *there*, breathing it all in, deciding for himself whether he liked this human world.

Because it was a part of her too.

Terjah stood up, exhaling a breath. "Then we'll try it. Do you give your consent?"

"I do."

Willingly being possessed, especially by a celestial being like Terjah, was something Seri was sure her family would never condone. She was definitely *not* telling her mother about this. Based on her experience of dealing with possession, the host would be in a fit of hysteria. She remembered Kamal, his eyes rolled back and limbs thrashing about, fighting against an unknown force within him.

They moved outside of the cave, where a few beings watched them curiously.

"Neither of you are going to die, right?" Nia asked, perched on a nearby tree. "This place would be boring if you do."

"Nothing like that will happen," Terjah told it firmly.

Terjah stepped forward, and she could feel his soft palm touching her forehead, felt his magic weave itself into her skin. She closed her eyes, steadying her breaths to calm her pounding heart, which was more nervous about their proximity than the act of possession itself.

Pictures flash through her mind like a fast-forwarded video—she saw magnificent spires made out of marble, the roars of dragons calling out to each other, her own voice screaming for help in the river, the steel weight of responsibility on Terjah's shoulders.

She was being pulled by the strong current of memories, and finally moored to where Terjah was hugging his knees on the river bank, alone and crying, a child abandoned. Then he looked up, hands reaching out for Seri's consciousness and holding onto it as she brought him home.

Seri had never been possessed before, so it took her a few minutes to get used to the feeling of a phantom latching onto her. What was more nerve-wracking, though, was taking Terjah away from Hutan Kilat. She half-expected something to happen to him the moment she stepped out of the portal.

Are you still there? she asked, internally.

Yeah. Terjah's voice floated in her mind. She sighed loudly, hand on her chest. *I guess the curse only meant to bind me physically.* Seri could feel his emotions gently grazing against hers; he was curious about the place she brought him to. *Where are we?*

On the rooftop of a building under construction, Seri explained to him. *It has the nicest view of the city. Look.*

She stared ahead so he could see through her eyes the dotted lights laid out before them. The city was crowded by tall buildings. From afar, the twin towers looked like lighthouses, and everything else revolved around them.

I come here sometimes, when I need to be alone, she continued.

The lights are pretty, Terjah observed. *I'm surprised you like it here.*

What do you mean?

It feels like you're breathing in smoke. There are too many towers, too many lights. You can't even see the stars.

The corners of Seri's mouth twitched downwards.

I'm sorry, Terjah added hastily. *But I'm only echoing what you feel.*

You're right, Seri laughed softly. *I come here because when I see those lights, I'm reminded that there are so many people out there, probably feeling the way I do.*

You feel lost.

Sometimes.

Terjah didn't push her to tell him why she felt that way. It was one of the many things she appreciated about him. He could let her be comfortably silent, and accepted her as she was.

There are so many humans, he said, after a while. *I forget about this sometimes.*

Seri chuckled, walking over to a small table where, earlier, she had laid out slices of cakes and a flask of tea.

If you can see what I see, does that mean you can taste what I eat? she asked, just to be sure.

I think so. We can try.

Terjah had always been picky about human food. One time, she visited him in Hutan Kilat bringing pisang goreng—her favourite kuih. "You humans are strange!" he had admonished, after taking a bite. "Why change something that's already perfect?"

It had put her off from trying again. Maybe it would be different this time—it was her birthday and he was possessing her.

She sat down on a foldable chair and picked up a piece of chocolate cake with a fork, tentatively putting it in her mouth.

It's delicious! Both of them thought at the same time. She could hear Terjah clearing his throat. *I mean, it can't compare to the fresh fruits we have in Hutan Kilat*, he tried to amend his words.

But she could feel his delight when she ate a slice of strawberry shortcake and declared that he would try to conjure these desserts with magic.

How did you find this place? he asked her.

Ha, it was infested by pontianak and langsuir. Remember the ones I brought to the forest for a while? They were from here.

I remember them. It was non-stop entertainment at the forest for weeks, Terjah deadpanned. *I almost lost my voice from so much singing.*

She giggled. *They really enjoyed themselves. You made them feel at home.*

Does your mother, or the other huntresses, know what you've been doing?

A little bit, Seri admitted. *She disapproves, but it's not like she can punish me.*

Can I be honest with you?

Seri gripped the mostly empty plastic cup. *Always.*

I don't think you want to be a huntress anymore.

She lowered her gaze to the ground. *But it's in my blood.*

All of us change as we grow. All of us are allowed to change our minds.

I used to think I wanted to be like my mother. Powerful. Undefeated. When she passed the keris to me, I knew what she wanted me to be. Instead I... Seri's mouth slanted into a lopsided smile. *Instead, I'm using it to create portals to bring the beings I'm meant to capture to safety.*

Do you like who you've become?

This wasn't what her mother wanted for her. Certainly, the generations of huntresses before her would be turning in their graves to know who she had become. She couldn't bring herself to hurt beings who only needed help. She couldn't picture herself in a home where she'd show off her hunting conquests.

What would it mean to quit being a huntress like her mother? A life of staring at computer screens every day, in a building surrounded by people she didn't care about?

She didn't want that either, and she wasn't sorry for knowing exactly what she desired.

I do. I like who I am.

Me too, Seri. Her hand rose, though it wasn't her doing, and the back of her hand touched her lips. *Happy birthday.*

There were words she wanted so much to speak into the night, to lay it out there for him to see. Maybe not yet. She wasn't ready.

Maybe I could take you somewhere else next time. Seri smiled, imagining bringing him to the sea, enjoying the view of the crashing waves, the sunset blanketing the horizon in orange.

The sea? Oh, apparently he could see her thoughts. Her cheeks felt warm. She wondered if he could sense that she was flustered. If he did, he didn't point it out. *I'd like that.*

ଔ
2016

The singing began when the moon took over the sky. Terjah wasn't used to celebrations in Hutan Kilat, but that was what the pontianak and langsuir brought to the forest. He stepped out of his cave just in time to narrowly avoid a pontianak colliding into him as she flew past.

"The Guardian of the Forest is here!" one of the women announced, while another dropped a crown of flowers neatly on his head. They had been doing this every night since they came.

It was disconcerting at first, but these women were starting to grow on him. They were funny, they sang and danced until daybreak as if nothing bothered them, and when they were hungry, they would fly off to hunt, returning with claws and mouths covered in animal blood from somewhere else. They knew not to harm anything in Hutan Kilat.

Most of them were naked, though some wore faded, dirtied batik around their bodies. Their dead, grey eyes gleamed with constant mischief. Seri told him that humans were scared of these women, made moving pictures of them (she called them 'movies' and promised to let him watch one next week), but she thought that all they wanted was a comfortable place to stay.

The pontianak and langsuir would tell stories through their songs. Most were about their desire to ruin the lives of those who wronged them. After all, the pontianak and langsuir were physical manifestations of their corrupted souls' desire for revenge.

Tonight, they listened to one of them sing about being killed by a lover and thrown into the river afterwards. She howled the things she would like to do to the man and his relatives who protected him; she would haunt them forever with her screams, until they lost their minds.

Once she finished, the women gathered her in their arms, holding her, whispering assurances that they would all, one day, be free of revenge. Then they would dance, their pale, lifeless limbs shining under the moonlight as they swayed to music only they could hear. There were no tears, no sadness; it was as if revenge turned into joy with company around.

"Where is the huntress that brought us here?" a pontianak who called herself Mira said, extending her hands for Terjah to take.

"She has a family dinner," Terjah explained, politely accepting her hands and letting her lead him into a dance—if you could call random movements one, anyway.

"Poor girl. I bet she has to eat *vegetables*. How horrid!" Mira gave a little twirl, and her long black hair fanned out around her. "We thought she lived here with you."

"Of course not." Terjah looked away, trying to hide the flush from his cheeks. "She's a human."

"And yet," Mira halted her dance, peering at his face, "I've lived long enough to see desire so visible in someone."

The flush deepened, and so did the need to exert his authority just so he could keep her from talking about his…feelings. "I'm—I'm the Guardian of Hutan Kilat. How *dare* you insinuate—"

"How *dare* I!" Mira threw her head back, laughing. "Ladies, did you hear him? Look at the Guardian, he's angry because of my harmless teasing!"

The women crowded around him, latching onto a new form of entertainment.

"Did you finally crack him open, Mira?"

"Spill all your feelings to us, O Mighty Guardian."

"It's none of your business." Terjah folded his arms, his eyes narrowed. "And I'll have you know that I could turn into a dragon now and eat all of you."

Nia spoke up from one of the trees, "He likes to say this to me, but has never done it."

"I'm not like her. We could never—I don't know if I can be *good* to her—"

Mercifully, before Terjah could keep spluttering and embarrassing himself further, Mira's cold hands cupped his face.

"We do not like love stories, Mighty Dragon of Hutan Kilat," Mira said, baring her fangs. "But we can offer you advice, so that the huntress doesn't end up like us."

Terjah sighed wearily. "Do I have a choice?"

She giggled, still holding his face. "Remember, Terjah, to always *ask* what she wants. Let her decide for herself what is good for her, and be at peace, whatever her decision may be." Mira let him go, and a flicker of sadness crossed her grey eyes. "If only the people who wronged us knew that, we would all still be alive."

☙

2019

Seri arrived at Hutan Kilat exhausted, her clothes covered in brown, oily slick that looked like blood. So it was understandable that when she entered Terjah's cave, he looked alarmed and immediately checked to see that she wasn't badly injured.

"Stop *fussing*," she said, batting his hands away as she sat down on the ground, catching her breath. She tossed the sheathed keris aside. "I'm fine."

It had been a violent night. She and her mother had freed five women who were kidnapped by orang minyak, cursed men who could turn themselves into slick. That was how they got to their victims. Nothing bad happened. The women were safe, traumatised but uninjured. If they hadn't gotten there in time though…

She opened her eyes to meet Terjah's golden gaze. This was where she always ended up returning to after a rough night of hunting, after narrowly avoiding death.

He had a small jar of salve in his hand. "You're hurt," he said in a low voice.

Seri glanced down at her arms and legs, covered in bruises. She didn't complain as he gently applied the salve on them. He was doing this so carefully, as if she were precious to him. When he was done, he stood up to bring over a wet cloth.

It was only natural that she unravelled her ponytail and let him wipe the slick off her hair.

"Do you love me?" she asked with a bite of impatience.

Terjah didn't draw back. He lifted his gaze to meet hers and said, "Yes."

"I meant romantic love, by the way," Seri added, a little flustered. She didn't want him to misunderstand. "Because that's how I feel about you."

He chuckled. "Yes, that's what I meant too."

"I want to stay here." She turned away, not wanting him to see her face because it would reveal too much. It was the first time she had ever told him what she desired. "If you'll have me, of course."

"I'm bound to Hutan Kilat," he said helplessly. "For as long as I live."

"That's not a problem."

"Your duties…"

She shrugged. "I'll figure it out. I just…" Seri took hold of his hand so that he'd stop trying to stop her. "I want this—to return to this place, to you, at the end of every day."

Terjah's hand trembled as he touched his cheek and brought their face closer, resting his warm forehead against hers.

"Only if it's what you want."

She smiled. "It is, my favourite dragon."

ABOUT THE AUTHORS

Collin Yeoh has wanted to be a writer all his life, and indeed has been writing professionally for 17 years. At some point, he remembered that advertising copy wasn't what he wanted to write growing up as a lonely bookworm kid. He now finds writing things that have plots, characters, themes, genres, and that won't be subject to notes like "please include more product benefits" a lot more fun. He lives in Kuala Lumpur.

Hamizah Adzmi is a storyteller and currently works as the Knowledge Mobilization Programme Officer for Musawah, an international women's rights NGO. She pursued a MA in Creative Writing under the Chevening scholarship in 2016/2017, where she focused on writing fiction revolving around Malaysian women. Previously, she was in the media industry and taught Creative Writing in universities. Her interests include books, writing, and feminism.

Ilnaz A. Faizal enjoys writing stories that cross between the genres of horror, fantasy, and romance. She also writes poetry and screenplays. Her favourite authors are Sarah Dessen and R.L Stine. When she's not writing, she can either be found reading, embroidering cartoon characters, or sleeping.

Ismim Putera (he/him) is a poet and writer from Sarawak, Malaysian Borneo. His works can be found in online journals as well as anthologised in *To Let the Light In Anthology of Life and Death*, *Instinct: Asian Speculative Poetry 2021*, *Colours of Tapestry 2: Stories from*

Asia, *Unsaid: An Asian Anthology*, and recently in *The Big Book of Malaysian Horror*. His poem "Durian Blossoms" won third place in the 7th Singapore Poetry Contest (2021) and "Jantina" was longlisted for the Malaysian Poetry Competition (2021).

Joni Chng is a writer and photographer based in Malaysia, born and raised in Kedah. She draws a lot of inspiration from diverse cultures around the world, particularly from the Far East and Southeast Asia, with speculative elements of her own invention thrown in for good measure. Her work has appeared in several anthologies and magazines, including *The Big Book of Malaysian Horror Stories* (Fixi Novo, 2022), *Night Terrors: Vol. 21* (Scare Street, 2022), *Tainted Love: Women in Horror* (Twisted Wing productions, 2021), and *NANG 3: Fiction* (2017).

Joshua Lim is a writer of speculative fiction. His work is published or forthcoming in *Fantasy Magazine* and in anthologies by Inklings Press, Fixi Novo, and Maya Press. Born and raised in Klang, he is currently a medical student who finds time in between classes to write stories and overthink his future. Find him on Instagram @joshualimwriter.

A medical officer and quality manager by profession, **Julia Alba** has been writing fiction since she was a teenager. She loves a great story no matter the genre or the medium, whether it's a book, a video game, an anime or a movie. Her bad habit is her inability to resist buying too much Harry Potter merchandise. She lives in Perak with her husband and daughter.

Rowan C is 22 years old and currently studying accounting, which inspired the title of this work. They're also heavily inspired by the D&D games they play, and they've always looked up to Neil Gaiman and the late Terry Pratchett. They hope, through their work, these interests of theirs can be shared with all of you.

Sharmilla Ganesan is a radio presenter, writer, and culture critic based in Kuala Lumpur, Malaysia. She was with The Star newspaper for over a decade; currently, she is attached to BFM 89.9, where she hosts shows on current affairs, the arts, books, and film. She has also written for The Atlantic, South China Morning Post, NewNaratif, and ArtsEquator.

Stuart Danker is a Malaysian author who's spent a decade writing across multiple genres and mediums, and that's after plying his trade in various industries such as hairdressing and accounting. His first novel, *Tinhead City, KL*, debuted in 2021. Find him at stuartdanker.com.

Syazwani Jefferdin is currently a 24-year-old PhD in English student at Nottingham University Malaysia. She has been writing since she was 9 and has been writing fantasy fiction since high school. Currently, she's working on her PhD creative work titled *God's Eyes*, a novel that will explore the Fantasy genre with Malaysian elements imbedded alongside classic western Fantasy elements.

Zufar Zeid lives in the morgue and tries to give a voice to the dead. In his free time, he pretends to write but is actually just daydreaming his life away.

About the Editor

Anna Tan writes fantasy stories and fairy tales, and helps people publish books at Teaspoon Publishing. She also wrangles writers and deadlines for the Malaysian Writers Society (MYWriters) and Penang Art District.

Anna has an MA in Creative Writing: The Novel under a Chevening scholarship and is the current President of MYWriters. She can be found tweeting as @natzers and forgetting to update annatsp.com.

Teaspoon Publishing

Just like a teaspoon of sugar sweetens your tea, Teaspoon Publishing adds a dash of something special to your words. Whether it's getting a dose of magic in your fiction, working magic with your words, or helping you find that magical balance of trad/indie/hybrid publishing, we hope you'll find what you're looking for here!

It's as simple as a **TSP**:

Traditional: where we source and publish fantasy works as a micro-press.

Services: where we provide writing-related freelance services such as editing, proofreading, and copywriting.

Publishing Hub: where we hold your hand(s) and let you decide how we can help you fulfil your publishing dreams.

Talk to us at info@teaspoonpublishing.com.my